The Seven Seals of Egypt

(Matt Drake #17)

By

David Leadbeater

Thriller, adventure, action, mystery, suspense, archaeological,
military, historical

Other Books by David Leadbeater:

The Matt Drake Series
The Bones of Odin (Matt Drake #1)
The Blood King Conspiracy (Matt Drake #2)
The Gates of Hell (Matt Drake 3)
The Tomb of the Gods (Matt Drake #4)
Brothers in Arms (Matt Drake #5)
The Swords of Babylon (Matt Drake #6)
Blood Vengeance (Matt Drake #7)
Last Man Standing (Matt Drake #8)
The Plagues of Pandora (Matt Drake #9)
The Lost Kingdom (Matt Drake #10)
The Ghost Ships of Arizona (Matt Drake #11)
The Last Bazaar (Matt Drake #12)
The Edge of Armageddon (Matt Drake #13)
The Treasures of Saint Germain (Matt Drake #14)
Inca Kings (Matt Drake #15)
The Four Corners of the Earth (Matt Drake #16)

The Alicia Myles Series
Aztec Gold (Alicia Myles #1)
Crusader's Gold (Alicia Myles #2)
Caribbean Gold (Alicia Myles #3)

The Torsten Dahl Thriller Series
Stand Your Ground (Dahl Thriller #1)

The Relic Hunters Series
The Relic Hunters (Relic Hunters #1)

The Disavowed Series:
The Razor's Edge (Disavowed #1)
In Harm's Way (Disavowed #2)
Threat Level: Red (Disavowed #3)

The Chosen Few Series
Chosen (The Chosen Trilogy #1)
Guardians (The Chosen Tribology #2)

Short Stories
Walking with Ghosts (A short story)
A Whispering of Ghosts (A short story)

Connect with the author on Twitter: @dleadbeater2011
Visit the author's website: www.davidleadbeater.com

All helpful, genuine comments are welcome. I would love to hear
from you.
davidleadbeater2011@hotmail.co.uk

The Seven Seals of Egypt

CHAPTER ONE

A dense fog swirled and thickened beyond the edge of town, seeping inside the blurred boundaries with questing fingers as cold as ice. The midnight darkness, already close to impenetrable, congealed until it resembled a living, breathing, shambling thing. All noise was muted, and the views across the valleys toward what they now knew was Dracula's castle were reduced to a creeping white mist pressed up against the window panes as if seeking a way inside.

A crackling fire warmed the inside of the large room, embers spitting in the hearth like angry demons, a chorus line of bright orange flames dancing along the walls and on the ceiling. The crackling pop and bang of timbers filled the room like gunshots, putting the gathering on edge.

"We can't stay here," Torsten Dahl said.

"We ain't going anywhere." Hayden nodded at the nearest window.

"Yeah, get a grip, Torsty," Alicia Myles croaked in a mock-frightened voice. "It's impossible to say what's lurking about in that mist."

The Swede shook his head slowly. "You've been reading too much Stephen King."

Alicia blinked. "Reading who? Do I *look* like I spend my time in bed reading?"

"You're the one afraid of ghosts."

"Dude." Alicia lowered her voice and stared around theatrically. "You know we're in Transylvania, right?"

The Swede ignored her. "A few days is fine. But ten Europeans staying at the same hotel for almost a week. Rarely leaving. Eating indoors. Staying together. Looking shifty—"

"One thing I do not look," Kenzie said, close to Dahl's right elbow, "is shifty."

"Maybe not. But I do. I know it's surprising—but Alicia does

1

have a point. We *don't* look like . . . civilians."

Alicia only nodded as if sharing wisdom. Kenzie took a moment to study the other faces in the room.

"And do you think we could ever be civilians?"

Matt Drake grunted and drank coffee. "I've been struggling with that one for years, love."

"You tried once, didn't you?"

"Yeah. Didn't work out so well."

"Which leaves us—" Hayden gestured at the four walls "—here."

It was the largest room in the guesthouse, where Drake and Alicia were staying. The carpet and the painted walls were tired-looking, the furniture shabby. The bed was small and uncomfortable. Black and white photographs on the wall portrayed several castles and were smeared and dusty. The baseboards and corners of the room were chipped and pitted, untouched for years.

"Where to next then?" Kinimaka asked.

It was a good question. The team had been mulling it over for days on end, exhausted all lines of conversation, and then started again. Information coming out of DC was scarce and unreliable. Hayden knew people that would fight for her; that would keep her in the loop, but the last thing she wanted was to compromise them.

"We know some high-level players in Washington burned us," Hayden said. "We can only speculate as to Kimberley Crowe's involvement. She's relatively new to the job and could have been railroaded. Or . . . she could be the instigator. We need to get closer, go higher. Somehow, we have to get back to DC."

Dahl shook his head. "We've been over all this," he said softly. "Those I care about are in DC. The girls . . . and Johanna." He covered the pause by talking fast. "We don't know the breadth of what we're up against and we can't risk my family being used against us."

"I can't believe they would sink that low," Kinimaka said.

The Swede didn't look at him. "They're politicians," he said.

"Yes, I know some are good. Some are trying to do the right thing. But as for the rest . . ."

He didn't finish. It had been said before.

"Keeping a low profile is best for now," Drake agreed.

"And the Sword of Mars?" Hayden pressed. "The longer that weapon of the gods stays in the wrong hands the worse I feel. It could be part of a longer-term venture."

"Like what?" Mai asked. "It's only just surfaced."

"No telling how long people have been looking for it."

"And who says Cambridge of the British SAS is the wrong hands?" Drake wondered.

"Well, don't forget it could also be with the Chinese Special Forces," Hayden reminded them. "That's a vast and deadly gulf between choices."

Drake acknowledged her words with a nod. "True."

Lauren, quiet until now, spoke up. "I should go back to DC. I wasn't with you in Peru when all the . . . shit happened. I wasn't there when Joshua died. I'm free."

"They'll interrogate you," Smyth said a little dismissively.

"What can they say?" Lauren protested. "I was on the phone to Crowe herself, gathering Intel and acting as the go-between. And it can be vouched for. Like I said, I'm free."

"Almost as if we set it up," Hayden said. "Or someone did."

"I don't know what that means," Lauren insisted. "But of all the people here I am the one that can go back to DC with ease, with impunity. Yeah, they'll question me and I'll tell them all I know. But the longer I hang around with you guys the longer it will take for them to believe me, and leave me alone to do my thing."

The entire team stared at her, thinking it through. It was true, almost as if had been set up right back at the beginning of the Inca operation. Lauren Fox was in the clear.

"They'll quiz you about the four corners mission, and why you didn't leave sooner," Smyth still protested.

"Yeah, and I'll say I kept my distance. Which I did, for the most part. This was my first real opportunity to leave. I'll tell them I slipped away in Transylvania and then recount everywhere else you've been. I'll tell them everything, quickly. Hope they check it out. Then . . ." She shrugged.

"They're trained for this kind of thing. They'll see through you," Kinimaka noted.

"You forget who I am." Lauren smiled. "And why I was initially recruited. My job is lying. My whole world was built around a lie. Jonathan initially recruited me for one thing— lying."

Again, the team sat back, more than a little impressed. Had Jonathan Gates envisioned a scenario like this, way back then? It was impossible, of course, but all bases had to be covered for all contingencies, and Lauren was the perfect actress and deceiver.

"Can't say I saw this coming," Drake said. "Nobody could. But Lauren does have a good point."

"They could keep her locked up for months," Smyth said. "Black-site her. Torture her. They could kill her and drop her down a well and we'd never know."

"All I need," Lauren said, "is one chance. One chance to get close to President Coburn. If I get that done—" she spread her arms "—all this goes away."

"Smyth does have a point," Hayden said. "I know how this shit works. They may keep her hidden away for a long time. Unofficial. Off the books. They may want all trace of SPEAR gone forever."

"Then I'll make if official," Lauren said. "I don't need my goddamn hand holding here. I'll walk right into the *New York Times* and give myself up."

Drake and the others regarded her with admiration. "It could work . . ." the Yorkshireman said.

"It will work," Lauren said. "I can do this for all of us." She coughed at the end of her last sentence, waving the help from Smyth away. "I'm fine."

"You've been coughing for days."

"Yeah, dickhead, it's called a cold."

"She's right," Alicia said. "I have one too. You never tried to hug the tits off me, Lancelot."

"And me," Drake put in.

"This is *Transylvania*," Dahl said seriously, with an accent. "There are far worse things out there than colds."

The team looked at him, surprised, and then all laughed together. It lightened the situation considerably and put a temporary end to Lauren's suggestions. As on every previous day, they would revisit all the diverse solutions later. It had become an unspoken agreement.

The team would stick together.

They watched without word as a whorl of mist seeped under the ill-fitting door and swirled around. The night pressed hard against the windows, the walls and the foundations of the house, as if representing the new enemy that hunted them.

Another enemy. So many, they had lost count.

"Y'know something," Hayden said. "I never mentioned this before. But winning, succeeding in whatever you do . . . simply paints you as a target. In many ways."

"Not just a target," Dahl said. "We could be on anyone's agenda, and used in a thousand ways. Even us, a team that supposedly does not exist."

Gravity was returning to the room, thick and fast. Alicia sensed it and all the morose gloom it brought; she rose quickly to her feet, and started to undress.

Pausing with her T-shirt raised above her head she looked around and said, "So, you guys gonna fuck off, or what? Drake promised to do the Time Warp on me tonight." She threw the shirt in the corner. "Now, I don't really know what that means, but I'm dying to find out."

She started on her jeans, unbuckling the belt.

The room emptied fast.

CHAPTER TWO

It was no coincidence that the shrewd, streetwise New Yorker, Lauren Fox, mentioned returning to DC that night. She'd thought it all through and planned it for days. She'd walked the roads, learned the routes, found out the time the first bus stopped by. In addition, she had scoped out a car that she knew how to hotwire. Leaving a double trail was better if they decided to follow.

Smyth would want to, maybe Mano too. Maybe even Dahl. But the others had seen right through to the core of her plan, considered her role and resolution, and saw that it might succeed. She was willing to accept whatever consequences came her way.

Wrapping up warm, cursing the cold she'd picked up, she left her room just before dawn when the night was still dark. The mist helped conceal her but also jabbed at her lungs. She managed to stifle another cough before moving on. Soon, she was clear of her room, walking a familiar path toward the center of town. Around her, though she could not see, homes were built atop the undulating slopes, all following the angles of the mountains and valleys. Some flickering lamps shone out against the darkness, sparse and bare, promising a safe haven, but Lauren pressed on through the wet murk, head down, and stuck to her pre-planned route.

Vague sounds caught her attention, sharp over her softly padding footsteps. A dog barking, a large bird taking flight. A car burbled over up ahead to the right, revealing that she wasn't the only one abroad in the chilling gloom, and offering an odd, small amount of comfort.

The long walk. The last walk. Would she ever see them all again? A team of strangers that had gradually become family. A bunch of misfits that had accepted her, befriended her and valued her opinion. She wasn't like them at all, wasn't built to fight and hunt and kill enemies. She hadn't even had much chance to showcase her skills, but when she did . . . they all respected her.

They would respect her again now.

Drake awoke to see Alicia staring out of the bedroom's single window, the glass foggy, a weak, stray beam of sunlight trying to find its way inside.

"Dawn?" he asked.

"A little after."

"Come back to bed. We have nothing to rush out for."

"Yeah, ain't that true."

Drake propped himself up on an elbow. Alicia was fully dressed as though prepared to head straight out on a mission. "Is something wrong?"

"It's all wrong. We should be out there. Fighting. Hunting. Putting the fear of the Devil into every would-be killer that crosses our path."

"Nobody asked for this."

"That's not the point."

He shifted a little. "Don't you . . . ache?"

She turned her head toward him, the blond of her hair catching the fragile light. "For what?"

"I don't mean mentally, Alicia, I mean physically. All the injuries, the wounds, the bruises; they add up."

"Of course I ache. I just get on with it."

"So take some time to heal."

Alicia shook her head. "Shit, Drakey, do you even know me?"

Of course he did. He knew her innermost thoughts and feelings, her fears and ambitions. He knew that right now she wanted nothing more than to keep moving, with friends; simply set her feet on a forward course. It was the inaction that hurt her.

"If it helps we're gonna have to leave here soon. We don't need more attention."

"How are the funds?"

"Not bad, love. Not bad. Yorgi appropriated a small fortune

from that safe near where they were keeping the Sword of Mars."

She managed a smile. "Ah, yes, well at least that promises another future adventure."

Drake climbed out of bed naked and padded over to her. "Plenty more to come."

"Are you trying to distract me?"

"Who?" Drake bent down to kiss her. "Me?"

The sudden knock at the door was like a grenade going off. Drake felt his heart leap into his mouth. Alicia was off her chair and taking cover just as a familiar voice rang out.

"You decent?"

"Smyth? What the fuck do you want?"

"We have a problem. Main room—two minutes."

Alicia wrenched the door open, sparing Drake no embarrassment, but Smyth was already gone, knocking hard on the next door.

Drake dressed quickly and followed Alicia to the meeting room. Most of the crew were already assembled, and within minutes the rest had joined them.

Hayden addressed the team.

"Lauren has taken off. Sometime during the night. We don't know how far away she is or how she's traveling."

Drake was surprised but spoke up immediately. "Bus station is a short walk."

"Tried it," Smyth said. "The first bus left two hours ago. We can catch up pretty easily."

Drake saw where this was going. "You want to catch her? Bring her back? And then what?"

Smyth stared as if he didn't understand the question. "What are you talking about?"

"She hasn't been kidnapped," Hayden said softly. "She wasn't coerced. Lauren left of her own free will. Do you want to be the one that *makes* her come back?"

Smyth bristled. "Well, well, yeah. If I have to. She can't . . . she can't just . . ." He ran out of steam.

"First of all," Mai said. "Are we sure she left of her own accord?"

Hayden shrugged. "Her room's tidy. Nothing amiss. Her luggage is all gone. Why would anyone just take Lauren? Oh, and we found this note."

She placed an A4 sheet on the table, on which were written just a few lines.

Don't come after me. I'll be in touch. It's my turn now.

Smyth looked away. Drake felt a rush of admiration for the New Yorker. "She's going to help us. Like *she* said—don't underestimate what she can do."

The team sat down, reflecting on what Lauren might have to endure. The outcome was entirely unknown, and she knew it.

"We should leave this place," Mai said. "Today."

"Sprite's right," Alicia said instantly, then. "Whoa, what did I just say?"

"Alicia," Mai glared at her. "We've been working together for what: five years now? And before that, on occasion. You really need to come up with a new and improved name."

"I do? Well, here's a few that roll right off the tip of my tongue—"

"Before we get to that," Drake hastily interrupted. "Shall we start packing? We should put a fair distance between us and Transylvania over the next few days."

Smyth looked unhappy. Hayden reminded him that Lauren was going to volunteer all the information. Hopefully Crowe would get involved.

Hopefully, they could trust Crowe.

Either way, they were in Lauren Fox's hands for a while now.

Drake walked over and took his first proper look out of the window that morning. The night mist had cleared away to reveal a rolling valley, dotted by trees and small houses, bright colors against the green and brown of nature. The skies were covered with gray clouds and a light drizzle greeted the rising dawn. People were moving out there, going about their business. Since they had chosen a guesthouse right on the edge of town they could see for miles—at least in two directions. The shambling old place also had the advantage of several egress and exit points.

"Meet at the cars in an hour?" he suggested.

A muted chorus of agreement met his ears. The team were rising when there came one more loud knock at the door.

Drake couldn't help but glance at Smyth.

"Don't look at me," the angry soldier snapped.

Hayden sprang to the side of the door; Mai sidling to the other side. Kinimaka took cover behind the sofa and then started to shout: "Who is it?" his head visible just above the cushions.

Hayden waved him down. They shouldn't reveal themselves yet.

Drake and the others edged to the sides of the room. No sound was heard inside or outside, and of course, there was a rear exit. Yorgi was already there, inching the door open a crack and Kenzie was right at his side.

The Israeli signaled that they keep quiet. Most of them rolled eyes back at her. Dahl was at her shoulder and then the three of them were gone.

Drake waited, imagining them creeping around the side of the house, vigilant in every direction. It shouldn't take long . . .

Another knock. Of course, anyone seeking to do them harm wouldn't be knocking, but it could be some kind of diversion. They could take nothing for granted.

"Hold it!" Kenzie's voice, commanding and harsh.

"Not a problem. Just don't shoot."

Drake frowned. That voice sounded familiar.

Alicia narrowed her eyes, staring at the front door. "I'm sure—"

"What do you want?" Kenzie asked. "Best be quick, old man. I haven't killed anyone for a week."

"I want you to take it easy," the familiar voice said. "And I want Drake and Alicia to get their arses out here."

"Bloody hell," Drake said. "I'd know that voice anywhere. Eventually."

Alicia used the comms system to stand Kenzie down in her unique manner. "Put it away, bitch."

Drake walked straight to the door and pulled it open. "Michael Crouch," he said. "Been a while, mate. How did you manage to find us?"

His old boss grinned. "You know me. Contacts everywhere. I don't like to reveal my secrets."

They dragged him inside, confronted him gravely. "This time," Dahl said, "you do."

"Alicia here—" the Englishman shrugged "—I have her personal number of course, for getting in touch when we need her help. I simply tracked it."

To a person, the entire team turned to stare at the blond woman.

"Are you kidding?" Drake said.

"What?" Alicia protested. "Only the chosen few have access to my personal number. Do you have it, Smyth? Kenzie? Mai? No, I rest my case."

"And what if they'd kidnapped this Crouch person?" Kenzie asked, staring at Alicia.

Drake managed to stifle a laugh. Alicia did no such thing. "Don't be a fool."

Crouch maneuvered his way to the center of the room. Though absent from their small circle for some time, Crouch had previously worked alongside them and separately with Alicia. His loyalty was absolute and unquestioned and it was a testament to the allegiance and trust he inspired that everyone in the room simply stood and listened to what he had to say.

"I need your help."

"That's easier said than done . . ." Hayden spoke fast and then deliberately let the sentence hang.

"I know your situation. I know what happened. Well . . . I've chosen to believe a certain one of the conflicting reports—let's put it that way. Someone across the pond is seriously pissed at you, my friends, and that needs taking care of."

"Is that why you're here?" Kinimaka asked.

"No. My mission is much more important."

Drake blinked. "What could be more important than unravelling a conspiracy that may stretch all the way to the President?" he asked.

"Egypt," Crouch said.

"Egypt?"

"Yeah, sandy place with a big river running through it. Turn left at the top of Saudi."

"All right, I know where Egypt is," Drake said. "What's the problem?"

Crouch reached for a glass of water, settling himself on one of the room's long, sagging sofas. "I wouldn't bother you if it weren't vital. And I do believe you'll hate what I have to say." He took a breath and another gulp of water.

"An ancient Egyptian tomb is about to be unsealed and unveiled to the public. Barely disturbed by the authorities except to make it safe, it will be unveiled with everything in-situ. The Egyptians are billing the event as top-level, all sorts of socialites, celebrities and well-known figures are attending. They're going to feed it across the Internet for maximum exposure."

Drake sighed. "And that's a problem why?"

Alicia smirked. "You weren't invited?"

Even Crouch cracked a smile. "Well, no. But that's not the worst of it. They will unveil that tomb and then they will go inside. They're planning to unseal an inner chamber on the night itself to ramp up the drama of it all."

Hayden shifted on her feet. "I still don't see where we come in."

"It's the first seal," Crouch said with some fear in his voice. "And when the first seal is broken the curse is unleashed."

"What curse?" Alicia looked around. "Is this something to do with a bloody mummy?"

"What are you looking for, Michael?" Mai wondered.

Alicia spoke first: "You know, the usual. Scarabs. Dead things wrapped in bandages. I don't like the sound of where this is going."

Dahl leaned over to whisper. "But can it be worse than sleeping just a few miles from Dracula's castle?"

"Shut the hell up."

"Listen." Crouch sounded genuinely shaken, which surprised Drake. He'd rarely seen his old boss so anxious.

"The curse simply points us toward the final seal, of which there are seven. All the seals need to be broken, but the seventh is literally—Armageddon. The problem is—" he gulped more water "—as explained, when they break the first seal the whole thing is going to play out, right down to the wire, right down to the seventh seal."

"You're talking an ancient Egyptian curse?" Hayden said doubtfully. "Kinda like Tutankhamen? They say his tomb was cursed."

"No," Crouch said. "Nothing like that. I'm not talking about a curse as described by Hollywood or sensationalist press. This curse is very, very real, and very, very deadly. Believe me when I say I need you on this. I need the best. Anything less . . ." he sighed and looked out the window.

"And we're doomed."

CHAPTER THREE

"Hold on, hold on," Dahl said. "I think this needs a little more explaining before we start purchasing plane tickets, don't you?"

Crouch nodded quickly. "Apologies, I'm very conscious of the time constraints. Of course, we're still learning about ancient Egypt, still discovering old scrolls and hieroglyphics and, in some cases, still trying to decipher an archaic language. Every day springs a new surprise. The amount of warnings, curses and caveats out there are enough to fill a library. We all know this supernatural stuff is pure bollocks." He paused. "Except Alicia, naturally, but a *curse* can have dozens of connotations. It could be a warning intended to *help* explorers; it could be a mischievous riddle; it could be part of a map that helps locate something carefully hidden from grave robbers. It all falls under the general label of 'curse.'"

Alicia put her feet up. "Can someone make the popcorn? I'm enjoying listening to Dad ramble on."

Crouch ignored her. "Luckily, you all know my lifelong passion for investigating ancient relics. My job—" he glanced at Drake "—with the SAS and other regiments got in the way for thirty years, but since I left the Army I have been thrown headlong into quite a few adventures."

"Yeah," Alicia said wistfully. "And most of them were cool."

Drake knew she was thinking about her last op as part of the Gold Team, where Zack Healey had been killed. The young man's death haunted her daily and, though she bore no guilt, a part of her had died that day too. Drake saw the same look in Michael Crouch's eyes. He cleared his throat gently. "Understood mate, we know you're one of the best in the world at this kind of stuff."

"Well, thanks. I try to keep abreast of everything that is happening in the relic hunter world." He shrugged. "What else do I have to do? Leads spring up weekly, but most of them pan out to nothing. Less than nothing." He gave another shrug. "They're a waste of time. But the curse associated with the Tomb of Amenhotep has existed for centuries along with uncountable others, not particularly famous but prominent enough to make certain people in certain circles take notice. Now, when the tomb was found and the unveiling announced I naturally sat forward and took notes."

"What makes you believe it's real?" Hayden asked, still unconvinced.

"It may not be," Crouch said. "But *if* this is the first seal and, inside, there's something that points toward a second—are you willing to take that chance?"

"I dunno," Kenzie said. "What *is* this curse?"

Crouch spoke from memory. "Translated into modern English it reads: Find the seven seals for seven tombs and settle the fate of men. Follow the lost symbol that entombs the Ancient Doomsday Machine. Break the seven seals of Egypt and start the End of Times."

"Crap," Drake said, shaking his head. "Even cast out as we are we still end up in the middle of it."

"I wouldn't have sought you out now, traveled all this way, if it weren't vital."

"I know that," Drake said. "But you're still playing a hunch."

"There's no gray area here," Crouch insisted. "The texts clearly state that the Tomb of Amenhotep guards the first seal. Nobody knew of this tomb until quite recently. The fact that we now know it exists gives credibility to the text and the seven seals curse."

"But an ancient doomsday machine?" Dahl said. "Come on, man."

Crouch shrugged. "I've seen less believable theories proved true. And so have you. I'm convinced we have to be there at the unveiling and get a look at this tomb before anyone else. We don't know what we're looking for, we don't know what we'll find there, but it's the 'better safe than sorry' principle I'm convinced we should follow."

"It may not even exist," Kenzie protested softly. "And you

want all of us to walk right in there?"

"I don't know you," Crouch studied the Israeli. "But I assume since you're here, you're good. I believe we—"

"Sorry," Alicia suddenly interrupted. "We forgot to introduce you. Kenzie, this is Michael Crouch, ex-SAS and Ninth Division commander. Michael, this is Bridget McKenzie, Dahl's new whore."

The Swede closed his eyes in resignation. Kenzie watched his reaction and then added no more. Crouch shook his head at Alicia.

"Still good at making friends, I see. As I was saying, I believe we need the whole team in place, ready, in case the so-called curse proves to be true. You can be assured there will be others present and prepared to hunt for this doomsday machine. You can be assured there will be corrupt organizations represented, with similar orders. Our enemies will be crawling all over this, folks. I think we need to look sharp about it too."

"You don't want to chance it that someone ancient planted a series of clues that leads to a terrible, hidden power," Hayden said. "I get that, and understand. But still . . . it's a risk. Even government-sanctioned SPEAR might not have been sent to this party."

"It's true," Mai said as Yorgi nodded. "Sometimes, we do find it hard to play well with others."

"Yeah, but that's because the others are assholes," Smyth growled. "All of 'em."

Mai nodded her agreement. "I do have a question for you, Michael. You say when the seal is broken we will find a clue to the second seal. How do we find the *first* seal?"

"It's part of the curse. 'Follow the lost symbol that entombs the Ancient Doomsday Machine.' It's saying the seals are the way to the machine, they *entomb* it. You have to break them all to find it."

"And the lost symbol?" Kinimaka asked.

"The most famous lost symbol of all time. Of all Egypt and quite possibly of the whole world. That is my guess."

Alicia grumbled. "Okay, just imagine for one second that I'm dumb. True, it's a tough job, but I'm sitting here trying to think of the most famous lost symbol of all time—" she shrugged "— and I'm coming up with a blank."

Surprisingly, nobody agreed with her. Drake saw even Kenzie was stumped. "Come on, Michael. What's the most famous lost symbol of Egypt?"

His ex-boss smiled. "Oh, if we weren't in such a hurry," he said. "I could have so much fun with this. Of course, it is the golden capstone that should top the Pyramid of Giza, which in itself is one of the most important and famous symbols in the world."

"Last surviving wonder of the world," Kenzie said.

Alicia tapped the arm of the sofa. "Until recently. I heard on the news they found another."

"None of that really matters," Crouch broke through. "The Pyramid of Giza is one of the most geometrically flawless structures ever built. Countless men and women have devoted their entire careers to studying it. But to newcomers, or if you look at a photo, one thing is plainly obvious. It has no top."

Drake sipped at a bottle of water and checked to make sure Kinimaka and Smyth were ready to check the perimeter. Hayden gave them a nod and they were out the door. No point playing the odds now.

Crouch continued. "It's the most famous missing treasure of Planet Earth."

Alicia coughed. "Now hold on a minute—"

"This month at least," Crouch amended with a small smile. "But the Giza capstone was reputed to be made of solid gold. Of course, it may have been looted; it may never have existed; it may be lying in a rich man's collection somewhere or even buried under tons of sand. In truth, the pyramid is a thirteen-acre, six-million-ton puzzle; larger than life and impossibly perfect."

"Looted?" Kenzie asked. "How on earth would anyone ever accomplish that?"

Alicia stared. "You're the expert. You tell us."

"But of course she is right." Crouch nodded. "The capstone

would have weighed many tons, even if it was smaller than many think. You see, I believe not only capstone is missing but several more layers of stones. It would have stood six to nine meters high atop the Giza pyramid . . ." He let that sink in for a while.

"Isn't the capstone one of the most important parts of a pyramid?" Dahl asked.

"Some would say the most important part," Crouch said. "Which is why it has to be the lost symbol. To my mind, it is also the ancient doomsday weapon."

Drake stared. "What? Why?"

"You said it yourself. It is the most important part of the pyramid. It has a power all its own. And it is the focal point of the curse. The lost symbol you must follow." He shrugged.

"But how could a capstone be so powerful?" Dahl asked.

"Well, maybe it isn't. I'm still looking into it. But all the clues point that way. And, Torsten, it was incredibly large."

Drake didn't want to commit before the team conferred, but knew time was short. "All we have to do is search this first tomb for a capstone symbol? And we're hoping we find bugger all, right-?"

"That's one way of putting it," Crouch said.

"The heathen way," Dahl groaned. "The moment I think I've managed to curb his ignorance we're back to square bloody one."

Drake gave him the finger.

"And we're back to the multi-million-dollar question," Mai said. "How can we all travel to Egypt and attend a star-studded gala whilst searching for a lost symbol?"

Drake frowned. "Yeah, it's not exactly an everyday question."

"So you're coming?" Crouch whistled his relief. "Thank you. I couldn't do this without you."

"Coming?" Alicia said. "Sounds like the party of the year to me, Michael. Just imagine all the booze we can drink in the knowledge that we're helping to keep the world safe."

Kenzie sidled close to Crouch. "Do you have access to a sword?"

CHAPTER FOUR

Kimberley Crowe, the United States Secretary of Defense, found herself once again seated in the dark, private, walnut-paneled room with two men she had begun to despise. General George Gleeson sat opposite and the CIA high-flyer, Mark Digby, sat to one side, right foot crossed over the left and wagging comfortably.

"Tempest," Digby said, smiling "That is the code name."

"You're official now?" Crowe asked quickly.

Digby winced. "I didn't say that. And don't you mean *we're* official?"

"So, what are we?" She so badly wanted to say *you* not *we,* but resisted. "And what is Tempest?"

The general diverted the questioning. "We are evaluating the recent efforts of SEAL Team 7. I was always doubtful about sending military men after military men. We need something different. If Tempest is to succeed we need an edge."

"How many . . ." Crowe hesitated, "know about Tempest?"

"Not many." Digby was deliberately vague. "A presidential aide is one of our better placed colleagues. But there are many working for us quite blindly. It's always the best way." He kicked his feet some more. "Better deniability for us."

Crowe didn't like where this was going. The two men seated in front of her had never been so open before about their secret operation and the circumstances behind SPEAR's disavowing. She wondered what the true nature of Tempest really was.

"In the end," she said. "SEAL Team 7 were unsanctioned. That should never have happened. I'm not entirely sure I'm on board with this, gentlemen,"

Digby sat forward sharply. "Then *get* on board, Madam Secretary. You're with us now, all the way. Just as culpable. Just as involved. Do not start acting the fucking angel now."

Crowe winced inside, but gave Digby a hard look. So there it was. Low down, dirty and mean. She was a part of this, as liable as they. Throughout her life she'd faced immeasurable odds; she'd overcome most and failed at a few. Now though, it appeared she would have to concede to get ahead.

She looked away from Digby, allowing him to win the staring battle. "And what of this seven seals problem? How do you see it benefiting Tempest?"

Gleeson fiddled with the buttons on his jacket as if impatient. "The tomb unveiling must be monitored. It may reveal some ancient weapon and we all know, after what happened a few years ago in Iceland and then the discovery of the tombs of the gods, that it may now directly link to Tempest and our ultimate goal. Everything we have worked for."

"And it may lead to nothing," Digby admitted. "But we have to be sure."

Crowe acquiesced. "Of course."

"Covert ops working indirectly for Tempest will be on hand," Gleeson told them. "If anything shows up they'll find it."

"And SPEAR?" Crowe steered the conversation to a place where she felt more comfortable. "What plans are you making for them?"

"What can we do?" Gleeson blustered, suddenly looking like he might throw a fit. "We helped create them. We helped them. Now . . . how do we stop them?"

"I think that's taking it a little too far, General," Crowe said. "They've saved this country countless times."

"Listen—" Digby waved that away with a flap of his hand "— right here, right now; this is what counts. History is for poets and has-beens. SPEAR are connected. They have a mix of first-rate skills. What we need is something totally different. Something they won't be expecting."

Crowe made sure she looked impressed. "Interesting. And that is?"

"A new section of Tempest," Digby said. "A very special team."

Crowe looked between the men. "Like SPEAR?" She tried to hide all traces of irony from her tone.

"To succeed Tempest will need to . . ." Digby picked his words carefully, "skirt the line, not stick to it. Walk through the shadows. It has to dwell between the dark and the light."

"Why?" Crowe had to challenge that.

"Because our long-term plan, to gather together all the weapons of the gods, will attract attention from every single part of the world—the good, the bad and, particularly, the ugly. We should be able to deal with that attention without . . . revealing ourselves. Our methods have to remain covert."

"The Central Intelligence Agency should be all over that," Crowe said.

"Well, that depends where we all want to end up."

Crowe was fully aware of everything Digby might mean, including a hole in the ground. She was aware that the cards were now well and truly laid out on the table. "I'm assuming you have already engaged this *different* solution?"

"Oh yeah." Gleeson showed positive animation for the first time. Even a little glee. "An old-fashioned, balls-out blood-warrior called Luther. Old style, no rules, no book. Luther has never used a computer in his life, nor anything bigger than a cellphone. You set this guy on someone's track and he's a fucking bloodhound. He'll track SPEAR down using just his nose and bury 'em all where they lie. Never to be found."

Crowe suppressed shock. She'd heard of Luther. Just the legend—but that was more than enough to give her nightmares.

"Luther and his team?" she breathed. "They're Judgment Day, for God's sake. You want real noise and destruction? You want catastrophe? Are you kidding me?"

"As far as I can tell," Gleeson gave her a heartfelt sigh, "they're the only kind of team that stands a chance of taking SPEAR out."

"Plus," Digby said, "every local authority around the world, when they hear Luther's involved, will get the hell out of the way."

Crowe breathed a tense breath. *Not everyone, but most.* Digby had it about right. Her own knowledge of Luther and his band of old-world misfits was purposely vague, but what she'd been able to pick up during her short term in office was enough to make her heart pound.

"You know," she said, "something doesn't smell exactly right. Luther is potentially worse for American relations than SPEAR. Yet, we've condemned them for the events in Peru that nobody except us knows much about." She held up her hands, seeing protest coming. "Now I know . . . I know it's all about Tempest. I'm not sure what your endgame involves for these weapons of the gods, but I do understand."

"America, leader of the free world, forever," Gleeson said with satisfaction.

"Based on what knowledge exactly?" Crowe asked, realizing they were getting side tracked but unable to stop fishing for a little more information.

"The Swords of Babylon," Gleeson said. "Remember that? Let me refresh your memory. All the power unleased from the tombs on that day came from the weapons of the gods. It destroyed the tombs. But we still have a list of weapons. Weapons that are still out there. The Sword of Mars, for instance. This Doomsday Machine in Egypt. This capstone, we believe, is endowed with the same power as the weapons of the gods. Perhaps it even was one. . ." he shrugged. "It makes sense, with all these other weapons appearing."

"Disappearing. . ." Crowe said drily.

"Well, yes, but we must find them. Find them all and use them for our own purposes. The Sword of Mars has now gone, but the great capstone is close at hand. Several others that were lost, stolen or traded. What can they do?" He gave her a grin of excitement. "I mean—*what can they do?*"

Crowe was momentarily shocked at his excitement. She also knew all about the old Tesla devices and how the brilliant engineer and inventor had created immense weapons out of seemingly nothing. Remembering more of the other mysteries from the ancient world she began to wonder just how many might be out there.

"We've proven that the old gods were once real," Digby said.

"No," Crowe said. "SPEAR did that."

"As you wish. But, if these gods were once men that inspired courage and leadership and did great deeds, elevating them to deities in the eyes of their fellow men, then maybe their weapons were powerful too. That's Tempest, Madam Secretary, and Luther is its cutting edge."

Crowe managed a nod. "You mean bludgeon, I assume?"

Digby smiled. "So long as he crushes whomever we tell him to crush, that's fine with me."

CHAPTER FIVE

Of course, FrameHub were gods, they all knew that. Not a single person but a collective, they ruled their kingdom with an iron rod, and their kingdom was the World Wide Web.

FrameHub looked out on the world through liquid crystal displays, monitoring in real time, taking anything and everything that they wanted to. This was the only world they cared about, not the ordinary day that existed above their carefully concealed bunker, beyond the hard concrete walls and outside the network of security systems, barriers, firewalls and next-generation tech that protected their environment.

FrameHub Fellow, codename: Piranha, spoke a word to grab the attention of the collective. It was a "hot word", something to make the group take notice, as normally they would never speak, lost in their data-filled world as they were.

He waited until they all paused in their work. "Today, is the day." He adjusted his glasses, feeling foolish, unused to social interaction and hating it. "I have your emails and messages." They all preferred to email, even those sitting beside each other. "Today, two assignments begin at once. The war games and the Egyptian tombs. I mean . . ." He couldn't stop a smile. "Isn't that cool?"

Seven similar-looking geeks grinned back at him: young, enthusiastic, utter geniuses in the computer field and consummate hackers.

Piranha went on: "First the Egyptian tombs game. The hired mercenaries are in place . . ." Several grins and chuckles at that. "We are hoping for success at the first seal, the first level, and hope to move on to the second. If government chatter is anything to go by this could be huge. So many people heading to the unveiling, so many *dangerous* people, it'll be fun. Remember when you played *Call of Duty* for the first time? This is that, in real life."

More chortling.

Piranha went sober for a moment. "Hiring these men as we do, online, is at best—chancy, but Vladimir, our man in charge, does appear up to the job. And he likes the money. But, of course, it's not our main mission."

"But it is a cool one," Codename: Manta spoke up. "Knowledge is power. And our ultimate goal is power. This is perfect."

"Agreed, Manta. We will follow the clues and own the machine. As you say, knowledge is power."

"We must stay hidden," Barracuda fretted. "Off the radar. At the moment, nobody knows we even exist."

"Of course, it's better that way. Don't worry, we will. And now for our real life war game."

They were interested, these vicious, distant gods. In one stroke they could cripple a town or a city, shut down a bank, lose a man's money, change a woman's entire life; but here they sat— eager and hopeful about the outcome of a new dream.

"Everything's in place, but we all play our part. Moray? You have Turkey. Orca and Manta, you have Greece. I'll take Egypt along with Barracuda and the rest are backup. All right?" He was desperate to get out of the mini-spotlight.

"There is one other," Moray said slowly. "The approach should be made quickly."

Piranha hesitated, caught off guard. "Karin Blake? I know we agreed to approach and offer her to be a part of this, but I don't agree that now is the right time."

"I do," Moray said.

The collective spoke up, as they rarely did, and came down on the side of Moray. The approach to Karin Blake would have to be made.

"Encrypt it well," Piranha said. "We want her because she's our equal. It will do no good to let her know who and where we are."

Moray glared as if insulted. Piranha realized what he'd said and shrugged in apology. He rushed ahead to get it finished and hopefully avoid any more physical confrontations.

"Let's go. Turkey, Greece and Egypt will be ransomed for our pleasure, our war game. Just for fun, because we are FrameHub and we do what the hell we want. Three countries threatened, the first to come up with the ransom wins. Are we ready?"

"Can't wait to see what happens to the ones that don't."

Barracuda rubbed his hands together happily.

Piranha stared. "They will be destroyed," he said carefully.

"We all agreed to that, Barracuda."

"I know, I know." Barracuda waved it away. "I was speaking metaphorically. Like . . . I can't wait to watch!"

"Me too," Mantra echoed.

As did the entire collective.

"The two losers will suffer total network destruction. Countrywide commotion. Uproar. Riots. Death. It will be war games, for real. Roads blocked, hospitals disrupted. Governments chasing ghosts. And when it's all done, we will be millionaires several times over."

He watched for reactions. There were none. This collective didn't need money. It had everything it needed right here in this room. Because the outside world didn't exist for them, the actions they perpetrated in it meant very little. Piranha knew this made them the most dangerous collective alive.

"FrameHub is go." He grinned. "Make ready the ransom demands. Don't forget, we expect them to ignore the initial communication and wait for something more . . . persuasive. Moray, you ready that. We'll need it prepared for short notice."

"And the Egyptian game?" Moray asked. "Are we fully prepped there?"

"Oh, yes. Along with the American government, the British, Mossad and China, it seems. Everyone wants a sniff inside Amenhotep's tomb. I imagine there will be others too— unknowns. Our mercenaries will surely earn their money."

"Joking aside," Barracuda said. "We should ready the secondary option. With so many players involved in the game tonight it will be messy even for us."

Piranha nodded. "Agreed. So . . . let the games begin."

CHAPTER SIX

Whilst Crouch arranged for a discreet flight out of Romania, the SPEAR team continued to debate the rights and wrongs of all that had happened and what they were about to do.

"This Crouch can facilitate us all?" Kenzie asked, watching the newcomer work.

Drake nodded firmly. "You haven't met him before, but I worked alongside him for years. Alicia too. He's the best connected person I've ever known. Someone once said he had more connections than British Telecom. I would say he's one of a handful of people in the world right now that could pull this off."

"And why didn't we call him first?"

Drake made a face. "It was on my mind, but we'd hardly settled on a plan yet."

"What of Lauren?" Smyth fretted gruffly. "You all happy with her leaving?"

Dahl squared up to the soldier. "We've been through this and more than once. If you feel so badly, Smyth—" he nodded toward the door "—go after her."

The other bits of conversation stuttered as people sensed conflict. Smyth's face was a clash of emotion; the soldier being pulled every which way. In the end though, surely nothing needed saying. Lauren had made her decision without duress; it was technically correct that she was innocent; also correct that their best chance lay with her being inside the capitol. Smyth didn't like it, but she had forced him to live with it.

"Crap." He walked over to the coffee machine and began to pour.

Drake watched Crouch make several calls. He trusted the man implicitly, despite Alicia's odd misgiving, or maybe because of them. It was an odd day when Alicia didn't show signs of mistrust. He saw now that she was happy to be moving on and wondered if, at her core, she really wanted to settle down with a soldier like him. The rest of the team were almost enjoying the anonymous break, he was sure, at least for a little while.

Maybe not Dahl. The Swede had been facing the toughest decision for a while. Johanna, his wife, was wavering between divorce and reconciliation, keeping Dahl guessing. Kenzie had taken a shine to the man, offering much more. Drake wouldn't get involved unless he was asked. It was the way with them.

As for the others—Hayden was trying again with Mano Kinimaka, aware that her words and actions of the past few months had been unnecessarily hurtful. The Hawaiian, always easy-going and loyal, took it in the best possible way whilst looking more than a little confused. Kenzie was being Kenzie—in the short time he'd known her, Drake had never fully trusted her, and whilst he saw her good heart and how useful she could be to the team he still couldn't bring himself to fully trust her. The deck on Kenzie had yet to be fully played.

Yorgi. The Russian thief was quiet as always; a part of the team but remaining aloof. He may have killed his parents in cold blood but Drake blamed them for the young thief's state of mind. He would never recover, but still a trip out to that ice-cold Russian field stood firmly in their future.

And then there was Mai Kitano. With her personal life settling of late along with her grief at being forced to kill a low-key Yakuza player and then confront his daughter, Mai was taking it easy. Drake thought she might be scared to show up on anyone's radar for fear of something else terrible happening to her or her family. Grace was fine though, living in Tokyo. Drake saw Mai passing time, probably hoping the next big event might finally turn out to be something good.

The team had been through hell these past years, no less recently with the attentions of Tyler Webb and his cache of secrets. Their current situation prevented them for searching for Webb's motherlode, and of the few he'd revealed all but one was out in the open.

One of you is dying.

The toughest one of all. Drake didn't want to believe it, but so far all of Webb's statements had proven correct. He shrugged the moment of pessimism away, looking over as Crouch finally finished up and walked to the center of the room.

"Now that's a mix of good and bad news," the man said. "If ever I've heard one."

The conversation died and every pair of eyes switched to him.

"Problem?" Dahl asked.

"Not immediate, but . . ." Crouch shook his head, clearly rattled. "First the good news. The plane is ready and fuelled close to Avram Airport. We have a private airfield nearby and a Cessna waiting. If we make haste now we can be in the air within the hour."

"Not sure if anyone has asked yet," Kinimaka said, "but when is this event?"

"Tomorrow night," Crouch said. "We have time to fly in and get settled. Buy you lot some nice threads."

"And the invites?" Drake imagined it would be hard rustling up ten invites at short notice.

"Already done," Crouch admitted. "Days ago."

"You know someone in the Egyptian secret service?" Dahl guessed. "And trust them completely? Our lives depend on it. We aren't paparazzi-plagued celebrities, but then I guess people *are* hunting us down."

"I covered it," Crouch told them. "My responsibility. So," he stared at Alicia. "Behave."

"You talking to me, bro?"

"Oh, yes I certainly am. My reputation is at stake."

Alicia made a point of staring askance at Kenzie. "It's not me you need to worry about. It's the sword maiden here."

Crouch held up a hand. "All right, we can discuss that later. I have to say I'm expecting this to work, hoping we can end this threat and then get our heads together to help you all return to the fold. I have contacts that whisper in the President's ear. I *was* hopeful."

Drake cleared his throat. "Is this the bad news, mate?"

"Until earlier today I was pretty confident I could help bail you idiots out," Crouch said. "Now . . . I'm wondering how many funerals I may have to attend."

Dahl sat up. "Excuse me?"

"Luther," Crouch said. "You may never have heard of him but the Americans have one giant ace up their sleeve. This man . . . he's retro dynamite. A throwback to the dark ages. A warrior in the old sense of the word."

"I've heard of Luther," Hayden said quietly. "You're saying they sent him after us?"

"I am. It's confirmed. Whatever this splinter group in the American government is planning, it must be huge. Game changing. Using Luther for anything less would be like throwing a wrecking ball at a wall made of foam."

"This Luther," Dahl said. "Can he be stopped?"

Hayden took a deep breath. "Unlikely. He's a bloodhound and doesn't stay on the grid. He'll receive no fresh updates, no communications. That's one of the reasons he's so dangerous and our government rarely resorts to using him. Luther will chase down his target, execute his orders, and then return home without making contact in between."

"Well," Drake said, "he doesn't know where we are now. We'll pop up in Egypt and then be gone." He shrugged. "I suggest we worry about him later."

Crouch gave him a look as if to say: "have you gone mad?", but then shrugged. "The die is cast," he agreed. "Sooner or later you will meet Luther and there's nothing we can do about it."

Alicia unfolded her legs, rising to her feet. "I do like the sound of this guy," she said. "He's my type. And if I'm being honest—his name rings a bell."

Drake stood with her. "Bloody hell, Alicia, do not tell me you've shagged him."

"Well . . ."

"That's a long list to sift through," Mai said. "Give her a few days."

"I'd remember," Alicia said. "I'm sure I'd remember a man like that. Does he have a—"

Drake quickly tuned her out, knowing from experience that she was about to get even more explicit. Crouch's reply: "how the hell should I know?" confirmed it. He wandered over to Dahl and met the Swede's eyes.

"You happy with all this?"

"Egypt? I think we have to. We're trusting Crouch's judgment but he hasn't steered us wrong before. Lauren will be on the inside in a day or two. I guess we should try to stay off this Luther's radar as long as we can."

"You scared of him?" Drake leaned in, playing a little mischief.

"Me?" Dahl protested. "I'm not even sure what the word means, pal."

Drake thought he was probably telling the truth. "You'd impress me more if you were at least a little scared."

"Fuck off, Drake."

Crouch motioned that they should get packing. The team split and then met up again ten minutes later, backpacks ready and faces set. Hayden led them out into the cold and toward the vehicles, most of them taking a last look around what had become, for them at least, the only quiet safe haven they'd known in years.

On the run we find peace, Drake thought with twisted irony. *What kind of soldiers have we become?*

A valley fell away before them, across which a brisk wind blew, bringing with it the scent of flower-strewn earth. Drake took it all in, and then they were inside the cars, fiddling with the heating and the satnav, settling in for a short drive during in which they were unable to relax.

Some time later they were in the air, not sad to leave Transylvania but unsettled as to what may happen next. As if the splinter group hadn't disturbed their lives enough there was now the threat of a supposed caveman called Luther. The plane rushed them all to Egypt, landing in an early darkness which couldn't have been planned better. Under the cover of night, they exited and ran down an empty runway to a quiet hangar.

Crouch called in for the car, which met them ten minutes later and transported them to a hotel in Cairo. Busy, hazardous and loud, the city streets were a harsh reminder of life after the tranquil peace they had experienced this last few days.

"A few hours' sleep," Crouch said, "and then we need to prep for tomorrow night. For the gala. Planning and research will be everything because, as we know, it's not just the whole world watching."

"It's Big Brother himself," Drake nodded, "in all his meanest guises."

"If anyone can do it, we can," Hayden said. "We're the best."

"Used to be," Smyth said. "Don't forget we're skating lightly now."

"That's one way of putting it," Alicia said. "And here's another—let's all fuck off to bed 'cause tomorrow's a bitch and to ride her properly, we're gonna need every ounce of energy." She turned away. "Night all."

Drake stared at the floor. "I have to sleep with that."

Alicia looked back. "We could always stick Yorgi down the middle."

The Russian looked terrified and quickly left the room. Drake fought to come to terms with the change of environment and the mounting pressure surrounding tomorrow night. Just like that, in an instant, they had to be at the top of their game.

This team, now more than ever, needed each other. Mentally as well as physically. In truth, he saw the upcoming gala as an interesting distraction provided they could fathom a foolproof escape. The team would gel, work for each other; they always did.

He watched Hayden and Kinimaka skirting around each other; Dahl and Kenzie strangely at odds whilst clicking; Smyth more worried and irascible than ever; Mai looking lonely as she wandered toward the stairs, cellphone in hand; Alicia still looking back at him and then surveying the room too.

"We'll be all right," she said. "All of us."

"I know that," Drake said quickly. "I know that."

He wished he felt as sure as he sounded.

CHAPTER SEVEN

Drake had been interested to see how the Egyptians would pull this off—a glitzy, high-profile show originating from a tomb with its contents in-situ, fortunately not too far from Cairo and the Giza plateau. It reminded him of the initial Odin show that the city of York had hosted, back when he was between careers. It reminded him of the danger-laden, ever-winding path his life had taken since.

The tomb entrance had been draped with enormous, velvet-red curtains, a stage erected outside and five steps constructed to lead up to that stage. A band played to one side, dressed in their finest suits, and high-profile glamorous guests mingled to the other, all pretending that the spotlights following their every move didn't exist. At the base of the stage stood rows of cameras and then a roped-off enclosure where members of the press and public were allowed to stand. A red carpet led straight through the middle.

Around the outside, the desert surroundings were untouched, dark and vast, but the television cameras wouldn't be focusing there. Behind the curtains, Drake saw nothing. The big unveiling was still a while away.

The team were hardly recognizable in their fashionable outfits. From suits in gray, black and deep blue for the men that fitted well and felt intensely uncomfortable, to gowns for the women that fitted even better but offered little freedom of movement. Crouch had begged them all to fit in with the general vogue tonight so as not to blow the op, but the sacrifices were large, as Alicia constantly reminded him.

They used the time before the event to vet the area and the gathering, splitting up into several groups to appear less conspicuous and achieve a better lay of the land. Drake and Alicia followed Dahl and Kenzie for a time, listening to the banter between them and wondering where the two were really at. For the Swede especially, the course of his life hung in the balance. Kenzie had already adjusted immensely, and tried harder every day. The dynamic between them was fluid and incredibly charged.

Hayden grabbed Kinimaka, much to the Hawaiian's surprise, and led the big man into the extravagant throng. Smyth, Mai and Yorgi took the outskirts, scanning for unwanted surprises.

"I'm seeing all the usual suspects," Alicia said to Drake. The team weren't using comms tonight for obvious reasons. "I see mercs, squeezed into their tight little jackets—" she paused for a second "—and trousers. Hello! A bit inappropriate, don't you think . . ."

Drake tried not to look. "C'mon, Alicia. Let's keep it professional."

Alicia gave him an innocent look. "When did we start that then?"

Just ahead, Kenzie and Dahl were having a similar conversation. "Three mercs right there," the Israeli said.

"Don't stare too hard," Dahl said.

"Why not? They'll assume I want to join them for ten minutes behind my boyfriend's back. That's all."

"That's all? Why would you think that?" Dahl hadn't even considered the option.

Kenzie laughed. "Because they're mercs, dummy."

"Ah, yes. I see now. Good point."

"I know them well. Their aspirations; goals; needs."

Dahl remembered Kenzie had commanded her own group of mercenaries for many years. "All the same?"

"No," Kenzie said. "Most wanted money, power and carnage but a few . . . there were a few that were different. Others just wanted to be led."

Dahl looked over. "And you were good at that?"

"Sure. I have no problems making a man do what I want."

Dahl lowered his voice. "See ahead? Definitely CIA. Undercover."

"Yeah, I was just about to say. Two more over there."

Dahl sought Crouch in the crowd. "I wonder what Michael

would say to that? Perhaps this splinter group have sent people too."

"Luther?" Kenzie asked.

"No. Judging from what I've heard Luther would simply surround and then assault this place with Howitzers."

"And the mercs?"

"Well, clearly Crouch isn't the only one in the know. I guess a third of the people here are government agents in some way."

"Unlike us," Kenzie said, then added: "Kinda sexy, huh?"

"What? What is?"

"Being disavowed. Hunted. Marked. I like it."

"Kenzie, you and I have very different perceptions of the word sexy."

"Really?" Kenzie moved closer so their hips came together. "I guess we could explore that later."

Dahl didn't move away, but didn't press forward either. The conflict battered him, making him lose focus for a moment. Then they came to the end of the stage and turned back, refusing yet another glass of champagne offered on a silver platter by a white-gloved waiter.

Drake and Alicia were a few steps behind.

"Looking at all the scattered Intelligence in here," the Yorkshireman said. "You can guarantee our location will be made known by the end of tonight."

"Worth the risk," Alicia came back. "If we do find the first seal."

Drake made a sound. "Depends on if we get caught, love."

She growled. "Listen to bloody Eeyore, here. If we weren't in this star-studded crowd I'd kick your arse off it."

"Star studded?" Drake whipped his head around. "Where?"

"Well, I saw someone who looked like that guy from Hawaii-Five-O earlier. Does that count?"

Drake frowned. "I was thinking more of the female variety."

"Oh, then no, just princesses and state wives I'm afraid."

"Bollocks."

"Check out the guards," Alicia said.

They veered away as they approached the curtain-covered

entrance to the tomb of Amenhotep. Two guards were standing to either side, carrying semi-automatic weapons and looking distinctly unimpressed. To the side of the stage stood a larger contingent, similarly armed and equipped for anything. Egypt itself was not the most stable country of late, and it seemed the Egyptians were prepared for the worst.

The time of the unveiling approached and the team came randomly together and gathered amidst the crowd as it grouped. An official stood before them, asking for quiet and then turning to face a particular set of cameras. He launched into a speech, explaining all about the tomb and how local archaeologists had discovered it. Excitement infused the air. Drake saw many guests almost hopping with glee at the thought of being allowed to enter a barely excavated, 'in-situ' tomb. The official went on to reassure them all that all they had done was to make it safe. *They* were the explorers, the archaeologists, the Howard Carters of today, and he asked for their cooperation in sharing any insights they might have.

Then, the curtains were thrown apart and the entrance revealed.

Drake saw exactly what he'd expected—a jagged entranceway bordered by hastily polished rocks and titivated with colorful embellishments. The entrance was lit by bright lamps and completely blocked any view of what was inside.

The official called forth the first batch of forty visitors. With help from Crouch's connections they were part of it and would be allowed twenty minutes inside before giving way to the next group. The tomb was large, it was whispered, and the way down narrow, so they wouldn't have too long to search.

Drake fell in line with Alicia like all the good civilians, making two rows behind four tour guides and more guards. Drake noted a couple of the mercenaries behind them and also several spies that had to be working for various undercover agencies.

"A regular convention," he whispered to Crouch. "Maybe make it a yearly meet."

"With all this *attention*," Crouch spoke the last word

meaningfully. "No one will be able to keep the findings secret."

"Unless they find and then destroy them . . ." Hayden put in ominously. "Keep your wits about you, guys."

Mai led their little group, paired with Yorgi. Drake came fourth in line and stared at the floor as the bright entrance lights filled their vision. He wanted as little adjustment time as possible. Happy chatter filled his ears, attesting that at least half of the first consignment were genuine civilians. *Thank the Lord for small mercies,* he thought. The spies he'd noted so far were good at their job, unnoticeable except to a highly trained eye. Many were in couples. The mercs, on the other hand, stood out like donkeys at a horse pageant, big and uncomfortable, sweating, smoking, not even pretending to listen to the historical sermon offered by their hosts, first by mouth and now as they moved into the top part of the tomb, by recorded voice.

"The tomb of the famous Amenhotep, thought lost to time, was recently discovered after a cave-in was triggered by archaeologists searching for something very different . . ."

Drake tuned it out as the passage came into focus. The walls were closer than he'd imagined, dusty, white and roughly hewn out of bare rock. Strings of lamps had been set up at their apex with the ceiling and these now led downward at a sharp angle.

"Step carefully," one of their guides said in English. "There is plenty of room to both sides so no need to worry about your cherished attire. Those with high heels should remove them, of course. Carry-bags are provided."

Drake bit his lip, unused to the pampering. Alicia checked to see if Yorgi was wearing heels. The small group moved down, a step at a time, taking care as some of the risers were uneven. Two minutes of shuffling passed and then they emerged onto a flat floor. Drake immediately felt the cloying, close atmosphere of the staircase fall away.

"How long have we got?" Hayden checked her watch.

The lead tour guide turned around and prepared to flick a switch.

"Welcome!" he said. "Welcome to the tomb of Amenhotep!"

CHAPTER EIGHT

With a plan already in place, as soon as the light came up, the team split and pretended to appear immensely impressed with the tomb. Drake did take a few moments to view the spectacle, taken aback by the sight. He'd seen his fair share of tombs before, but the Egyptians never failed to impress.

High, arched walls were adorned by multicoloured murals and stretched a few hundred feet back, where a slightly smaller arched door led to another part of the tomb. The lighting down here was better, provided by spotlights. Drake dropped several steps down into the tomb and started studying wall space.

The murals were large and plentiful, well-detailed, ranging from life-sized Egyptian figures in full regalia to smaller depictions of scarabs and animals. A murmur sprang up among the crowd, echoing loudly inside what was essentially a tunnel with a single exit. Drake saw the others split up and then followed what he thought were a pair of CIA spies to the left-hand side. Alicia pulled him along gently; the drawings were large here, but Drake wondered if the capstone—if it was here at all—might be disguised within the pattern of a sleeve or the design across a cup.

"Roped off area," Alicia muttered, nodding ahead. "Suspicious."

"If the Egyptians knew about the seal," Drake said, "we wouldn't be here. They wouldn't risk it."

"Unless they already removed it," Alicia said.

"I guess that's possible." Drake saw no signs of tampering so far, though the wall decorations were already starting to confuse his eyes. He blinked and stepped back.

Dahl, behind them, placed a hand on his shoulder. "Need your reading glasses?"

"Funny man." Drake sighed. "Try to keep your eyes on the walls and off your bird for five minutes, eh?"

"My bird?" The Swede struggled for a moment. "Oh, come on—"

Alicia grunted. "You'd have more luck asking his bitch to stop swinging swords around."

"She's not my bi—"

"Kids," Crouch hissed from a few feet away. "*Focus.*"

Alicia stared at Drake. "Yes, Dad." But they returned their attention to the walls, noting the potential CIA spies had moved ahead and were now studying the ceiling in earnest. All around the tomb, people were gazing at pictures and the tour guides answered questions up ahead. The SPEAR team cruised slowly down the length of the passage, taking everything in.

When they reached the end, Crouch turned, eyes expectant.

"Nothing," Hayden spoke for them all.

Crouch almost looked happy. "For once, finding nothing is a good thing."

Mai motioned toward the next door. "We haven't finished yet."

"I know, I know. Just feeling hopeful."

The Japanese woman inclined her head. "It's not easy," she acknowledged. "Always running, chasing, stopping bad things from happening to good people. But Michael, we've just endured almost a week of retirement. Believe me, *that's* harder."

"For some." Crouch nodded. "For others, it's a breath of fresh air."

He turned toward the next door as Alicia vocalized the incredulity that she might agree with Mai for once. Kenzie joined in and Drake envisioned a group hug occurring before they suddenly remembered where they were. Others were gathering at the next entrance and the tour guide was ready to move on. Through they went, a few at a time. Drake studied the doorway carefully as he stepped past but it was unadorned, nothing but crumbly white rock, stark under the bright lights. The dust drifting through the air caused him to sneeze and he heard an older man complaining to his wife in an undertone that he'd simply have to throw the suit away at the end of the night. Even *their* housemaid wouldn't be able to adequately remove all the dust.

The spies were three paces in front, along with another potential couple. No mercs were among them though, so Drake breathed easier. The next part of the tomb was slightly smaller and narrower, also containing a door, this time set into the right wall. Drake saw a sarcophagus, set low to the ground, roped off at this time. He moved to study the hieroglyphics upon its surface and those on the wall behind. Maybe one of those represented a capstone.

The strange search continued. Drake knew the spies and mercs above were probably unaware of SPEAR, and used that knowledge to remain highly visible, taking in every inch of the place. He smiled when he saw Kinimaka giving the sarcophagus plenty of space as he walked past. Knowing the Hawaiian, he'd brush against it and trigger an ancient trap, entombing everyone inside. The party split now, some entering the door set in the right wall and then another after that. A guide shouted that they had only eight minutes left. Drake saw dozens of murals and pictures, and tried to study each and every one, but saw nothing like the symbol he was looking for. He kept an eye on the spies too, noting them disappearing into the far part of the tomb.

"Three minutes," the helpful tour guide said.

Drake dragged Alicia through the final door, anxious to check the entire place before they whisked themselves off back into hiding again. It hadn't escaped their attention that television or press cameras might capture their faces, but as soon as they were clear they intended to leave Egypt far behind in the proverbial dust.

The final room was small, square and bare apart from more wall art. One of the tour guides told them that the lack of objects was due to ancient grave robbers, prevalent in their time, though one or two items had been 'liberated' and would soon be on display. Drake scanned the walls. Alicia glared up at the ceiling.

"Birds, beetles," she said. "Queens, slaves. There's even a bloody monkey up there."

"But no capstone," Drake murmured under his breath. "For once, I think, we've caught a lucky break."

"You really think so?" Crouch walked up to them, nodding at

the far corner of the far wall. "Check down there."

Drake closed his eyes momentarily. "You're taking the piss, right?"

"Just look. You tell me."

They drifted over, aware that the tour guides were already ushering people out. The mural that adorned the far wall was dark, composed of dusky golds, browns and blacks. It depicted two tall figures with Egyptian headdresses, staring at each other; one holding a club and the other a spear. They were seated on low stools and, as Drake bent down to get a better look, a tour guide patted him on the back.

"Sir? Time to leave and allow the next party down."

Drake stared from him to Alicia, trying to communicate silently.

"What?" the Englishwoman said. "You want me to *distract* him." She waggled her eyebrows.

"Shit," Drake spluttered. "No. I—"

"Happy to take one for the team," Alicia smiled brightly at the tour guide. "Now tell me. What's the Egyptian version of the Kama Sutra?"

Drake rose fast, put an arm around her shoulders, and whisked her away from an embarrassed looking escort. "Wait," Alicia protested. "Don't you need a look at the thingy?"

"No, Alicia. Crouch got a look at it."

"Oh, so why are we back here then?"

"Good question. I think we need to catch up."

They hustled out of the tomb, leaving the guide behind. Before they reached the exit staircase Drake had caught up to the ex-SAS commander.

"Didn't get chance," he huffed. "What did you see?"

Crouch made an improvised sign for 'walls have ears' and screwed his face up. "It's not good."

With that, they climbed the stairs and emerged once more into the fresh air. It was Crouch that stopped quickly and motioned to the ominous line-up of mercs and spies, scattered liberally among the civilians and preparing to go down next.

"Once that happens," he said. "The race will be on and the world will be a lot less safe."

"So it's real?" Drake asked.

"Oh, it's real," Crouch cursed quietly. "It's very real."

"In what form?"

"Explain later," Crouch stalled as they were ushered aside. "Basically, a depiction of the capstone set above the picture of another tomb, with a tiny set of specific hieroglyphics."

"You're sure it's genuine?" Kinimaka asked.

"As much as I can be out here, right now. But finding the second seal and another symbol will confirm it."

"And you think we should minimize the number of people that are about to see it?" Smyth said. "What do you want us to do? We're criminals right now, bud."

"I have an idea," Alicia said.

Drake and Dahl whipped their heads around, suddenly scared.

"Noo—"

CHAPTER NINE

Alicia raised her dress slightly and strutted over, bold as brass, to the forty-strong group that awaited permission to head down to view Amenhotep's tomb.

"Oy!" she shouted. "Is that you?"

Heads shot around and eyes darted in her direction. A tour guide stopped his spiel. Strangely, several men began to look uncomfortable.

Alicia zeroed in on her target. "It *is* you? Gavin! Gavin Lucas, you bastard!"

Dahl held Drake back from running after her. "Don't worry," the Swede said. "She's chosen the daftest looking mammal. Just get ready."

Alicia walked right up to the edge of the crowd, ignoring the whispers and stares of the closest civilians and the new attention of the guards. One of the tour guides started to wander over.

"Look at me!" Alicia glowered at her victim—a large, hard-faced man of thirty or so, bulging muscles threatening to rip his shirt at the seams and pant legs riding up over his socks due to the width of his thighs.

Everyone saw the huge specimen mouth 'me?' and an anxious look fall across his face.

"Yeah, you. Don't you remember?" She turned to a nearby older woman looking splendid in her jewels and finery. "Thick as a tree trunk, but rode me harder than John Wayne on full gallop."

The older woman looked over with interest. Alicia held out her hands. "C'mere, Gavy-boy. C'mere. Let's reacquaint."

The merc looked ready to start pushing his way toward her until one of his comrades leaned over and whispered into his ear. Immediately, a cloud of doubt settled over his features.

"Yeah, my name ain't Gavin."

Alicia laughed. "Don't be a goose. You have that tattoo, don't you? The one on your ass?"

Now the man's comrades were staring at him with more than just boredom.

"What?"

"You broke my heart!" Alicia pushed her way toward the man, largely to escape the attentions of the guide and the oncoming guards that just wanted to calm the scene. Alicia stood in front of the merc, looking up.

"Don't you remember me?"

"Nah, girl, but I sure wish I did. You ain't a bad looking bitch."

"I'm a what now?"

"Get rid of the damn whore," another merc spoke up, probably the leader of their little group. "We're headed down."

Alicia shook her head. "Excuse me? Just one sec." She held a finger in front of the newly arrived tour guide and his guard. "You need to apologize."

Laughter rang out from the mercs. Civilians all around looked embarrassed. Drake and the team were close now, ranged around Alicia and trying to look impartial.

"I demand an apology!" Alicia cried in a high voice.

The merc Alicia had picked on still looked uncertain, but the rest assumed their nastiest faces. Drake watched the spies in the crowd taking it all in without drawing attention.

"Fuck off, whore," one said.

People gathered around gasped. Drake saw some of the men start to protest. This was about as far as they should go. Nobody wanted innocent civilians dragged into their mess.

Then, everything changed. One of the mercs, unable to restrain himself, pushed 'Gavin' aside and shouted a string of curses into Alicia's face. She reacted predictably with a knee to the groin, a jab to the sternum and a punch to the throat. Her abuser said no more, but went down gurgling, clutching his neck, tottering on his knees.

Alicia placed a finger on his forehead. "There's a free lesson for you," she whispered and pushed him over. "Don't treat women like that."

His friends were coming now, barging the crowd aside, vision filled with nothing but red mist. Alicia backed off into a tour guide and one of the guards, and gave them a look of apology. "I'd call in backup," she said.

Drake had been tracking the leader. Just before Alicia toppled the abuser he saw him make the tell-tale sign of an incoming communication—a finger placed to the ear. The leader then fixed Alicia with a clearer gaze before staring over at Drake.

Oh shit, that was quick. Someone knows their way around the Internet and facial recognition software.

Which begged the question: Why were they using such low-rent mercs?

Drake was moving even as each successive thought materialized, and so were the rest of the team. The guard, apparently unaware that he had any form of nearby backup, raised his gun and began to shout. The crowd panicked. Men and women started crying out and looking to flee. An air of panic quickly set in.

Dahl pulled the guard free and set him aside, yelling that he should call for backup. Drake didn't know whether to be annoyed at Alicia or happy with what she'd done. The flow of people into the tomb had definitely been altered, but the outcome of tonight was still in jeopardy.

"Not good." Crouch pointed at the tomb's entrance. Many were still heading down.

"We can't stop that," Hayden said. "We need to leave. Now."

The mercenaries reached Drake, Dahl and Alicia. A tussle broke out, with fists flying. The three tried to contain the advance of the mercs but found themselves forced back by weight of numbers. Civilians still cried and stood all around. Some fell to the floor, knocked aside by the mercs.

Drake saw guards formed of the Egyptian military beginning to assemble.

"Out," he shouted.

They spun and ran, joined the bulk of their group and then hastened toward the edge of the stage. The mercs followed, sensing blood and victory rather than a sensible retreat and a chance to get to safety. They didn't see the guards coming.

Plus they forgot their orders, Drake thought. *Bonus for us.*

Still, they had to assume other factions knew what they knew. He wanted to get hold of Crouch and extract the exact information but that would have to wait. He leapt from the stage amidst the SPEAR team at full flow, landing sprightly and turning it into a sprint. The guards wouldn't pursue—they hadn't done anything wrong.

But the mercs knew them.

For a moment he wondered if whoever was pulling their strings had now decided to deliberately send them after SPEAR, forgoing the tomb. But no, that just didn't make sense. They left the stage area behind, pounding across a patch of desert now as they raced toward the parking areas. Here stood many coaches and private taxis used to ferry guests to and from the event. The road passed close by. Drake checked the rear whilst Hayden and Kinimaka scoped out the best exit.

"Cairo," Crouch said.

"Yeah, already on it," Hayden said. "Back to the safe house?"

"Yes, it will be good for a short while."

Drake saw the mercs barging people off the stage, causing injuries as they neared its edge. The guards were in pursuit, coming around the side. Hayden urged them to a mini-van where the driver sat waiting, the engine ticking.

"Sorry," he said in poor English. "I . . . have . . . already . . . fare . . ."

"Double." Crouch stuck his head through the passenger window. "We'll pay double. And make it quick, we have another party to get to!"

"Ah! What the hell are you waiting for? Get on in!" Suddenly, he understood English just fine.

Drake saw they barely had time, but didn't want to draw attention to the pursuit. The team jumped in, told their driver to get a move on and then they were speeding across a flat piece of desert toward the main road. Drake, squashed in the back beside Smyth and Yorgi, stuck his nose against the rear pane of glass.

"They're slow," he said. "But, I think still coming."

"Move it," Crouch said.

"I am going as fast as she can," the driver told them. "What's the rush, man? Party can wait."

"We're hungry," Alicia said bluntly. "Now speed *her* up before I start chomping on yer arm."

Drake and Smyth were assessing the pursuit. "Looks like half the mercs made it away," Smyth said. "The rest stopped by guards. I guess that's still about eight though."

"You think they'll have weapons?" Yorgi asked.

Kenzie barked a laugh. "Mercs? They're never more than a mile from their stash, my Russian friend. No doubt buried their guns in the desert. What's our head start?"

Drake shrugged. "Five, six, minutes if they stop."

"They'll stop."

"How long to Cairo?" Mai asked.

"Big pyramid over there." The driver pointed out the window. "Five minute drive."

"And then *our* arms are twenty minutes away," Smyth pointed out.

"It's gonna be tricky," Drake said. "Real tricky."

CHAPTER TEN

Between them, Alicia and Kenzie kept the driver at close to full speed the entire way. Even so the mercs were closing in by the time the outskirts of Cairo came into view. Drake breathed a sigh of relief to see the packed, mostly paved streets; the various homes with sheets draped outside windows and across small balconies, the impromptu stalls set up in street corners and tiny niches; all dusty and dirty from the desert, the rain and the circumstances. The pathways were uneven, rocky, strewn with rubbish. Their taxi driver veered toward the nearest, accepted cash, and waited for them to evacuate the car.

Drake jumped into night-time Cairo. A general hubbub filled the air, shouts and catcalls punctuating the background noise. The air smelled of rotting rubbish laced with spice and other things Drake couldn't identify—a complex smorgasbord of odors.

They started walking swiftly, Smyth checking back to work out the progress of the following mercs. Each building here was built almost atop the next, with an ancient, sculpted church sitting alongside a new wooden-fronted, gray-blocked structure with no visible gap in between. The road twisted and turned, passing cafes and carpet and jewelry shops. Hayden took point, with Kinimaka and Crouch just a step behind. The ambient light was minimal, enshrouding narrow passages, sunken shopfronts and anything that might be trespassing there.

Smyth caught up. "Best pick up the pace. They're right behind us."

The dull drone of queuing motor cars and the high-pitched squeak of scooters came from the right. A deeper quiet came from the left. Hayden used her cellphone's GPS to follow a winding path to the busy street, hoping it would help them disappear.

Drake dropped back, making sure Smyth was not alone at the rear of the group.

Mai went with him. The mercs were visible now, jogging and waving their guns carelessly. One of them spotted Drake and gave a shout.

Instantly, he ducked aside. A shot rang out, passing between Mai and him. Smyth ducked into the shadows and quickly climbed a rickety ladder onto a balcony, then crouched down to wait. Drake slunk back, seeking half-light. Mai leapt atop a nearby stall, hoping it would hold for at least a minute.

"Saw them," a man shouted. "Swear down I did."

Five men appeared, walking carefully now; the other three in their party probably taking an alternative route. Drake waited for Smyth to make his move.

A warm wind drifted up the passageway between buildings, stirring litter and making eddies in the piles of sand. Smyth leapt into their midst just as it died away.

Landing feet first, his right elbow slammed down onto a merc's neck with crushing force. The man collapsed instantly. Smyth kicked out at the next, keeping his balance. A gun flew through the air. Mai dived off the unsteady stall, losing a perfect target because the shaky supports collapsed just as she leapt. Still, she adjusted and came down in front of her adversary, taking him out with two blows. A merc spun quickly, bringing his elbows up to block her next attack, then pushed her away. Mai lost her footing on the uneven ground, went down to one knee. The merc, if he'd pressed ahead with his attack might have won, but the focus of his thoughts centered only on his weapon.

Lifting the gun took several seconds.

Mai balanced her weight on one hand and kicked out with both legs, taking him at the shins and watching him crash to the floor. His gun hit concrete and then she was upon him, a flashing blur in the dim, golden glow of the single light.

Drake slunk out and came up behind the lead merc just as the man turned and took aim upon an embattled Smyth. The soldier's back was turned; he would never have known. Drake snapped the man's wrist without mercy and caught the gun before it fell to the floor.

"You were once a soldier," the Yorkshireman whispered. "What happened?"

He didn't wait for answer, smashing the man about the temples and seeing him stagger away. Two mercs were down, motionless, the other three struggling and bleeding.

Drake waved at his colleagues. "C'mon, folks. Show mercy to these wankers. Maybe it'll persuade them to get another job."

They melted away quickly, all three conscious that it would take a while to catch up. Mai slipped out her own cellphone and they ran hard, following the path they thought Hayden would have taken.

Drake stayed on the lookout for the three rogue mercs as well as the ones they'd spared, knowing in his blood that men like that were far from being able to learn new lessons. Already, he knew, they'd be back in the chase.

Smyth kept an eye to the rear, Mai to the front. Drake called Alicia.

"Where are you?"

She explained. Drake guessed they were just a few minutes apart.

"Three to five unaccounted for," he said. "Possibly tracking you."

"Understood."

They ended the call, both focused fully on their colleagues and surroundings. Drake, Mai and Smyth ran across a busy road, weaving between cars and around people, darting back into the shadows on the other side. They were only eight minutes from their safe house now but couldn't afford to lead the mercs there.

"I see Yorgi and Kenzie," Mai said. "Up ahead."

Drake squinted, barely able to make them out, and was reminded briefly of Dahl's comment about needing glasses. Were his eyes failing or was it the dull light?

Just ignore the mad bastard.

That usually worked. Drake checked around once more, seeing nothing untoward. Bit by bit, they caught up to the rest of the team who were moving at half pace.

Hayden looked back. "All good?"

"Yeah. Two taken out. Rest probably still coming."

"We've seen no sign of enemies," Kinimaka said.

"They're here though," Kenzie said. "Close by."

Alicia stopped. "How can you—"

They came from the side street, three at first and then the ragtag remnants of the earlier tussle. Alicia, Kinimaka and Hayden saw them coming and immediately jumped in to prevent any gun-play. Drake, Mai and Alicia ranged around as the rest of the team engaged.

A shot rang out, the barrel of the gun forced toward the ground, the bullet striking and glancing away. Dahl kicked the offender hard in the face, sending him smashing back into a brick wall. Kenzie jumped in feet-first, pushing another man into a wooden structure, watching as the timbers fell all around and buried him. With a wry grin she picked up the sharpest spar of wood.

Then spotted a lone gunman, hovering at the back of the mercs. She used another's back to leap into action, and brought the spar down upon the man's face. He raised an arm to block the blow and the gun went off, the bullet shooting high into the night. Kenzie swung twice more, drawing blood and forcing the man down.

Behind, in the general melee, the rest of the team were taking on opponents. Drake used his environment; throwing a merc against a low balcony and then watching him fall into a narrow opening, unconscious. The next he brought down a line of washing upon, tangling and blinding the man. A few well-placed punches left him wrapped in a heap, groaning. Drake stood aside as another leapt in, then watched him trip headlong over the wrapped-up bundle on the floor. Another gun went skidding from another hand, rattling across the concrete and ending up at the base of a wall. Drake picked it up not just for protection but to prevent some civilian stumbling across it tomorrow.

Mercs swung wildly. Dahl climbed a balcony to leap from, came down like a mountain on two mercs, and rendered them unconscious. Kenzie found herself on a similar balcony, a merc having followed her up there; then prodded him with the spar. The man caught it, wrenched it away but unbalanced and fell, arm pin wheeling, onto the concrete below. Kenzie dropped in his wake and saw blood seeping from the back of his head. She scooped the spar up, jabbed at another enemy.

Alicia punched hard and evaded, finding she'd run out of enemies after just a few minutes. Casting around, it seemed a little rude to just barge in on Hayden's brawl, but with a loud cough and a little wave she caught the merc's attention and brought him over to her side. Eight seconds later he was down.

"You're welcome," she told Hayden.

"I had that."

"I know, but Hay, you haven't been shot in a while. Thought I'd take that chance right off the table."

The mercs fought doggedly, handing out bruises and bleeding mouths but failing to stop the SPEAR team for more than a few minutes. When they were groaning, lying practically motionless, their leader dead, Hayden signaled a final sprint for the safe house.

"We all good?"

Crouch and Yorgi came back from the shadows. The pair had never pretended to be fighters, but had taken weapons to use in case they were needed, a plan so well executed the mercs never even knew about the spare backup. Crouch took point now and led them through darker streets, and the team used Smyth and Kenzie to check for any signs of pursuit.

There were none. But there was something else. A brooding darkness lying over the less traveled streets of Cairo, a menace unseen but heavily present. Something that offered violence and fire and the chance of turmoil. Drake had felt it before many times—close to war zones and inside cities fighting for their lives. At border crossings that might be subject to attack. The Middle East was a roiling cauldron of ferocity, madness and religious hatred. *Is anywhere safe?*

Drake and Alicia checked the side alleys. Mai took a quick sprint across the rooftops.

"Clear."

Together, they headed to safety.

CHAPTER ELEVEN

FrameHub were both pleased and dubious. Their army of mercenaries had secured the first clue set right at the back of the first seal, but had come across a problem larger than they had anticipated. FrameHub weren't entirely sure how to process the information, or how best to react.

They were IT gods, not military captains.

The man on the conference call was the leader of the mercs. He called himself Vladimir and spoke with a Russian accent.

"It is an American Special Forces unit called Team SPEAR. They're off the books, specialists in everything you could name and many things you couldn't. Taken down some of the world's worst."

"It sounds like you admire them," Piranha said.

"They're soldiers, and pretend to be nothing else. One time— we were all like that. At least, most of us were. They took out enough of my men to force me to recruit even more." Vladimir sighed.

"The timetable must not be compromised," Barracuda said in a robotic computer-generated voice.

"It won't be. You employed me because I have good connections and get the job done when and how you specify, not for my shocking good looks and bowling arm."

"Ahh, okay." Barracuda's uncertainty made the mechanical voice absurd.

"What do you know of this . . . SPEAR?" Piranha tried to cover for him.

"Too much to retell," Vladimir said. "There's about ten of them, I guess. Mix of nationalities. Here's the interesting thing— the American government recently disavowed them. These guys're acting on their own."

Piranha was confused and didn't try to hide it this time. "What are you saying?"

"It is too early to know but I do believe they're acting on their own. That puts them in our territory and easier to kill. No backup, limited tech. All this helps. Also, if the American's *have* disavowed SPEAR they will have someone hunting them down, but I haven't found any details yet. Perhaps you guys could help?"

Piranha weighed and judged the request instantly. "We can find that information, but how will it help?"

"It will tell me the worst of what we're up against."

"Okay, I understand. I'll have the information within the hour."

"Within the . . ." Vladimir sounded shocked and doubtful. "Something like that will be deeply classified. It's hidden behind so many—"

"Please," Piranha murmured. "I said an hour because we have a retro office Galaga challenge planned. That will take forty-five minutes."

Vladimir remained silent.

"Did you find out *why* this team were disavowed?" Manta asked. "That could help."

"Couldn't say. Usually though, these things have little to do with a team's actions and much to do with political maneuvering. I doubt the real reason will be on file."

"It's fine," Piranha said. "Please concentrate on the tombs and the seven seals. This knowledge is vital to our future and thus to yours. We can make you rich, Mr. Vladimir. Just work with us to find that seventh seal. That is your sole and only goal right now."

"Understood. The seals are crucial. They're also front and center on many men's radars right now. What are you boys gonna do about that?"

Piranha smiled at the screen. "Something huge. You will hear about it, be assured."

Manta snorted. "A Tibetan monk will hear of it."

Moray glanced at him. "They have Wi-Fi in Tibet, idiot."

"Yeah, I know that. It was a figure of speech, asshat."

"Right," Vladimir cut in. "I'll let you boys get on with it. Keep me updated."

"We're not *boys*," Piranha said. "Well, not all of us. Rest assured we have a method to distract the entire world from the seven seals of Egypt."

"You said that already. I'll be watching and listening."

"Good," Piranha said, unable to come up with anything witty. They needed Vladimir though—somebody out there in the real world dealing with real-world problems and situations. None of them had seen sunlight for months. They were too busy following their mandate: Knowledge is power. Down here they could accumulate vast amounts on everyone and anything, but if the curse of the seven seals was right and led to an incredible doomsday weapon . . .

FrameHub thought that was ultra-cool.

Vladimir signed off. Piranha shook his head at the entire group and called for FrameHub to reorder. It was bordering on an extremely momentous time.

"Tell me, FrameHub, are we ready?"

"We are ready," the collective agreed.

"Shall we make them fear us?"

"We shall."

"Shall we make them cower?"

"We will."

"Press that start button then," Piranha said. "It's game on."

Piranha arranged his thoughts. With the first seal broken and the clue discovered, the mercs would handle the second seal. Some kind of abandoned tomb according to Vladimir. FrameHub had been formulating a plan for some time now, a game plan, to bring three nations to their knees, and then two of them to collapse. It was a test and a warning, something to make the rest of the world sit up and beg.

Literally.

They were connected worldwide through the computer network. And not just to the Internet but every single thing on earth that required any kind of mainframe or processor. The best hackers of their time had become a divine and superhuman collective, and the world was about to find out what they could do.

Piranha watched proceedings. In their real-life war game three countries would be threatened, all by email message. The first to capitulate to their demands would win, the other two would be destroyed. It was pure gaming rules.

"We expect them to ignore the first demand," Piranha said. "So prepare the second. We need to be taken seriously."

A desire he'd felt his whole life.

FrameHub had researched carefully and identified the right agency, the right branch of that agency and even the correct person to send the threat to. It would be registered, so that when the second was received the level would be escalated. There was a procedure to go through and because FrameHub needed the time and the lengthy distraction they would happily adhere to and not force it.

Their rules. Their game.

Piranha ran it through his head. "The governments of Egypt, Turkey and Greece have twenty four hours to meet our demands, those being the delivery of three hundred million dollars to an account of our choosing. Failure to meet these demands will result in a catastrophic failure of your entire infrastructure, sending you back to the Dark Ages. You will face famine, disease, war and utter bankruptcy. Only one country will be allowed to meet these demands—the very first to do so. The other two will crumble. Do we—FrameHub—have your attention? Good, you have our demands. Take them seriously or perish."

It would be analyzed, traced, taken apart. It would be subject to a deep data dive, an Interpol investigation—all kinds of scrutiny. It would do them no good. FrameHub had inserted several clever reroutes into the transmission that would force the authorities' tech guys to attest to their genius and sincerity.

The rest would no doubt rely on the second demand, where a demonstration would be in order. *Good. Really, I can't wait.* Piranha had never set off a real live missile. The difference between game theory and real life would be interesting to see.

"Message sent," Orca said.

Piranha grinned at the collective, unable to hide his glee. "Just twenty four hours," he said excitedly. "And we get to do this shit for real!"

A cheer echoed around the underground bunker.

CHAPTER TWELVE

Hayden Jaye finished her call and threw the cell on the table. The room was cramped. To the left Kinimaka twitched at the gap in the curtains, checking out the street below. Every three minutes he gave a shake of his head, signaling all was quiet. Drake and the rest of the team sat or stood around the small area, drinking water and coffee, checking and cleaning weapons which they would now keep with them at all times.

"That was Claudia from the DC office. Old friend. She says Lauren arrived safely."

The team immediately took note, sitting up and focusing.

"What else did she say?" Smyth asked, his voice thick with anxiety.

"Not much. Lauren's being questioned right now. The buzz is that she's in the clear, but they're taking no chances."

"As we thought," Kinimaka rumbled. "Everyone involved covering their ass."

"Yeah. Lauren played it just right though. Another few days and she can get started."

Smyth coughed. "Maybe."

Hayden tried a commiserating look, realized it wasn't working and gave up. Lauren had indeed done the right thing in her opinion, but everything she did from here on in—at least for a while—would be under scrutiny. She was intelligent, street-smart, and hopefully working with a crew like theirs for the last few years would have a positive effect on her.

Lauren would come through.

Hayden stretched her weary muscles, opened a bottle of water, and took a long gulp. The room was stifling. Sweat ran freely down her face. Outside, the streets were noisy and packed, just another day for the locals. She wondered what had happened to the mercs.

"Let's get this done," she said. "Then we can get the hell out of this oven. First, this ransom demand from a new group calling themselves FrameHub. Opinions are divided. Some say it's a childish prank, others that the countries involved should be placed on the highest alerts."

Drake looked interested but Hayden held up a hand. "That's the kind of job Team SPEAR would have been given," she said.

"We're not Team SPEAR anymore. At least not in the eyes of the government."

An air of despondency settled across the room. Dahl wiped sweat from his brow. "We may still want to monitor it."

Crouch drained a bottle of water. "I can do that," he said. "My people at Interpol and other European agencies will be watching closely."

Hayden accepted with a nod. "All right. If you can . . . gather something together. One of the countries involved is Egypt so it could affect us all."

Crouch nodded. "Speaking of Egypt, what do we do next?"

"Hey, you're the boss," Alicia said. "You tell us."

"I thought Hayden was the boss," Kinimaka spoke up.

"Shit," Drake looked around innocently. "I thought I was."

Hayden laughed. "Nobody's the boss here, guys. It's just a family now."

"We have to be the oddest family in all of history." Mai looked around. "From the mad, the bad and the incredibly ugly to the pretty, the witty and the ultra-dumb. What a motley crew."

"Umm," Alicia frowned. "Which is which?"

Mai laughed. "Oh, I'm sure you can work it out."

Kenzie put an arm around Dahl. "The mad and the bad are sitting right here."

Dahl shrugged it off. "Back to business. What do we know about the second tomb, Michael?"

Crouch took a breath. "As I said before, finding the second tomb and locating or not locating the second symbol will confirm if the so-called curse is real. If there's a second clue then we have to work on the theory that we're really searching for the actual capstone and that the ancient doomsday machine exists."

"More tombs? More buried treasure?" Alicia looked gloomy. "More running from the authorities? I'm sick of going underground."

"Nice. The clue I found back at Amenhotep's tomb was a depiction of the capstone along with a drawing of a tomb. I recognize the sculptures depicted, with the three pillars outside, but haven't been able to place it in my memory. But that's not a problem—we can look it up. The problem is this . . . we're not the only ones chasing this."

"Not by a long shot," Mai said.

Hayden listened for a moment, taking in the mood of the team. In so many ways this was different for them—a guard at the window, a back-street hotel, and a cramped little room, limited tech support, having to look out for authorities rather than encourage them, always worried they may be spotted—but they were now relying on each other more than ever before and the actual mission parameters were the same. Of course, due to intense situations such as theirs, personal issues were sidelined.

Not necessarily a bad thing.

Time away from private relationships helped put them into perspective, it seemed. Her position as leader removed her from deeper feelings. Now that they were all on a par, she saw how badly she'd upset Mano. Whatever words she'd said had been purely manufactured to give her space—but the friendly Hawaiian didn't know that. She watched him now as he watched the street, wondering if there was any way back.

Crouch continued: "We have to be fast and faultless. If others found that capstone symbol they could be heading to the second tomb as we speak."

"We have to assume they did," Kenzie said.

"Definitely. So let's break out that laptop."

Mai took it from a backpack and handed it over to Alicia.

The Englishwoman regarded it with horror. "What the hell are you doing? Don't bring that thing near me."

"You can't type, Taz?"

"I don't do geek. Yogi, my boy? C'mere. Wrap your mitts around this."

The Russian looked confused but grabbed the laptop anyway. Following Crouch's descriptions, he began to trawl a path through images.

"All this talk about curses," Alicia said. "Makes you wonder, doesn't it? I remember Tutankhamun's tomb was said to be cursed."

"Well, a curse is pretty much all-encompassing over here. Any person that disturbs an Egyptian body, be it a mummy or a pharaoh, can be affected. There are no differentiations. Thieves, kids, archaeologists, holidaymakers. You name it. You're all fair game. Some Egyptian tombs contain curses, some don't. Most commonly, the mistaken one is Tutankhamun's. His resting place contained no curse."

Dahl grunted. "A curse can be distorted into anything you want," he said. "They're usually rather vague."

"And it normally mentions disease," Crouch said. "Which, when one disturbs a corpse, is not out of the question."

"No seven plagues then?" Alicia threw a glance at the window as if expecting hordes of flies and locusts gathering there.

"No, and that was different, as you know. That was God's wrath. But the whole 'curse' commotion was thrown back into the light when Howard Carter discovered Tutankhamun. Carter's canary died in the mouth of a cobra, thus inciting the locals to fear the onset of a curse. Later, Lord Carnarvon died, after becoming infected by a mosquito bite. A letter was written two weeks prior to his death, and published in the *New York World* magazine, in which Marie Corelli asserted that 'dire punishment' would fall upon anyone that desecrated a tomb. Mussolini, who some time before had accepted a mummy as a gift, ordered it removed. Next, and incredibly, Sir Arthur Conan Doyle became entangled in it, suggesting that 'elementals' created by ancient priests were involved and had caused Carnarvon's death."

Alicia shivered in the heat. "You can stop there if you like."

But Crouch was on a roll, in his own element and talking about the very thing he loved most in the world. "Soon after, a man called Sir Bruce Ingram, who had been gifted by Carter a mummified hand with a bracelet that bore the inscription 'cursed be he who moves my body. To him shall come water, fire and pestilence', saw his house burned down and then, after it was rebuilt, suffered a flood."

"Shit, you couldn't make this up." Kenzie laughed.

"Surely you have come across curses in your line of work?" Crouch asked her.

"My line . . . ? Well, I guess as a relic smuggler you'd think so," Kenzie was taken a little aback by the direct question. "But believe me, the only curses I come across are those I speak and those uttered by my men when I make them work."

Alicia looked over. "Yeah, Drake's like that."

"Hey!"

"Howard Carter himself was hugely skeptical of the curse," Crouch went on. "But he did write about an unsettling occurrence—when in the desert he saw jackals of the same type as Anubis for the first time in almost forty years."

Alicia gulped. "And you want us to go out there?"

"Of the fifty eight people present when Carter opened the tomb, only eight died in the following years. Six of those could be attributed in some way to disease." Crouch shrugged. "You make your own theories, my friends."

"I'm more interested in mummies to be honest," Alicia said. "Those guys always seem to be angry."

"Yeah, so Hollywood tells us," Hayden said. "But if your internal organs were removed, your body washed out with spices, your brain liquefied, all over a period of forty days, and then your dried-out body was wrapped in linen, you wouldn't exactly be feeling perky now, would you?"

Alicia screwed her face up. "Uh, nope."

"I have it," Yorgi said, swiveling the laptop around to face the room.

Crouch stared and then nodded. "That's it. Meritamun's tomb, discovered in the nineteenth century. It's small, insignificant, and came with all the usual objects. Sarcophagi. Canopic jars for internal organs. Amulets. The Book of the Dead. Household furniture of a sort. Ushabti figurines to work for the dead in the afterlife. Food. Wall paintings. Statues and carvings. And, of course, wall-painted spells. Nothing out of the ordinary. Over sixty tombs have been found and most are similar, not unremarkable, but nothing on the scale of Tutankhamun and just a few others. The tomb of Nefertiti has never been found."

"What are you saying?" Hayden broke in, sensing Crouch might wander off on still another tangent.

"That this tomb, in this place, will have been largely forgotten over the last couple of centuries. It's dry now. Protected yes, but forgotten. If we looked hard enough we might even find an inventory of tomb photographs online, but I strongly suggest we attend in person."

"There's no suggestion about it, pal," Drake said. "We're going."

Hayden watched the team rise up and make ready, and a feeling of pride swelled in her chest. Beaten down as they were, hunted by the most powerful nation on earth, they were still trying their best to work together to save it.

Team SPEAR would never die. Do to it what you would.

"You okay, Hay?" Mano was beside her, looking a bit worried. "You seem out of it."

"No, no." She snapped out of it. "Just thinking how, despite everything that's happening, there are no other people on earth I'd rather be standing in this sweaty room with right now. That's it."

Kinimaka smiled. "Me too, Hay. Me too."

She grinned up at him.

CHAPTER THIRTEEN

Drake always imagined an Egyptian tomb would come with a sense of awe, of wonder and majesty; just like the first they'd visited, but the tomb of Meritamun was a narrow opening close to the ground. High pillars stood outside, adorning the entrance, but Drake got the sense that nobody really cared anymore.

The day was stifling, a hot, dry wind blowing across the desert. The vista was open to the right, broken by a series of low hills to the left. Their jeeps had left long, conspicuous tire tracks in the relatively short stretch of sand they'd covered since leaving the road. The team wore hiking gear, with as few clothes as possible, but carried all the weapons and tech they had. Nobody expected this to be easy today and a confrontation was all but certain. Everyone wore a hat except Kenzie, the ex-Mossad agent well-used to heat and even complaining that the odd gust of wind raised gooseflesh.

Drake, sweating enough to fill a pint-pot, took the GPS and marked the coordinates. "Well, this is the place. The tomb of Meritamun. Looks peaceful."

Dahl bared his teeth. "Now that's a proper dumb thing to say."

Crouch sized up the entrance. "Let's get this done quickly. Maybe we can be in and out before company arrives."

"There again," Dahl complained. "*Inviting* disaster."

"Well personally," Alicia said. "I'm more worried about heading down a mummy's black hole. Who knows what we'll find down there?"

Drake broke out the flashlights and other equipment they might need. The Jeeps stayed where they were, parked behind a series of low mounds but almost impossible to hide. Crouch, unable to conceal his excitement, muscled to the front and headed in first.

Alicia shook her head and followed. The rest filed in after.

Kinimaka and Smyth stayed back to guard the entrance and the surrounding area. Kenzie ranged further afield, finding a position to watch the road and the desert.

"Something tells me that girl's as at home in the desert as a scorpion," Alicia said. "And still as nasty."

"I think she likes that," Dahl said wistfully.

"Being nasty?"

"Yeah." He paused. "I mean there's being nasty and then there's being *nasty.*" He enunciated both words, one with more feeling than the other.

Alicia sighed. "I remember those days."

"Until Drake tamed you?" Dahl asked innocently.

"Torstyyyyy . . ." Alicia said in a warning tone. "Any more of that and you'll be wearing your wedding tackle for earrings."

Even Drake winced. The tunnel continued at a steady decline, burrowing into the earth, leading them away from the baking heat. Drake felt the sweat turn cool and breathed a little easier. He wondered briefly about the curse and the seven seals. If all this really was leading to some kind of incredible weapon how had it stayed hidden all these years? If it was ancient and apocalyptic, shouldn't it also be large? Nobody had invented a miniature doomsday device yet. His thoughts drifted directly from there to the splinter cell operating within the American government. It was truly incredible how fast and how completely people's lives could be destroyed by those in power. Criminal, really. Those that cast aside 'innocent until proven guilty' and took the law into their own hands were surely just exacerbating the problem. But he was a soldier through and through; never having many aspirations other than living a good, positive life . . .

And becoming world table tennis champion.

That reminded him—Dahl and he still hadn't properly concluded their rivalry there. Who was Team SPEAR's premier ping pong player?

The comms burst into life. "All clear up here," Kenzie said. "Great day. I can see for miles around."

Alicia, confronted with a pinprick of light in utter darkness, grunted. "Bitch."

Soon, the tunnel ended and they reached flat ground. The earth was solid and dry, the walls of the tomb strong. Crouch flicked his flashlight around and so did the others, everyone highlighting something different. Drake saw colorful wall paintings and a place where the sarcophagus had been; recesses in the walls for jars and treasures. He saw empty ledges and vacant spaces and concluded they were standing in one medium-sized hollow void.

"Nothing here," he said.

"That's the good thing about murals and hieroglyphics," Crouch said. "For the most part, they stay in place."

He moved over to the nearest wall, directing the rest of the team to carefully scan the others, not forgetting the ceiling. Dahl got straight to business, finding the furthest, darkest corner, hoping for a repeat of Amenhotep's tomb. Within moments the entire team was peering at the wall space and into corners, craning their necks high, all searching for anything that might resemble a capstone.

"You mentioned that you might be able to find photos of this tomb on the Internet," Alicia grumbled, rising and brushing her knees off. "Next time, Crouchy, let's do that."

"I prefer my archaeology first hand," the ex-Ninth Division boss said distractedly.

"Any agencies are most likely doing just that," Hayden told Alicia. "I'm pretty sure we would have."

"And we still can't be sure who knows what," Yorgi said.

Hayden and then Mai shouted out a couple of false alarms and then, again, it was Crouch that spotted the motherlode.

"I think I have it."

Drake was close and inched over. "I can barely see that, mate."

"Glasses," Dahl said, then squinted himself. "Whoa, that's nicely hidden away."

The capstone depiction sat at the base of a man's foot, just below the sole and a few millimeters above the earth. Anyone not looking for the symbol would never have noticed it, and even those cataloguing the tomb would barely have given it a second glance.

"The second seal," Crouch breathed. "The capstone and the ancient doomsday weapon."

"What the hell is that?" Drake leaned in even closer.

Alicia leant on his back. "You haven't see one before? That's an impressive erection, Drake."

"It's an obelisk," Crouch said. "Built by the Egyptians and a hundred other cultures. Only half of the world's Egyptian obelisks remain here in Egypt; the rest are scattered from Paris to London and America. This one—" he took several photos with his phone "—I have to assume remains in the country."

Dahl also took pictures as back up. "Let's hope so."

"Can we go now?" Alicia asked.

"Yes. We can identify the obelisk up top."

"Cool, and look at that: no trouble whatsoever. You know, this freelance game seems easier than working for the government. Less dangerous."

"Watch her," Mai said. "She'll be wanting to bring a picnic along next."

"Domesticated," Dahl added, sliding his phone away.

Alicia ignored them, heading now toward the exit and dragging Drake along. It was at that moment, as they all started back, that Kenzie's voice broke over the comms.

"Oh, no. That's not good."

Drake immediately started walking faster and keyed the comms. "What? Say again?"

"Choppers," Kenzie said bluntly. "Two headed this way and at speed. You have less than three minutes."

Without a word, they ran.

CHAPTER FOURTEEN

Drake slipped his Maglite into his mouth and pounded back up the tunnel. The way was worn and strewn with debris; mostly piles of sand. The close-set walls impeded him at every step. Twice he rebounded from left to right. At his back the grunts and groans attested to almost everyone else having a similar problem.

"Have you stopped for takeaway?" Mai asked from the back.

"Shut it." Drake ran hard, feeling the heat increase with each step. Every instinct screamed at him to pull out a weapon and make it ready but the way up was just too unpredictable, treacherous. He counted a minute of running and then the temperature rose sharply. The tunnel walls lightened.

"Heads up!" he cried and pulled up hard close to the exit.

Kenzie came over the comms. "They've seen the Jeeps. Kinimaka and Smyth are already there. Where are you people?"

"Here." Drake stepped out into the glaring daylight and headed straight for the transport. He could see two helicopters now, diving out of the sky, men hanging out of the sides.

"Taking fire!"

He rolled to the side as the choppers swooped. A burst of gunfire sounded and then a blast of raucous laughter. The second chopper targeted the Jeeps, raking the area with bullets. Kenzie was returning fire from her perch atop a sandy mound, giving both helicopters something to think about. The first veered away sharply, one of its gunners shouting a protest. The second dove even lower behind the mound, slipping lightly over the desert sands, throwing up mini dust-tails in its wake.

Again, the team ran for the Jeeps, everyone firing and giving the choppers full warning of their firepower and how they intended to use it. Bullets pinged off metal and broke windows, some even thudding into seatbacks. Both choppers were in some disarray, probably full of ego-laden mercs and not expecting the retaliation.

Kinimaka and Smyth climbed behind the steering wheels of the Jeeps and started them up, trusting their comrades to keep the gunfire off them. Drake saw the first chopper swinging back around, this time with some serious weapons poking out of it.

He stopped, fell to one knee, and lined the aggressors up.

A line of bullets stitched the ground near his right knee, traveling well past. Alicia dropped to the other side of it, weapon aimed.

"Make 'em count," she said.

Drake fired without stopping, targeting every face and window he could see. Glass exploded and metal ripped away. Alicia's bullets hit the mark too, and one man fell out of the chopper and tumbled to the floor. The bird thundered overhead, rotors whirling, a nightmare sound under fire. Drake turned with it, tracking it toward the nearby mounds.

"That'll make him think twice," Alicia said.

Drake saw the rest of the tomb's structure now, not having been in the right place or even particularly interested earlier. It was a rectangular, flat-topped, stone-built structure, at least half of which was crumbled away, but the overall shape was still noticeable. This structure covered the deep shaft leading to the tomb itself. Cut into the bedrock, it would have taken a significant amount of determined men to fashion.

There would be others around. Many of these tombs were built close to one another. A thought to bear in mind.

The second chopper decided to come back around for more. The rest of the team were in position around the Jeeps by now, giving Drake and Alicia time to run up to them. Volleys of gunfire surrounded their arrival. The men in the choppers, despite their height advantage, were being handicapped by the clumsy maneuvering and turbulence, and even by the chopper's own structure.

"Easy pickings," Mai said.

The Jeeps were running, primed to go. Drake saw no advantage to leaving, though, whilst the helicopters were in the air. Doing so would only turn the disadvantage right around.

As they waited, Crouch's phone started to ring. The man

ignored it, watching the choppers hovering and trying to figure out what to do.

"Tricky one even if they weren't packed full of mercs," Alicia said ungraciously. "It's mostly flat ground out here. Just those low mounds. We'd be picking each other off for days."

"Good point," Crouch said. "A shame we can't contact them."

"What? Why?"

"It's a stalemate. Time for quid pro quo."

"They will land," Mai said quietly. "It's the only sane thing to do."

Smyth pursed his lips. "They're mercs. Nothing sane about it."

"Move the vehicles," Dahl said, unable to keep the glint from his eyes. "A short way. Then get ready to jump out and finish this."

Crouch's phone rang again. He ignored it. Drake gave the Swede a shake of the head. "Crazy idea, pal, but I like it."

Smyth gunned the first Jeep. "Me too."

Tires slewed and skidded over the sand as Smyth and Kinimaka flung the vehicles around. Dust mushroomed into the air. All of the windows were open so Drake heard the choppers the moment they started to move.

"Here they come!"

The jeeps rolled forward as most of their occupants rolled out of the side doors. Dahl was first, two rolls and up into a kneeling position. He caught the first chopper as it came after them, nose down. He emptied a clip into the oncoming beast, changed mags in record time, and started on the second. To left and right the rest of the team did the same, a nonstop onslaught of lead. The cockpit glass shattered, the pilots shot several times. Drake saw other men scrambling to take charge of the controls.

But the choppers came on.

The first at a sharp angle, slightly erratic, mercs still trying to get a bead on the enemy. The second swooped to the side, losing altitude very quickly. Mercs leapt out of both sides as it approached the ground. It hit once, bounced, and then hit again, listing badly. Men scrambled out from underneath its bulk, terrified, weapons left behind. After a moment it settled back onto its skids, a broken beast.

The first chopper righted itself in the air and came on, straight along the path the Jeeps had taken. Drake moved his position, aiming along the side. The black mass flew above him again, forcing him to stare into its underbelly. The updraft was huge, forming a small cyclone of sand and dust particles, mixed with rock. Drake dived out of the way, keeping his head down. He coughed, face in the sand.

Now, survivors from the first crash were headed their way.

"Time to leave!" The comms were full of advice these days.

Kenzie had hotfooted it across the mounds and was now approaching from the right, headed for the slow-rolling Jeeps. She jumped in on the fly. Others fired more and more lead at the chopper, making it gain altitude before trying to turn.

"Ammo running low," Mai said.

"Save it," Crouch said. "Jump in, people."

At that moment the chopper above lost control. Maybe it was a random bullet, a pilot error or a fatality, but something vital changed. It literally fell right out of the sky, straight down toward the lead Jeep.

Kinimaka was at the wheel, eyes on the desert ahead and the upcoming roadway. He knew nothing until Kenzie roared out a warning.

"Move it! Move! Sky! Chopper!"

Whatever she meant, it galvanized the Hawaiian. Instantly, his enormous right foot rammed down hard on the gas pedal, making the jeep lurch forward. More sand sprayed. The engine roared. The tires gained traction and the vehicle shot forward. A great shadow hung overhead, falling fast. Drake watched with his heart in his mouth, the blood pounding hard in his ears. A bullet passed close to his ribcage, traveling on into the desert. He never noticed. Everything else was forgotten.

Hayden screamed over the comms. "Move, move, fucking move!"

Kinimaka wrenched the wheel hard, trying to evade. A deafening, all-encompassing roar filled the world of everyone inside the Jeep—Kenzie, Yorgi and Mai. For once, there was nothing any of them could do. This was a game of chance.

"C'mon, Mano," Alicia breathed again and again. "C'mon, Mano. C'mon."

As the jeep dodged frantically, the helicopter crashed hard, its heavy structure striking the desert with such force that it shook the earth. Metal shrieked and twisted. Drake, from this vantage point, couldn't tell whether the Jeep was running on the other side or crushed underneath. A vast sand-curtain billowed up, obscuring everything and everyone.

The licking flames pinpointed the helicopter.

Drake picked himself up, moved back and then ran around the fallen beast, Alicia and Dahl at his side. Their hearts were in their mouths, their hopes displayed on their stricken faces. Crouch and Hayden were with them a second later, running in from a different position.

As one they came around the wreckage.

It exploded; a concussive wave expanding fast and once more causing the ground to shake. Drake fell forward onto one knee, didn't stop moving, and managed to recoil back into an upright position, still progressing forward. Alicia landed on her left hip, crying out, but was up again in less than a second. The rest followed. A few chunks of debris flew around them, some flapping in the gust. A portion of the sand that had flown upward began to rain back down.

"You there?" Hayden cried frantically. "Mano? Mai?"

Her plaintive call went unanswered.

Drake cleared the fiery remains, still running into a curtain of dust, finally seeing it beginning to thin out. He saw tail lights then, and at last Kinimaka's Jeep, now coasting and stopping a few hundred yards beyond the wreck.

"Mai?"

"Comms are out," Alicia said. "At least theirs are."

Hayden was running past them, approaching the Jeep and wrenching at the doors. Kinimaka brought it to a stop, a look of surprise on the big Hawaiian's face as they all came alongside.

"Whassup, brah?" he asked. "Did I hit something?"

Drake laughed and clapped him on the shoulder. "Yeah, a fucking great bird. Well done, mate. Bloody well done."

Hayden was alongside him in the passenger seat, reaching out, grabbing his shoulders for a hug. Mano went right in, arms engulfing her. Drake took in the back seat and the relieved faces there.

"All good?"

Smyth came alongside in the second Jeep. "We gotta hurry. Some of those idiots are still coming."

"Don't they know the tomb is theirs?" Mai asked.

"I'd be amazed if they knew their mother's name."

Crouch's cellphone rang once more, the tiny sound barely discernible. "Jump inside." He waved everyone into the Jeeps and climbed in last. Drake kept an eye out to the rear but saw nothing beyond the burning chopper.

"Go," Hayden said finally. "Just go. We'll sort ourselves out later."

The Jeeps pealed out, heading for the tarmacked road.

Finally, Crouch answered his phone. "*What?*"

It was only because Drake was looking straight at his old boss that he noticed the quick variation of expressions. Like changing seasons Crouch's face went from relieved to surprised to shocked and then, surprisingly, to fearful.

Drake had never seen Michael Crouch looking scared before.

"Are . . . are you sure?" The voice came out low, just a croak.

Someone spoke for another twenty seconds.

"All . . . right . . . oh, my . . . all right . . ." Crouch's voice cracked with almost every word.

Drake sat forward, consumed with worry.

"You okay?"

Crouch ignored him and finished the call. For an entire minute he stared down at the floor and then managed to collect himself. He looked up at those in the Jeep.

"We have big, big trouble," he said. "I almost wish I'd never started this now."

"What trouble?" Alicia asked. "What's wrong, Michael?"

"I really don't see how any of us can survive this."

Drake almost gulped, affected by how Crouch was acting. "Tell us, mate."

"It's Luther," Crouch breathed, voice barely a whisper and strained to maximum. "He's here, in Egypt and locked on to our trail. We're done."

Drake frowned at him. "We're *never* done. Not this team. Besides, we're trying to stop an apocalypse here."

"Luther *is* the apocalypse," Crouch said. "With arms and legs. We can't stop him. Can't beat him. I'm sorry, my friends, but it's just a matter of time until he finds and then kills us. All of us."

Drake looked away from the already beaten gaze, stared at the desert skies and drifting clouds. Somewhere out there was a retro warrior, gunning for them with only one mission on his mind, one goal, removed from all communications, closing in by the minute. He could almost hear the approaching footsteps.

Judgment day was coming.

CHAPTER FIFTEEN

Crouch had the presence of mind to put them on the road to Thebes.

Drake lounged back in his seat, eyes half-closed, lulled by the gentle rocking and rolling of the vehicle with the air-conditioning set just so. It was an odd thing to be told, after everything he'd accomplished, that a balls-out blood-warrior was coming to kill him and that he'd probably die, but he tried to make the best of it.

"We have a head start on the mercs," he said brightly.

"A two-hour drive to our obelisk." Crouch had recovered slightly by now and told them he'd recognized the next clue. "We should still beat them there."

"What do we know about it?" Alicia asked. Drake guessed she was attempting to settle Crouch by getting him to talk about the stuff he loved.

"Oh, it's hard to say. This giant monolithic obelisk tops out at twenty meters high, the tip is covered in a gold-silver alloy electrum to catch the first rays of the morning sun. It was fashioned in one piece of red granite from Aswan and has been moved twice since its initial placement in front of a temple gateway, south of Thebes. Luckily this particular obelisk remained in Egypt. Augustus and other early Roman emperors had many removed. The Roman emperors commissioned the first new obelisks since the twenty-sixth dynasty, they were so fanatical about them. But ours . . . ours is pretty standard fare, I'm afraid. Nothing spectacular about it."

"But that's the norm for this quest," Alicia said. "Clues left where they will remain. Inconspicuous, low-profile."

"She has a good point," Drake said. "Even the curse was barely known until Amenhotep's tomb was found."

"Does it have a name, this obelisk?" Smyth asked.

"What—like George?" Alicia wise-cracked. "I doubt that."

"No, no, don't be a wiseass. Usually these things have titles. The Obelisk of Amun-Ra, or some such."

"It is believed to be the obelisk of Pharaoh Menes, but as I said it moved around. Most recently, and we're talking many, many years ago now, it was taken as a symbol of an ancient church." He smiled. "I'm not quite sure what came first. The church or the obelisk. Most ancient churches in Egypt are Christian and *not* based around Cairo, as most think. Many of these churches are built on sacred ground, where it was believed the baby Jesus and family stopped. Others, like the one associated with the obelisk, are secluded, out of the way, because they were built when the Christian religion had been forbidden by the Roman Empire." He shook his head. "Yeah, in those days there was even conflict between eastern and western Christians. Most of the churches are unusual, some even built in caves." He paused as his phone started to ring again and glanced quickly at the screen.

"A contact," he said with relief. "I asked for more information regarding this FrameHub fiasco."

Drake rolled easily with the bumps and the bends, closing his eyes against the glare that filled the windows. He'd lost his sunglasses back in the desert, a calamity to be sure but probably not the last time he'd ever do it.

Crouch sighed and pulled himself upright using the seat back. "Okay, okay, this FrameHub could be a credible threat. They're threatening a demonstration if the countries don't reply soon. The demand has been re-sent, re-evaluated. We don't like the look of what they're doing. Don't like the look of it at all."

"Any clues as to who this FrameHub crew are?" Hayden's voice came over the comms system loud and clear since all the damaged units had been replaced.

Crouch sighed once more. "Basically, they're a myth. No, they're *the* myth. Half a dozen of the world's greatest ever hackers joined together, planning mayhem. And not just of the digital kind. They're looking to change reality."

Drake shifted position. "Why?"

"Well, that's the question isn't it? Clearly, it's not for the money. They could skim a million bank accounts and we'd never know. It's not for the recognition. They're basement gods. Best guess at the moment . . . it's because they're whacko."

Alicia nodded. "That covers most of our enemies."

Drake looked over at Crouch. "Is that it? So we know nothing." It was a statement.

"We're not dealing with ghosts here," Crouch said. "We're dealing with the vaguest impression that a ghost passed by once. Give them some time."

"Try telling that to Greece, Turkey and Egypt," Dahl said, "when that deadline approaches."

"I want to approach the elephant in the . . . car," Hayden said. "Luther. Everything I know is hearsay, possibly sensationalized. You know how office rumors go. He's real, for sure. I saw some basic reports years ago. What I want to know is—what can we expect?"

Crouch looked at Alicia. The Englishwoman looked away. "I remember him," she said. "From one mission a long time ago. Our unit infiltrated a highly organized, highly dangerous terrorist cell in Eastern Europe, received good Intel on when to take it down, and worked hard to hone a takedown plan. We watched, we waited, we manipulated every member of that cell so they were there, inside, that day. All we needed was our contact to get out. Three minutes before the agreed time an American team hit that place." She exhaled. "Talk about the fourth of July. They lit not only the terrorists' apartment up, but the entire building. The block. They ran in there with semi-autos, grenades and even RPGs. It was hell on earth when a sniper would have made do. It was utter havoc when it should have been a quiet assassination. They wanted no remains, not even bones. That—" she looked back at Crouch again "—was the one and only time I met Luther."

Drake now sat upright. "So you did meet him?"

"I wasn't gonna let that go. Such disregard. I chased the bastard down. Confronted him. He was . . ." She frowned. "Savage. Like you might imagine a Native American to be when they ruled the plains. All he said was 'orders' and then turned away, wearing his American military swagger like a fucking cape, full of himself and full of loyalty too, I guess."

"You think he was manipulated back then too?"

Alicia shrugged. "Oh, I don't know. Soldiers carry out their orders and don't ask questions. This was more about the man—the beast, if you like. I've never seen such ferociousness. It stopped me in my tracks. The only time that's ever happened."

A silence panned out, punctuated by the road noise and the whistling air-con. In the end it was broken in the best, inimitable way of the Mad Swede.

"Kenzie," he said quietly into the silence with the comms on. "Please remove your hand from my lap."

Drake laughed. Even Alicia smiled. Smyth took the chance to tell everyone they were twenty minutes out and to start loading up. Their supply of ammo and other military gear was dwindling rapidly. If they didn't top up soon, they'd be out before the next seal presented itself. Drake knew Crouch could probably take care of that, but didn't want to rely solely on his ex-boss.

A small town appeared up ahead; dusty, sandy and shining under the sun. Most of the buildings were dull browns and beiges, but some of the taller ones glimmered and more than one faux-gold capstone twinkled. Smyth made his way through until they were a block from the obelisk and then pulled up. Dust surrounded the vehicle as he stopped.

"Reccy time," Hayden said. "Don't forget we have more than just mercenaries looking for the seals, and now Luther too. Bring your A game, guys."

Drake and Yorgi moved off to the left as the rest of the team split. The heat outside was unrelenting, beating down at his scalp, but at least there wasn't the slightest breath of wind to stir the sand up. With a quick look he confirmed the others were on their way, Alicia and Mai together—surprise there. Dahl and Kenzie joined at the hip—no shock there. Drake worried for the big Swede, but getting personal was not his place. Half an hour later they all met up.

"All clear," Crouch said.

"Seems so," Alicia said.

The obelisk stood less than a hundred meters before them, rising straight and high, and pointing right up at the heavens, at the sun. It was sandy in color, imposing in height and covered in pictures and hieroglyphics.

"Y'know," Alicia said with a laugh. "What the hell are we gonna do if the picture's above head fucking height?"

Drake blinked. He hadn't thought that far ahead. It now became clear that their headlong flight across Egypt wasn't exactly conducive to clear thought. Also, the stress caused by being on the run felt like a blanket, shrouding and blocking plain, sharp judgment. Crouch though, gave a short laugh.

"No worries," he said. "We zoom in with these." He patted a pair of field glasses. "Great magnification and photo option included."

The obelisk stood in a tiny square, paving all around. To the left sat a low huddle of homes and to the right a hodgepodge chain of ugly buildings.

Alicia stared at the perpendicular object. "Stands out like a sore—"

"Alicia," Drake warned her. "There are people around."

"What?"

Those few passing by were locals, judging by their look and clothing. No tourists over here. Drake studied alleys and windows but saw no furtive movement. Crouch started forward.

"Best get started."

Drake saw pictures he'd become used to now: large and small hieroglyphics. It didn't take long for most of the team to scan the obelisk whilst two stayed on watch. After that it was Crouch using his binoculars to study each side. The capstone portrayal was at the very top and on the back of the obelisk, just underneath its own shining pinnacle. Crouch struggled to get a good photo because of the position of the sun, but came away after ten minutes of trying.

"I think I have it." He rotated a wheel, zooming in on the screen's image. Four pairs of eyes crowded around to get a better look.

"Is there anything to confirm it's the doomsday device?" Kenzie asked.

"No, but what else could it be? There was once talk of the Giza pyramid itself being built for such a purpose but it's all too fantastical. Passageways hewn at just the right angle could amplify and cohere energy emissions using highly sophisticated crystal technology. It's all a little too farfetched for me. I'm backing simple weapon, simple technology. It's the capstone. But now . . . that's interesting . . . the new depiction is the mortuary temple of Hatshepsut," Crouch said with awe. "That's easy to find and enter. Very famous. But, oh hell, it's bloody huge."

"Bigger than the tomb?" Alicia asked.

"Many, many times."

"Good job there are so many of us," Kenzie said positively. "We'll get the job done."

"But no chance of destroying or even hiding the picture." Dahl gazed up at the topmost heights of the obelisk. "Which I think we *should* do with at least one of these clues."

Hayden clapped Kinimaka on the back. "We could always ask Mano here to lean up against it."

Drake smiled. "Or just walk past it."

"Hey, cool it, brah. Or I might just *walk past* you."

Drake studied the terrain for the dozenth time. "Abba is right though," he said. "We do have to slow our pursuers."

The roar of a powerful engine and the grinding of large tires reached their ears.

Drake keyed the mic. "Smyth?"

"We got two fully laden military vehicles headed right toward us. Full-on velocity too. They're taking no prisoners."

Crouch went sheet-white. "No. Not now. We can't—"

Drake felt a strange trickle of trepidation drip down his spine. "Luther?"

"Well, none of them trucks got a name," Smyth said. "But the way, even on approach, there's men hanging out the windows with RPGs I'd say that's a pretty safe bet."

Judgment, Drake thought.

Their judgment was here.

And it had brought the motherfucking fire.

CHAPTER SIXTEEN

Flight or flight? Drake thought. *Fight or flight?*

Ordinarily, the choice was clear but today it had a number of cloudy alternatives. In the end there was no choice. Crouch was already running for the lead car.

"Outgunned. Outplayed. They have superior vehicles, backup and drones. Just run." The man's voice was calm over the comms.

Hayden's decision had to be split-second. "Go."

They crowded back into the cars, waiting twenty seconds for Smyth and Kenzie, and then gunned it down one of the tributaries that led away from the town. Even inside the cars they could hear the roar of Luther's transport, hear it growing closer and closer. The man knew exactly where they were, possibly aided by the drones, but now Drake remembered something.

"You said Luther was old school," he said. "He won't have backup or eyes in the sky."

"I know," Crouch said seriously. "But we had to move. We could never have held that square as we were."

"So he's what . . ." Alicia asked. "Sniffing us out?"

"Doesn't matter," Crouch said. "He's here now!"

Ahead, two military Hummers swung into the street, traveling two-abreast. Drake's mouth fell open in shock as they began to pick up speed.

"Do not play chicken with this maniac!" the Yorkshireman cried.

Crouch swung the wheel right, followed by Kinimaka in the second vehicle. "I don't intend to. I don't have a death wish, Drake." He jammed his foot to the floor, pouring on the speed.

Drake turned around, saw Kinimaka's vehicle almost kissing their rear fender and then, storming around the sharp corner, both of Luther's Hummers, bouncing off potholes and walls alike.

"He's not holding back."

"And neither will we." Hayden was breaking out the rear window in the following car, preparing to shoot.

"Wait," Dahl said. "This man, notwithstanding his reputation, is a government employee, sent by the Americans, carrying out a mission. Do we know his orders are to kill, or capture? Do we know who sent him? Certainly not President Coburn. Do we know if he wants to talk, or shoot?"

Drake tended to agree with the Swede. Luther was a soldier under orders, not a mercenary taking dollars for blood.

"Meatballs has a point," he said. "Surprisingly."

"Call me one more Swedish export and I'll set Kenzie on you."

"Ooh," Drake cackled. "Promises, promises. Ow!"

Alicia removed her fist from his ribs. "Careful, boy."

"Shit, I can't even crack jokes anymore?"

"Listen," Crouch cut across them. "Let's have the verdict. What are we going to do?"

Dahl took a careful squint through the rear window. "I have an idea."

Drake threw a hand up to either side of his face. "God, no."

"Believe me," Dahl smiled, "you'll like it."

With that he told Crouch and Kinimaka to stamp on the brake pedals. Both vehicles came to a quick stop, jarring the occupants. The chasing Hummers slammed on too, the closest impacting gently with Kinimaka's rear trunk lid.

Dahl was out of the car, the others bemoaning the sanity of the plan but forced to follow. The Swede chose to climb up onto their Jeep's hood, then climbed the windscreen and ran across the top of the car.

Jumped onto Kinimaka's, still running.

Drake followed, and then Alicia. The others chose the low route, using the roadway. Dahl jumped onto the second Jeep's roof and ran harder. Doors were opening further back, four men with weapons climbing out. By then Dahl was leaping through thin air, hitting the first Hummer's hood with both boots and continuing his run. Drake was three steps behind. At floor level the rest of the team were keeping pace, weapons kept low but at the ready.

"Hold there!" a voice boomed out, augmented by some kind of tannoy system built into the Hummer.

Dahl, atop the vehicle, paused. Drake stopped outside the windshield, staring in at the speaker himself.

Luther.

Their eyeballs fused, unable to wrench one from the other. Drake saw a muscle-bound man in his early forties, a man with a head as big as a bear's, with a millimeter of bristle for hair, with hard, purposeful black eyes and with a well-lined face set with formidable, granite-like determination. A terrible white scar ran from his lips to his temple.

"Hold right there," Luther spoke into a radio. "Turn yourselves in. We're taking you in, Drake. Dahl. All of you. Put down your arms and surrender."

Drake had to try even though he guessed it would be hopeless. "You're being manipulated, mate. We're not the enemy they're painting us to be. And this . . . this is a really bad time."

"Not my call," Luther boomed. "I gotta deliver every last one of you, dead or alive. Now . . . lay down your arms."

Dahl glanced at Drake; they had their answer. Alicia jammed a finger into her right ear. "Wow, man, even your *voice* is loud."

"Sorry, dude," Drake said. "But we're laying down nothing."

Dahl leapt from the roof on top of a soldier, bringing a forearm across the bridge of the man's nose. He went down, groaning. Dahl wrestled his weapon away and threw it up to Drake.

Drake threw it back to Hayden.

One more to the tally.

Alicia rushed to help Dahl. A shot sounded, loud in the narrow road, signaling Luther's lack of knowledge or respect for all they had previously accomplished. Drake slammed a boot on the windshield right in front of Luther's face.

"Get your old, moldy ass out here," he said. "I got a beating for you."

Luther unfolded his body from the car seat, slammed the door open, and jumped out. Drake met him head on, giving no mercy because he knew none would be given. Luther was a rock, a solid rack of beef. Drake's knuckles jarred as punches landed. Up close, he put the gun away and tried to take Luther down.

The huge soldier was fast, as fast as Drake and stronger. He took the punches without flinching. As he fought he kept an eye on his men, on Drake's team, and much of the terrain around. Drake found no weaknesses. The Hummers disgorged five figures in total, four men and one woman who all immediately fought nose to nose against Drake's team.

Hayden came over the top, dropped down and implored Luther with a gaze. "We're the good guys. You gotta listen to us!"

Luther simply turned his back on the fight, even took a punch to the kidneys, and shouted at his own team.

"Turn it up a level."

All hell broke loose.

A soldier slammed a door into Smyth's face, forcing him away, reached inside the Hummer and took out a fully prepped rocket launcher. On the far side of the car another man did the same, using Crouch as a punch bag. Two RPGs lined up on opposite high walls that bordered the street.

"No!" Alicia's cry was in vain.

Grenades flew from the small barrels, streaking across the small space. A loud explosion filled the street and concrete debris showered down on top of the Jeeps. A large chunk buckled the hood of one and a persistent cascade shattered the windshield of another. Blocks bounced off onto the floor. Debris blocked the road.

"Light 'em up," Luther yelled.

Drake leapt hard at him, striking the bull-like neck and pushing him face-first into the very wall he'd just ordered bombed, drawing forth a grunt. Drake pushed in hard but Luther used his own forehead to lever away from the wall. He slammed an elbow around, first to the left and then the right, catching Drake, then again and again. Hayden stepped in, but Luther leaned to the side and kicked out, smashing a boot into her chest and stopping her in her tracks, gasping for breath.

From his pocket he produced a Glock.

Drake jabbed at the hand, raining punches down until Luther

dropped the gun, flexing bruised fingers and revealing that the gun had been a ruse. A knife appeared in his other hand and jabbed hard at Drake, completely fooling his defenses. The six-inch blade struck without any obstruction, hitting hard.

Drake grunted and fell back. Hayden saw it and jumped in, her own Glock leveled at Luther's face.

"Drop—"

The man moved faster than she could see; her Glock there one minute and falling to the floor the next. Blood trickled down between her fingers.

Drake, on his knees, somehow managed to collect both fallen weapons then scramble back. The knife had struck his stab vest, saving his life, but jarring and throbbing so much he was seeing double. A bullet hammered into the wall above Luther's head, another close to Hayden. Dahl threw a man at the wall, and was shocked to see him bounce right back with a flying front kick. Mai tripped her female opponent and turned for the knockout blow, only to find a backhand slamming her across the face. Kinimaka's face was bloody. Smyth tried to pick himself up off the floor. Only Kenzie looked in control, and that was because she fought with wild abandon, shaking the blood off in a stream of droplets and diving, snarling, right back for more.

"More!" Luther snarled.

Drake brought a flying elbow down on the man's neck, finally staggering him. The returning punch stopped him though, making him wheeze. Hands on knees, bent over, the two regarded each other.

"Give it up, Drake."

"I . . . can't. Too much at stake."

"We're taking you to justice."

"The people you work for haven't a clue about justice." Drake's chest eased and his breathing began to come a little easier. "When Coburn finds out, it will put them and anyone that has helped them in the firing line."

"The President doesn't know half of what happens out here," Luther growled. "And that's for his own good. Don't try to manipulate me or my team."

"Another time, another place, we would have been team*mates.*"

"Maybe. I read about SPEAR. Shit, I followed you in three times, though you never knew. Babylon." He nodded. "Hawaii, and New York. I was part of your backup." He dropped his eyes. "I knew Komodo. Good soldier."

"And still you think we're rogue? I don't get it."

"Not me. I admit I was surprised, but you're going down, Drake. You and the rest of SPEAR."

"Not today."

Drake raised both guns and aimed them at Luther. "Even that mountain you call a head wouldn't deflect a bullet."

Luther stared impassively and then turned his head slightly. "2015."

Drake found it hard not to gawp, impressed, at the fifty-millimeter scar. "Shit. But do you wanna gamble on that pony twice?"

Luther went to back away, but Dahl was at his rear, also a gun in each hand, one of which lodged into the small of Luther's back. The battle was at a stalemate, guns aimed, nobody giving an inch. It was entirely clear to Drake that Luther would never concede out loud.

"We're leaving," he said. "Catch us later."

Crouch called over from the far side. "Can't go forward."

Drake waved a gun. "We're taking the Hummer."

Steadily, with incredible care, the team inched their way inside the oversized military vehicle, weapons unwavering. Luther and his team didn't give an inch, never said a word, but made no aggressive moves.

"Now that's spooky," Alicia whispered over the comms. "What is that? Extra sensory perception?"

Nobody spoke, trying not to break the spell. Crouch found the starter and checked the rearview.

"Moving now," he murmured. "Stay frosty."

Drake realized his eyes were still welded with Luther's. He watched the larger-than-life figure until they were out of sight and saw not one flicker in the man's frame, not a single movement.

Apart from the eyes. They spoke a grim and dangerous vocabulary.

Crouch heaved a huge sigh as they drove away. "Everyone okay?"

Affirmatives were received, so the team settled in a little, combing the Hummer for useful items.

"He'll find out where we're going," Crouch said.

"You said yourself—it's huge," Hayden said. "We'll be careful."

Crouch looked unconvinced.

Drake, beside him in the front seat, said: "Now I know what you mean."

"That the guy's a walking apocalypse?"

"Yeah. He's relentless; crazy; clever. I can see why the Americans send him in."

"Good guy to have at your side."

"Oh yeah, and a monster to have at your back."

Drake stared out the window, wondering how they could possibly hope to deal with the new threat, especially on top of those that already existed. Luther was acting on orders, but if the guy threw any more missiles at them Drake knew they would retaliate in kind. *Not* to do so would be fatal.

"You know something," he said. "When Lauren left to carry out her plan I wasn't entirely sure it was the right thing to do. But now . . . now . . ."

Hayden nodded in agreement. "She feels like our last hope."

"Depends on the bloodhound." Alicia pointed her thumb back at the town. "And how far he wants to take it."

"Don't be fooled," Mai said. "He'll follow your own creed, Taz. He'll go all the way, every time, hard in, as often as he can. And he'll take no prisoners."

Drake saw worry even in Dahl's eyes.

It was reflected in his own.

CHAPTER SEVENTEEN

Another hour of the day and another safe house—this one in the center of Luxor City, as close as prudence would allow to Hatshepsut's temple. Once the capital of Ancient Egypt, Luxor, then called Thebes, was situated close to many of the famous sites—Karnak, Hatshepsut's Temple, and the Valley of the Kings. The main city was modern and shining bright under the midday sun as the team arrived; with wide through-roads lined with rows of trees and a variety of transport. In sharp contrast, within the contemporary environs lay the remains of the old city, the temple ruins of Karnak and Luxor still standing inside the new city. Before they arrived Crouch told them he had visited Luxor many times, likening the city to one large open-air museum, a fantasy theme park for an old archaeologist like him.

The Nile cut through, and across the west bank Necropolis lay the Valley of the Kings, and the Valley of the Queens.

"Feels even hotter down here." Alicia fanned her face, trying to bask in the air-conditioning.

"It doesn't get much hotter than this," Crouch agreed. "Or sunnier. We'll be at the safe house soon."

"Please tell me it has air-con," Smyth pleaded.

"Well, it has decent sized windows."

"Crap."

Ten minutes later they were ensconced in their apartment, a modern block this time with three different rooms and a modicum of comfort. Hayden walked over to the TV and switched it on, searching for a news channel.

"I was hoping this would be prime news." She threw the remote down.

On screen, a reporter spoke live from the streets of Cairo, a government building in the background. It was a BBC broadcast and came across in English.

"With the deadline fast approaching, officials in Egypt,

Turkey and Greece remain steadfast but nervous. A terrorist organization that call themselves FrameHub continue to hold these countries hostage, reiterating just an hour ago that the first country to capitulate wins." The reporter enunciated the last word and the picture cut to an image medley of each country as a robotic, unidentified voice spoke over the top.

"We will send the other two countries back to the dark ages. Your missile sites will be used against you. Network disruption will cripple you; roads, hospitals and all crucial services will be rendered useless. You have two hours to comply or we will be happy to give you a small taste of what *we* can accomplish."

Hayden sat down heavily, still watching as the picture cut back to the reporter. Most of the team watched with her as they rechecked weapons and reloaded. Drake changed his stab vest; the team wiping sweat away with towels. Kinimaka found the air-con unit and switched it on; though the feeble machine barely managed to huff out a decent blast of air.

"Awful, brahs," he complained. "If we got Lancelot Smyth upset we'd get better airflow."

Smyth was studying his cell and quickly returned it to his pocket. The look on his face told them he hadn't heard Kinimaka—his mind was in an entirely different place. Dahl shrugged back into his gear, eyeing the covering T-shirt with trepidation.

"Just once," he said. "I'd like to step out of the door in a hot country in just my T-shirt."

Alicia raised a brow. "Really? I'd pay to see that."

Dahl sighed. "You know what I mean."

"Cool it," Drake intervened. "That's my bird you're stirring up there."

"She wants to see a real man." Dahl flexed a few muscles. "Leave the poor girl alone."

"And they're mine," Kenzie said with a salacious smile. "Or soon will be."

Dahl found a space to sit and watch the TV. "Don't bet on it, Kenzie."

Hayden raised a hand to shush them as the reporter wound up.

"So here we are; just a few hours until this unknown group threaten to unleash some kind of warning attack on the countries of Egypt, Turkey and Greece. A source in the Egyptian government tells us that, so far, they have been unable to unearth any information on the so-called FrameHub organization threatening to send at least two countries back to the dark ages."

Hayden checked her own weapons. "That's what we'd be involved with if we were still operational."

"Don't fret," Dahl said. "I'm sure they'll have someone working on it. Another team."

"That's what worries me too," Hayden said. "They shut us down, disavowed us all. How many other teams have they disowned?"

Drake hadn't thought of that. "You're think there may be more?"

"Well, we surely can't think we're the only ones. That'd be naïve. I'm thinking if we could contact them . . ." She let the idea hang.

Crouch was listening. "I could help with that," he said. "I haven't heard anything that supports such a theory, but I agree it's unwise to assume you are the only ones. I'll make some calls." He slid out his cell and flicked at the screen a few times.

"Well a little more information now. As you know I tasked a couple of contacts with finding out more of this FrameHub. They might be new to the world, but they're an old unit, together at least two years. Apparently they're made up of super-geeks and, by turns, considered myths and then supposedly proven bona fide. Nobody has ever proven their existence. Nobody has even met anyone involved—" Crouch paused, looked up with an expression of exasperation on his face. "Nobody has ever met anybody who's *met* anybody involved. They're ghosts, people, just ghosts."

"Put 'em on a shelf," Alicia said. "And we'll exorcize 'em later. Is everyone ready?"

Crouch's face changed instantly to excitement. "Moving out?"

"Yeah, and let's make this one quick. The last thing we want is those mercs turning up in such a busy place. And the same goes for Luther."

The team grabbed water and snacks and headed straight for the door.

CHAPTER EIGHTEEN

Hatshepsut's Temple is an ancient funerary shrine situated on the west bank of the Nile, close to the Valley of the Kings and dedicated to Amun, the Egyptian sun god. Its beauty is unmatched, one of the most outstanding monuments that remains on the earth today. Drake heard Crouch state all this and more, but didn't fully understand until he saw it with his own eyes.

He stopped in his tracks, stunned. First, he noticed the enormous cliffs rearing up behind, sandy colored, as if tasked to protect the ancient shrine. The building itself, whilst huge, was dwarfed by the cliffs and the bright blue spread of sky above. Drake saw three levels, a wide ramp leading up to the second. Rows and rows of pillars fronted the shrine, evoking a sense of classical architecture. The ramp and the second level were crammed with tourists and the noise level swelled as they approached.

"Any ideas where to look?" Kinimaka asked.

Crouch shook his head. "We may only get one crack at this. Time is short. Don't rush, just cover every square inch, and—" he tapped the side of his head "—call in the moment you find something."

Drake took a moment to stand at the top of the ramp, turn, and study the crowd behind them. Nothing suspicious presented himself so he turned toward the pillars and the darker, cooler areas within. It took a while for his eyes to adjust and then he started paying close attention to the walls, the ceiling, the pillars, just as before. The area back there was narrow, thankfully so as it gave them less ground to cover. The floor consisted of smooth, seemingly haphazard paving, gray in color, and what few depictions there were on the bodies of the pillars were worn and hard to make out. Still, Drake saw nothing even remotely looking like a capstone.

The team completed the outer sweep and moved into the

inner courtyard, seeing another row of pillars and tired, sandy walls full of depictions. Again they split up and walked across to study every inch.

Drake kept an eye on the tourists and the locals, noting that Smyth and Kenzie were doing the same. The atmosphere inside was low-key and pleasant, everyone knowing what to expect and quietly awed by the ancient construction. The day stretched out ahead of them.

"Is this weird?" Alicia asked.

Drake frowned. "Is what weird?"

"Us. Like this. I mean . . . fugitives? Really? I know I've been on the run most of my life but not like this. Every uniform, every cop I see, even the sound of an approaching siren—it's all suddenly a concern, you know?"

"I get it." Drake nodded. "And if it wasn't for Michael needing our help we'd be on top of it by now. I'm sure we would, love—"

"We don't even know who burned us," she interrupted. "Or why. Crowe would be a good place to start."

"True, but I don't think she's behind it all. At worst, she's compliant. Either way, they need taking down. Especially, as Hayden suggested, there may be more teams."

Alicia nodded at that. "It would be naïve to think we're the only ones affected."

"We'll get there," Drake assured her with a clear, open look. "We will."

"I know." Alicia turned her attention to the wall and the pictures there. Drake stayed close, again scanning the crowd. A quick flick of the comms and a chat assured him that everyone was where they should be.

Crouch spoke up then. "Nothing here, I'm afraid. We should head down. Try the lower level."

The team agreed, heading for the ramp again with its central stairs. It was mid-afternoon by now, the tourists out in full flow and the sunshine as hot as it was going to get. They took their time descending, broke out water and snacks, then looked at the lower row of pillars that stood before them.

A few minutes later they were in that shade again, searching, hoping to find the lost symbol.

Drake heard a distant roar, dull at first but gradually growing louder. It wasn't the approach of anything airborne, nor a powerful car. It was something else.

"You hear that?" He turned and shaded his eyes, staring back toward the road and parking areas.

The approaching roar was not alone. Several engine notes could be heard.

"My ears tell me that's a Ducati Panigale," Drake said. "Anyone else?"

"It's a *motorbike,* Drake." Alicia shook her head. "You're such a child sometimes."

"Hey . . ."

Crouch was alongside him now. "It is a Panigale," he said. "And an MV Augusta if I'm not mistaken. Others too. And they're headed straight for the bloody ramp!"

Drake knew it couldn't be a coincidence. The riders were large, double-teamed, the bikes the fastest of their kind on the planet that day. Five of them—ten men—and they were headed straight across the car park directly through two masses of tourists, sending them diving and screaming out of the way.

"What is this?" Hayden asked in surprise. "An assault? Here? Surely not."

"Well, whatever it is, we should prepare." Crouch unslung his backpack.

Drake scanned for guards, knowing the Egyptians would be entirely on their toes when it came to something like this. "The security?" he breathed. "It's all gone. There were armed police there." He pointed. "And there. A couple of undercovers I spotted too. But . . . now . . ."

"It begs the question," Dahl grunted. "Who on earth are the mercs working for?"

"Someone with the capability to pull the guards away," Hayden said.

Drake watched all five bikes, their helmeted riders and passengers using the machines to a great degree of their potential, approach the base of the ramp. Quickly, they slowed. Civilians dashed to and fro, desperate to get away from the area. Their screams were almost enough to drown out the roar of the

Kawasaki Ninja that Drake had his eye on, but not quite.

"Let's make 'em pay for this."

He stepped out of the shade, around a column, and one of the bikers saw him. Shouts went up and helmet visors were raised. One man gunned the engine of a Honda Fireblade, the other opened the throttle of the Ninja. Both bikes spurted toward him.

The SPEAR team spread out around the far side of the bottom level of Hatshepsut's temple, stood in the heat and beneath the cloudless blue sky, weapons ready, studying the terrain and the scene. Civilians were beyond the oncoming bikes and nobody would risk a stray bullet at this stage.

The fifth bike in the procession—Drake recognized it as an Aprilia RSV—also veered off the path and darted across the dried-out desert, closing the gap at rapid pace. Two bikes remained near the ramp, their occupants staring over at Drake and the team through black visors, surrounded now by angry, mystified people. The bikers ignored everything; they just stared.

Drake and the others had no choice; as the bikes powered closer, engines roaring, they raised weapons. *Still no sign of the cops. What the hell is going on?*

He sighted the Ninja's rider, the very center of his pitch-black helmet. What were they up to? Something smelled decidedly off about the entire attack.

"I have a feeling we've been outthought," Dahl said.

Then the Ninja's rider held up a hand, slowing before Drake and Dahl. He stopped and then waited a moment, dust swirling around him. The other bikes pulled up too, all six riders holding gloved hands in the air.

The first rider climbed off his bike. Alicia held up her own right hand. "What the fuck is going on, CHiPs?"

The man took a moment to remove his helmet. A hard, Eastern European face presented itself, pockmarked and forever bereft of smiles. This man had grown up hard and had only known hardship.

"Who is your leader?" The accent was thick, the English perplexing at best.

"I am." Hayden stepped forward.

At the same time, Drake said: "Me."

And Crouch coughed. "Well, I guess you could say—"

"Stop!" the biker snarled. His colleagues were in the process of dismounting and gathering threateningly at his back.

"We're an unconventional crew." Mai smiled.

"It does not matter!" the man shouted.

"Then why did you ask?" Alicia said innocently. "C'mon, Barry Sheene, it's too hot out here for foreplay. Give it to me right between the eyes."

"You come with us." The man took a breath and wiped his streaming brow. "You all come with us now."

Drake stared. "I don't think so, pal."

"Then you will cause the death of all these people." The merc couldn't keep a vicious smile from lighting his eyes. "I do not care either way."

Drake and Dahl indicated their gun hands. "You're the one standing in the sights."

"Maybe." The merc pulled out a phone and turned the screen toward the SPEAR team. "Watch."

Drake squinted as the rest crowded around. Slowly, the potential scenario became clear and Drake felt an ice-cold torrent of horror drop straight through his body.

"No," he breathed. "You . . . you can't do that."

The merc smiled nastily.

CHAPTER NINETEEN

Drake couldn't tear his eyes from the screen.

It showed the final two bikes, the ones that had remained near the ramp. The riders remained in place but their passengers had climbed down. Now, a man was taking a live video of those passengers and the bombs that were strapped to their waists underneath their thick jackets.

"Choice is yours," the merc said. "But make it quick."

Drake restrained a desire to lash out. Alicia couldn't. She moved fast, but Dahl was ready. His right arm came out as she moved, encircling the top of her chest and holding her back.

"Don't."

Alicia fought, but Dahl held on. Smyth was also walking forward, hatred and hellfire plastered across his face. Mai stepped in front of him, pushed him backward, and caught a swipe of his arm. She twisted it back, stopping the soldier in his tracks. Kinimaka was red-faced, puffing, but unable to say a single word.

Crouch caught the merc's attention. "Just stay calm. There's no need for violence. What exactly do you want from us?"

"You come now. All of you. Right now. No more talking. Or the first bomber goes in."

Drake let his Glock fall, dangling below his hand. Dahl did the same. The team stood down. Perhaps it was all a bluff, but the probability was that it wasn't. Better Intel would have been great, but for now they were flying blind.

"You looked like tourists once. Do it again. Walk with us."

Under the intense heat the SPEAR team walked alongside the bikes. Soon they joined the others, passenger-less now since they had joined the crowd. The initial appearance of the bikers seemed to have been taken as a prank. Tourists were laughing again and taking pictures, though Drake saw no evidence of locals.

"What's this about? Who are you?"

"No questions. No answers. You will find out what they want when we get there."

Drake glanced at Dahl. What *they* want?

"They're mercs," Dahl said. "Basically slaves."

Drake nodded. He hated that they'd been forced into capitulation by a horrific but ingenious plan of attack. Nobody hurt, not even close. But the bombers were still back there, and the authorities, judging by distant sirens, seemed to have their hands full with something else.

Presently they reached the parking area and were joined by all the bikes, minus the two bombers. Drake cast his eyes over the powerful machines, ticking in the heat. A gray van was indicated and its rear doors thrown open.

"Get in," the leader said.

"You're really gonna regret this," Kenzie said.

"Crap," Alicia said between gritted teeth. "I normally don't get into the back of a van like this. Not without first being treated to a glass of Lambrusco."

The team climbed up and sat around the dirty, gritty floor. A moment before the rear doors were slammed shut the lead merc made another appearance.

"So you know, bombers will remain in place until we reach destination. Understand?"

Drake nodded. The doors closed.

"Shit," Alicia said. "It's like a bloody oven in here."

"Don't worry," Drake patted her leg, "we can treat this as a reconnaissance mission. Let's get some valuable info."

"Don't touch me." Alicia swatted his hand away. "You're all sweaty."

"I thought you liked that."

"Not this kind of sweat."

"Oh, there are different kinds?"

"Damn right there are."

Drake stared around. The others all sat in repose, resting, conserving their energy and wondering where they'd end up, and who might confront them. It wouldn't be Luther, Drake was sure. But another player. A big player.

"Well," Kinimaka said to make conversation. "I guess this is the first team sauna."

Drake found it interesting that they hadn't been stripped of weapons or even searched. The threat of a man wearing a bomb-suit was enough. They were free to talk, plan, execute.

"What do we think this is all about?" he asked.

"I've been thinking that too," Crouch said. "Unfortunately, there are a dozen possibilities. The US government, looking for you. Old enemies of any one of us. It could be linked to the FrameHub situation. A rival team. More likely though, it has something to do with the seven seals."

"Wouldn't they have waited until we found the fourth clue?" Mai asked.

"Yes, they would. That's another thing bothering me."

The van bounced and rattled its way toward an unknown destination, the team holding on as best they could. Several times it slowed, but then sped up again, and soon the sounds of the city were left behind. It felt like they were out in the middle of nowhere—not a single sound outside the truck could be heard.

"They're taking us into the desert," Hayden said.

"No good ever came out of a forced trip to the desert," Kenzie said. "Believe me, I know."

Dahl shifted beside her. "Do you *know* any of these guys?"

"Me? Why? You think they might be relic smugglers?"

The Swede shrugged. "Good place for it."

"I don't recognize anyone, but if I do—you'll be the first to know."

"I am sorry, Kenzie," Dahl said into the silence. "I know how hard you're trying to leave that life behind."

"It's like . . . kicking a drug habit. Losing that sense of intense danger, excitement, satisfaction. It's like losing a whole part of yourself that you love."

"Hey, we're not exactly the Brighouse and Rastrick Brass Band," Drake grumbled.

Kenzie nodded and smiled. "Of course, I know. The danger

though . . ." She clicked her tongue. "It's different. Very different. It calls me. It wants me. And, if I'm being honest, sometimes I want it all back."

"I know this sounds unlikely, but I know what she means," Alicia said quietly. "Being on the other side for a while—it has an effect you can't shake off. It calls. Always."

Kenzie gave Alicia a grateful look and then huddled down. Drake had thought she'd already kicked the bad habit. What did she need to get past it? Listening to them, it seemed that Alicia, Kenzie's arch-enemy, might even be able to help.

At last, the van slowed and then came to an abrupt stop, throwing both Yorgi and Smyth, who had been standing, to their knees. Men started shouting, many men, and some came running around to the back of the van.

The sound of weapons priming was loud and ominous.

"You come quietly," the merc leader shouted again. "We have many men and bomber still in Luxor. You hear?"

Drake shouted a compliant reply.

The back doors opened. Drake saw darker skies, full of sunset and glaring lights illuminating a rough paddock, bordered by a fence. At least a dozen men had weapons trained on them.

The merc leader grinned. "Now. You come with us."

CHAPTER TWENTY

"Scream as loud as you like. In the desert, nobody will hear you."

That had been the advice of just one of their endearing guards, all of whom were filthy and foul-looking. They were inside a prison, just inside the entrance to a network of caves. The prison was makeshift but it was strong, made up of two mountain walls and strong, thick four-by-four that had been hammered and then concreted into the already sturdy floor. Laths of two by two made up the horizontal braces, giving the guards something to rest the barrels of their guns on when they wanted to have a little fun.

To the prisoners' left they could see the entrance to the cave system, softly illuminated as the night drew in. To the right the wide passage ran on into darkness, the way marked by flickering torches.

Alicia just watched the guards.

This had been such a terribly confusing few weeks. For her. For them all. It showed the measure to which any kind of powerful authority held their prize employees. It was repeated in all walks of life. In the end you were just a number, only as good as your last failure. The wins only helped those already in front of you. She shook her head violently to dispel the negative thoughts. Stuff like that could get you killed.

So her concentration went, fully, to the guards. There were eight of them at any one time. Others came and went. They didn't appear to have any structure, any balance. Just animals with weapons and a small slice of power. She figured they'd been incarcerated for the best part of two hours now and had learned zilch. Twice, Crouch and Drake had spoken up, asking why they were here.

The guards snarled like desperate, rabid, grimy dogs and rested their guns on the slats. Once, they fired, the bullet passing in between Drake and Yorgi, and slamming into the mountain wall. Everyone outside the cell laughed. What a great joke.

Alicia loved these people. They were her weakness. Being alone and focusing every day on a new horizon had its drawbacks, yes, but it damn well had its perks too. Caring about nobody, having nobody, meant your heart and your mind and your emotions could never be held hostage. The thought of having loved ones scared her more than any other event in her life.

The thought of losing loved ones was unadulterated hell.

But she turned to her strengths now, knowing they held the best chance of getting everyone out of here alive. It would help to know *why* they were here, but escape was the priority.

The situation was grim. The team had no weapons, no comms. They hadn't been offered food or water. Every man outside those wooden bars held a reliable weapon. They were being watched twenty-four-seven. And it was getting cold now, the desert night drawing in. The extra clothes they'd been forced to wear earlier—to conceal Kevlar and weapons—were welcome now, though the bulletproof jackets had been taken from them.

There will be a chance. We just need to be ready, to recognize it.

The guards watched her watch them. To be fair, they weren't half bad, a few always standing well back, away from the bars, overseeing all and remaining indistinct. Alicia wanted to bait them, to anger them, force them into a mistake, but unfortunately it appeared none of them spoke English, which took the wind well and truly out of her sails. All she could do was transmit her disdain through her gaze and, to her credit, she thought she was doing a pretty good job.

Alicia shifted, accidentally kicking Yorgi. This was another problem. They were cramped, thrown side by side in this small cell and then chained together. Chained to the wall. Chained by the legs and the wrists.

A knocking sound echoed through the cell, drawing everyone's attention. A new man stood there, Uzi poised across the slate, the barrel inching from target to target.

"My name is Saint." He laughed. "I know! Crazy, huh? I'm your jailer, your new direct boss. What I say, you do. When I say it, you jump, or bend, or crawl. You drink when I tell you. Eat when I tell you. Sleep if I let you." He paused. "Is that clear?"

Alicia glared back with utter contempt.

Drake said, "Why are we here?"

Saint shook his head very slowly. "You don't listen. I *knew* you wouldn't listen. All right, then. Here's lesson number one."

He shot Yorgi.

The Russian thief screamed, scrambling in the dirt on the floor of the cave. Kinimaka and Smyth, the closest to him, leaned over to steady his writhing body. Chained together, he pulled on all of them, making the rough iron chafe and bloody their wrists and ankles, pulling their limbs to and fro.

Yorgi took an enormous breath, tried to steady himself. The bullet had grazed his thigh, traveling by. Smyth's hand staunched the blood loss.

"In case you're wondering," Saint said. "My aim isn't off. It's perfect. I could take an eyebrow off a stag at a thousand yards. I could take your nose off—" he nodded at Drake "—or shoot one up your ass. Perfect." He looked to Alicia. "I know you don't wanna be here. But you are. And I'm in charge, so get fucking used to it."

"Yessir, boss." Smyth couldn't help himself. "Whatever you say."

Saint whipped out a wicked looking knife, letting the serrated blade glint in the light. "I'm also good with this," he said softly. "In fact, I skinned a man alive just last night. Right here. Took me hours. But then," he looked up, "practice makes perfect, eh?"

Nobody spoke.

"Well, that's a little better. I don't expect answers. I know who you are. *What* you are. Team SPEAR." He laughed. "What a prize. If only my orders were different I'd have half the world's terrorists on their way down here, ready to make a highest bid for you. I'd make a fortune. But—" he sighed "—that's just a wet dream. And speaking of wet dreams," his black eyes moved across the women, "I see four right here."

Alicia knew it was a test, a provocation issued to see if they needed another demonstration. For now, nobody did and Saint took it as another sign of acquiescence.

"Good, good," he said, tapping first his gun and then his knife against the bars. "I see we're gonna get along. Now I do realize you have no idea what's going on. I do realize you're all dying to find out. And I do realize you're all hungry, thirsty and uncomfortable." He let out a peal of laughter. "So . . . on that note, I'll bid you goodnight."

He turned away, speaking quite clearly to the guards as he went.

"No food. No water. And keep it unpleasant."

Spoken in Romanian, Kenzie translated for the team. "They have to be the mercs from the first tomb," she said. "Or part of them. I wonder what they want."

"Well, we did kill a lot of them." Dahl watched Yorgi.

"It is okay." The young thief noticed everyone's concern. "It burns, but is only a flesh wound."

"Wrap it cleanly," Hayden said. "I'm guessing infection down here is rife."

"I will."

"I'm not liking this," Crouch said. "Revenge? Maybe. But who do they bloody work for? It almost feels like a CIA op."

Hayden stared at him without emotion. "You know, I guess anything is possible. There are more off-the-books ops these days than sanctioned ones."

A machine-gun ratcheted, the noise cutting through the cave. When Alicia looked to the bars she saw a grinning man with jagged yellow and black teeth. Slowly, he held a finger up to his mouth, revealing bleeding gums.

"Shhh."

Water came creeping into the cell, soaking the floor. Alicia rose with the others, the process incredibly complicated with them being chained together. She guessed this was more of the 'unpleasant'.

Forced to stand, the team passed a few more hours.

The night was long. The guards came and went, seemingly

randomly, joined by those that just wanted to take a look. The random aspect to things only made it all the harder. Alicia saw no way out—at least no way without taking casualties. Real casualties.

"If we thought being on the run was grim," she said. "It was a walk in Hyde park compared to this."

"Shhh!"

"Oh, go snog a sand spider."

The guards attacked the bars then, sticking long knives through and jabbing at the captives. Alicia took a blow to the bicep, felt the blood flow. Hayden cried out from a deeper cut; Dahl from a longer slash. The team rattled their way to the center of the cell, sloshing in water, only a hand's length away from the hacking blades.

Yorgi bit his lip until it bled, already suffering.

"Nice work, shit-for-brains," Kenzie whispered in Alicia's ear.

Alicia studied her wound. "Yeah, I was hoping they'd just stab you."

Then Saint returned, calling the guards back from the bars, laughing to see their predicament. "Well, well, the SPEAR team humbled. I do love seeing this. Wait, just wait . . ." He rushed off, returning in half a minute.

"Hold that pose."

He took a photo on his cellphone, chuckling all the while. The laughter turned incredibly evil toward the end.

"And this is only the beginning," he said. "The night before the storm. The calm before the thunder and violence. Oh, how I look forward to tomorrow!"

He skipped away, happy.

Alicia closed her mind away for a while, unwilling to accept this situation. *It won't last.* They had several of the best leaders, soldiers and fighters in the world among them.

But tomorrow was always going to come.

CHAPTER TWENTY ONE

Morning dawned outside the cave network, throwing lustrous rays through the opening and onto the dusty floor. Alicia had given up standing the night before, along with all the others, and now sat in a slurry of dirt, soaked through, her back against the mountain wall, as far away from the guards as was possible. The rest of the team were seated around her, arrayed as best and as restfully as they could be under the circumstances.

During the night, the guards had broken out several small toys. One, a mini-crossbow like a child's toy, could fire toothpicks, small nails, stones and other sharp implements at a fast and bruising rate. The guards appeared to start gambling on who could make the best shot, elicit the loudest cry of anger, strike certain areas.

It all fuelled Alicia's fire.

She restrained it, nurtured it, made ready to release it all when that chance arose.

Saint arrived half an hour later.

"Oh, hey." He looked around and then back the way he'd just come. "They didn't bring your breakfast? No coffee and bacon? Oh, shit, well, never mind that. I came with news. Who wants a bit of fun interrogation?"

The team generally ignored him, but those that were watching didn't let their eyes waver.

"C'mon, kids. It's all good. A finger here, a toe there. I promise to be precise. No ragged edges . . ." He grinned and spread his arms. "Or you could just talk to me."

"You need to make your mind up," Smyth growled. "They've been telling us to shut up all night."

"Ah, well, I am in charge after all. Not you. Anyway, was that a volunteer?"

Smyth grinned back. "Whatever, man."

"I see you had a nice cool night. Don't worry, it'll start to warm up again soon. And I mean really warm up. The temperature in here can rise to a dangerous level. Luckily though—" he swigged from a plastic bottle "—we all have more than enough water."

He poured the remainder onto the floor before their eyes.

Alicia unglued her tongue from the roof of her mouth. "You do know a time will come when we get out of here?"

"Oh, yeah, Alicia Myles, I really do. In fact, that's gonna be later today. And then the games really will start!"

He turned away as another man came running up, clearly more than just a colleague to Saint.

"Bud, you gotta come and look. They fired us an email across, showing us what happened. FrameHub, I mean. They launched their demonstration, just a dose of what they're capable of."

Crouch leaned into the chained circle. "FrameHub? I don't get it. Why are they interested in us and what does it have to do with the seals? Shit, what are we missing?"

"Hey, Liam," Saint said. "What did they do?"

"Stopped a vital dam working in Egypt. Poisoned some kids in the isolation ward in a hospital in Greece. Suffocated six workers in Turkey. All CPU-based shit."

Saint was grinning now. "This, I gotta see. Give me a moment, bro, I'm trying to decide which one of these assholes I start snipping."

Liam gawked. "Gotta be one of the hotties, bro. Let the guys pass her around a while; soften her up."

"You can fucking try." Alicia was up and at the bars faster than the new merc could blink, her sudden adrenalin dragging the others with her. With the small space she created, she took the opportunity to jab three stiffened fingers at his eyes.

Liam squealed and staggered back, holding his face. Saint shook his head in bewilderment. "Bro, you are a fucking pussy. And not too bright. Get the hell outta here. I'll be up in a minute."

Liam staggered away, moaning.

Saint affected a look of embarrassment. "Yeah, I know, I know. And he's one of the brightest. So look, we gonna do this the hard way or the fun way?"

Alicia gripped the wooden bars, trying to see more of the cave system. The entrance seemed composed of only a brash brightness that left imprints on her eyeballs. The way that led further into the system vanished into darkness, inadequately lit.

Drake and Dahl came forward a little, dragging Kinimaka with them, the three making a formidable wedge at the front of the little chain-gang.

"You may have taken our weapons," Dahl said. "But, since you're such a nice, chatty jailor, I have to warn you. We're not defenseless."

Alicia also knew what everyone else knew. They were required alive. If not, they'd be rotting in a hole in the desert by now.

"Oh, really?" Saint boomed. "Thanks for that wonderful moment of insight. I'll promise to be careful. Now . . . see how we do things."

He turned to the gathered guards. "I want the old one there. Near the bars. Bring him to me now."

Alicia saw they meant Crouch and felt a stab of anguish. The doors were opened and the team crowded around. Guns were leveled at them, some wavering. Drake and Dahl bunched at the front, with Kinimaka covering Crouch. The others all bunched in.

"All right," Saint came inside, "we do it the fun way."

He held up a Walther, aimed it at Mai's leg and fired. The bullet flashed a millimeter past, the burn singeing her pants leg. He fired another in-between Dahl's legs, higher than was comfortable, the bullet missing and then burying itself into the ground.

He whipped his knife around, slicing Alicia and Drake, darted back, and raised the Walther again.

"I can do this shit all day."

"You do that," Dahl hissed. "Just get the hell out of our house."

He kicked out, catching a guard in the ribs. The man folded and Drake reached down for the discarded weapon, only to be brought up short by his chains. Dahl tried to bend too, but the steel was just too short and tight.

"All right. Just take the old fool." Saint backed out.

More guards flooded into the cell until movement was hard. They tugged on the chains, two, three at a time, shuffling Drake and Dahl to where they wanted them. Punches and kicks were meted out. Kinimaka was stabbed in the thigh until he fell, blood flowing from the wound. Hayden cried out and fell to her knees beside him, dragging Kenzie with her. The movements upset the chain and sent everyone tottering, steel scraping skin, and chains pressing into bone. Rifle butts were used too, on exposed heads and without mercy. Drake could not move as a gun was smashed over his skull, three times.

More guards squeezed by the scene of the punishment and grabbed hold of Crouch. They removed his manacles from the chain and dragged him clear; their colleagues still fighting with Dahl, Smyth and the others. Alicia could barely move but managed to trip a guard and hook a hand around his throat when he fell.

She gripped the larynx, crushed it as hard as she could. His gun was trapped beneath his body, inaccessible to Alicia. Such were the breaks.

A boot smashed down onto her cheek and stayed there, pushing her face into the hard dirt, exerting more pressure until the blood pounded in her brain. In the end she gave up her grip on the larynx, preferring to fight another day. Still the boot pressed down and another pounded on her back for a while. Someone bruised Drake, because she heard him cry out.

At last, the pressure eased and the guards went away. She looked up, hurting, to see Saint still standing outside their cell.

Crouch stood at his side, hands cuffed behind his back, a gun at his temple.

"You see?" Saint said pleasantly. "I hate to say I told you so, kids. But I did, and I guess that's why I earn the big bucks. I could pop this prick right now, blow his brains out. You want that?"

Alicia felt her heart lurch, tried to move. The others did the same. Chains rattled and restraints clinked.

"You see? A soldier loses his edge when he loves. That's how it is."

"I'd say—" Dahl grunted and heaved as he rose to his knees, dragging three others with him "—quite the opposite."

"They call you the Mad Swede, am I right? I can see why. Now, simmer down for a while. Conserve your energy 'cause you're gonna need it."

"Where are you taking him?" Alicia asked. "Why?"

"Just up a ways," Saint answered. "Don't worry, you'll be able to hear him. This prick's gonna get a very *sharp* talking to."

CHAPTER TWENTY TWO

"Come on. Come on!" Alicia berated them all. "Come up with a damn plan. They're torturing him up there!"

The screams had endured for the best part of half an hour now, with little let up. They could hear Saint laughing, shouting, cajoling. Drake had dragged them all around the cell, ignoring the guards and their torments, searching for a weak spot. They found nothing. Now, those in the middle of their huddle were attempting to find a fault in their chains.

A guard shouted at them in Arabic. Alicia spun and hurled a rock at him. The missile struck the bars but made him jump back in shock. No weapons were raised. Again, the temperature was their enemy, rising by the minute and making everything more uncomfortable. Crouch's screams were unrelenting, and Alicia knew he was once a trained soldier.

Retired, living his life more hassle-free.

They should never have gotten involved. Crouch was living a fantasy and they were on the hoof, runaways. Hunted. Where would it all end?

FrameHub were chasing something, not just conflict between nations. The American splinter cell were chasing something, not just the downfall of SPEAR. Luther was chasing something, not just death and destruction. The Chinese and the British were chasing something, not just the Sword of Mars. And now she, and all her friends, were caught in the middle.

The only way out was to finish it. End it all so they could come out the other side and taste the freedom once more.

Then Crouch's screams abruptly stopped. A strangled cry rang out, and then nothing. Alicia stared fearfully up the passage.

A guard spoke in Arabic, laughing. Kenzie translated it: "We return him to you later. A part every hour."

Then Alicia saw them gathering—a dozen guards and then

more. Guns were poised and so were other weapons. Some held clubs, baseball bats and even rocks. Others brandished steel bars and one, a heavy leather whip. Alicia rose slowly as she sensed something big was happening.

Drake and Dahl shushed the others, everyone rising to their feet as a silence settled. Alicia got the impression that they were about to find out exactly why they were here.

Saint came rushing up. "Hey, hey," he called. "I'd forget my own head if it were loose."

"What have you done to Michael?" Alicia asked.

"Urm, he's helping us with our enquiries. Or he *was*. But never mind that. You people have far worse problems to worry about."

Alicia bit her tongue, tensing every muscle in her body. The rage was waiting to be unleashed.

"We're taking you out of there. Now, we doing it the fun away like before or are you gonna come quietly?"

"Looking forward to cracking your skull." Dahl rolled both shoulders.

The guards attacked as before. This time Kinimaka smashed an opponent's skull, leaving him prone and unmoving. Dahl rendered two more unconscious, but still the range of movement was crippling, the confines thwarting every attempt to gain an advantage. The guards had weapons, fresh hands. They had once been soldiers themselves.

Five minutes and Alicia was outside the cell, her hands cuffed at her back, legs hampered by more manacles set at a length that hindered movement. The others waited at her back, dripping blood and flesh torn. They were all soaked through, sweating freely and filthy. Alicia was glad to see heads held high and faces unflinching.

To a person, they were plotting escape.

Saint no doubt knew that too. He was careful, clever. He positioned men away from the line and every four meters or so, always with line of sight. He put other men with automatic weapons at the front and rear of the line. He made sure every member of the SPEAR team knew there was a personal sight lined up on them.

"Go."

As one they shuffled off, arms already aching from the tight restraints. The passage led deeper into the cave system inside the mountain—or hill as it may be—they hadn't seen it clearly from the outside. Every meter a dull torch glowed. Ahead, Alicia saw nothing but an arched passage leading somewhere unknown. The guards were all around them.

They passed an internal cave, a niche in the wall, where Crouch surely had to be, but saw nothing of the man. Alicia saw blood on the floor though and her old boss's watch lying on a table.

Saint shouted out. "Keep the line going. Nothing to see there."

Alicia stopped, peering closer. A guard flew at her face and she headbutted him away. She saw blood pooling around Michael's watch, and dripping to the floor. She saw a mound of something thrown into a corner but, in truth, it could have been anything.

A heavy club came down on her back, staggering her. She moved on, still being beaten. The cave passed by. Ahead, after a while, and through a haze of pain, she saw light. Bright light. The passage started to lean in a downward direction as it headed straight for the unsettling glare.

Alicia stopped walking right at the edge of the light, a guard's hand held upright and palm outward in the recognized gesture. It gave her a moment to study what was on the other side.

Saint came alongside. "Welcome to *our* inferno, boys and girls. They might not treat you well here, but I doubt you'll complain overmuch."

Alicia was awestruck. The cave system branched off here to a vast, stepped hole set in its very center. An inverted dome, open to the skies, but surrounded by the mountain so that nobody ever knew it existed.

Nobody except FrameHub, maybe.

The walls were uneven, offering seating, and the almost perfectly round floor was flat. Pure, undiluted sunshine flooded the entire inverted dome, making it fry. Alicia saw hundreds of men already seated around the sides, stripped to the waist, bottles of beer held in their hands, an assortment of guns and other weapons lying casually across their laps. When one of them saw Alicia at the entrance he pointed, and caught the attention of others, and soon all eyes were looking upward.

A cheer went up, almost a roar.

Saint propped an elbow on her shoulder. "Show us your mettle, Alicia," he said. "It's time to shine."

He pushed her forward and the whole chained-together line started off once more, shuffling along at a steady pace. Just as slowly, the arena they were entering took greater shape. The large, round ring of sky; the sun starting to rise over the eastern tip of the bowl. More and more mercenaries sat waiting, eager and animated. Threats were called out, issued as fast as junk mail. Saint pointed Alicia to a narrow channel that had been hewn into the rock.

"You want me to walk down that? Chained together like this we'll all be skating."

"I don't care how you do it or what happens to you. Just get down before I push you down."

Alicia clenched her fists, barely able to stop herself launching an attack at Saint right now. It was the presence of her friends chained at her back and the unpredictability of the outcome that poured ice-water on her fury. When she regarded the channel again she saw it had a large amount of uneven footing which, in this instance, would help.

"You coming?" she asked Saint.

Their jailer grinned. "All the way."

They inched down the slope, urged on by the beer-swilling mercs, all the way to the bottom. It was much hotter down here. Alicia recalling seeing people frying eggs in this kind of heat.

Saint mopped his brow as they came to a halt, scooped up a bottle of water from a completely incongruous cool-bag resting on the floor by his feet. It was bright blue and sported a pattern of stars around the top.

"You're fighting for water," Saint said, then swigged half the bottle. He threw the other half into Alicia's face which, in truth, was a blessing.

Saint turned to a guard. "Untie Myles. She's up first."

Alicia felt her chains loosened and then she was free of the restraints and the chain. Instantly she lunged at Saint, but the man stepped back fast and a guard with a gun nipped in at her side. His weapon was pointed at her legs.

"Your choice." Saint smirked. "Either way, you're gonna fight."

Alicia saw sense and backed off. Guards were everywhere and stationed around the floor of the bowl in a rough circle. Guns were held ready, not easily. Saint made it clear he would only unchain one person at a time.

She saw no way out of this.

She wiped her face, getting the last droplets of water and transferring them into her mouth. Since they had taken her Kevlar and jacket, she was left with a white T-shirt and combat trousers. The direct sun burned her exposed skin.

Saint raised his hands and stilled the crowd. He turned three hundred and sixty degrees, grin flashing, stubble gleaming with sweat.

"First bout," he said. "Alicia Myles versus the MMC."

A cheer went up. Men and women in the crowd stamped their feet and tapped their rifle butts against the floor. Some whistled. Many more called for blood.

"You killed some of their friends," Saint whispered out of the corner of his mouth. "Our bosses thought this a good way for you to go out. We did too."

He backed away, the eternal laugh piping out of his mouth. Alicia didn't take her eyes from him. "What's the MMC?"

"Oh, just a pet name. It stands for massive meaty chap. There's always one in every fight. Enjoy!"

Alicia stood on the floor of the arena, vision full of blinding sunlight. Grit scraped beneath her boots as she shifted stance. Sweat coated her entire body and dripped off her face. She was ready to fight, focused, determined to help her friends by winning; by always looking ahead and never back.

From an alcove across the other side of the ring a shadow moved. It came around the corner—large, bulky, moving at a slow pace. Alicia waited for it to emerge, then saw a man the size of Kinimaka, but with added muscle and a little more height. His face was hard and crisscrossed with scars. When he set eyes on Alicia he boomed out a peal of laughter.

"This?" he bellowed. "All you bring me is this?"

Alicia harnessed her rage. Here, finally, was a target she could unleash on. And size had never bothered her. *Truth be told,* she mused. *In some instances it had its advantages.* Or so experience told her.

Saint shrugged. "She is the first. She did us all wrong. Do not make it quick."

The MMC slapped his bare chest. "It will be hard with such a twig, but I will do my best."

Alicia stalked to the center of the arena. "Twig? What . . . are ya trying to date me?"

"Date?" The MMC looked startled. "Never, I prefer my women with more meat on their bones."

"Really? To me, you look like you prefer men."

The MMC roared. Saint held up a long, bloodied machete, ready to start proceedings. "Maybe don't talk to her," he suggested calmly. "This ain't Jimmy fucking Fallon."

The machete carved a slice of air.

Alicia planted her feet in the center of the arena.

Her adversary charged.

CHAPTER TWENTY THREE

Alicia skipped aside, using her pace. The MMC lumbered by, an arm outstretched which Alicia saw coming a mile off. Easily, she ducked past that and came back around. Beyond the slobbering monster she saw her team, all watching with worry, agonizing over the outcome, heavily guarded. It was also dreadfully clear that the arena was going to be the place they died, one by one, on this day or another.

Alicia darted one way, then the other, upsetting her big opponent, and managed to leave a trailing leg as she passed him by. She hoped he'd trip, but all he did was bark her shin with his huge ankle bone, making her curse aloud.

The crowd laughed, enjoying her pain. Alicia looked up into the bright sky for a moment then immediately wished she hadn't.

The MMC charged and her retina was just pure white light. She skipped back, stumbled on a rock and fell. The MMC was over her. He roared and kicked out, the blow glancing off her ribs as she twisted away. She rolled, kept her eyes shut to help clear her vision, then snapped them open and leapt to her feet.

The MMC was right in front of her.

"Strike one!" Saint shouted.

His feet struck her stomach, doubling her over. Alicia felt pain; but where normally she would summon a surge of power and agility to get her the hell out of there, today the lack of food and water was taking its toll.

She fell to her knees. The MMC placed a hand on top of her head and mimed something at the crowd, to which they all burst out laughing. Alicia heard it and the callous hatred that surrounded her, found the inner fury and embraced it.

She rose fast, a fist clenched and punching up right into the MMC's scrotum. The man howled and then staggered, cupping the area and blowing hard. Alicia saw her only opportunity.

She struck out with lightning blows, each a devastating strike. The MMC took them all, barely flinching. Red marks crossed his chest, neck and face. The pain in his groin made him throw up into the dust. The crowd jeered and Saint couldn't stop the laughter. She heard encouragement from Dahl and Drake. She worked her way around to the back of the enormous slab of beef, wondering where the sweet spot was.

Having already tried most of the nerve clusters, she was slightly at a loss. But she was sprightly and unharmed, apart from a deep pain in her stomach. The MMC lashed out, an elbow catching her waist. Pain exploded. Alicia backed off. He lashed out again, this time striking only hot air.

He panted, rose to his feet, head hanging. Liquid poured off him in torrents and his black hair hung lankly. He came forward. Alicia bent, grabbed two handfuls of dust and flung them into his eyes. He stood there, rubbing them, blind for a moment.

Alicia ran in, leaped and landed a stunning front kick to his kidneys, followed it with multiple strikes. The MMC groaned and finally flinched. The effort had drained her though, drained her considerably.

She moved back, panting, exhausted.

Saint kicked her in the small of the black, sending her sprawling into the dirt. Drake and Dahl cried out in anger and rushed forward, but warning gunshots into the air stopped their advance. It hardly mattered for now. The MMC was still clearing the dust from his eyes and Alicia used the time to take a breather.

"I guess it's time for some blood," Saint said.

He threw a club into the arena, a club studded with nails on every side. The weapon bounced across the ground and came to a rest at the MMC's feet.

He grinned down at it.

"Old friend."

Alicia unleashed it all; every ounce of rage she'd stored up over the last twenty four hours. She sprinted like a cheetah chasing lunch, threw herself feet first through the dirt, straight toward the club, but ignoring the actual weapon. Dust and gravel spun up to both sides of her, marking the path of her slide. Her momentum saw her through and as the MMC reached down to grab the club her boots were in perfect line with the top of his skull. She kicked out, still sliding, saw him rear back and passed between his legs.

On the way through she snagged the club with her left hand.

She came up on his rear side, planted her feet and rose. Spun with the club now in both hands, and brought it crashing down onto the MMC's exposed back. The nails struck and lodged. The MMC arched his back and howled. Alicia kicked him down into the dirt.

She looked over to the Saint as the man fell.

"Finish it."

"No."

"Your funeral. He will be back."

She skirted the groaning figure, now prone and alien-like—the club with its nails sprouting from his back. Blood ran freely into the dirt as men ran on to help him away.

Saint threw Alicia a bottle of water and then turned to the rest of the SPEAR team.

"Guess who's next?"

Matt Drake took a small swig from the water bottle that Alicia handed round to everyone. Saint watched him walk to the center of the arena as several mercs took aim and cocked their weapons.

Saint held up a hand. "It appears they know you?"

Drake looked up into the stands. "We probably attend the same Yorkshire Pride conventions."

A shot rang out; the bullet kicked dirt up at Drake's feet. Saint laughed and gave the stands an indulgent look. "Go on then. Take your shot. Just one, mind."

Several gunshots rang out. Bullets hammered all around Drake, glancing off the floor, traveling across the arena. He stood immobile, without flinching. Even the slightest show of fear would tell them they'd won.

Saint bellowed for quiet. "Here we go then. Fight number two."

Drake watched the alcove as a shadow moved. A man came out, dressed in a dark blue suit and wearing a red tie and white shirt. He carried a briefcase, which he laid carefully on the ground, unzipped and then pulled out a meat cleaver.

Drake couldn't help but shake his head at Saint. "What the fu—"

"The Gentleman." Saint grinned. "Now Drake, whatever else you do remember what your mom used to say." He backed off. "Enjoy yourself!"

Drake sidestepped around the arena. The Gentleman kept a light grip on the cleaver, rotating it occasionally in his hand, allowing the bright, clean blade to catch the light. The briefcase lay where he'd left it. Drake was less than three feet from it when The Gentleman attacked.

Blade slashing in downward arcs, left and right and left, he came fast. Drake side-stepped and backed away and then darted past, coming up to the briefcase now and darting a look inside.

The Gentleman stopped, reached a hand into his inside jacket pocket and pulled out a small black device with one large yellow button. He pressed it immediately, catching Drake cold as the small explosive he'd left in the briefcase detonated.

The blast knocked Drake off his feet, and sent sharp fragments flying into his body. He landed hard, on his back, the wind knocked out of him. The Gentleman loomed through the smoke, tall and dark and swinging the cleaver.

Drake thrust up his hands, catching the cleaver as it came slicing down. He managed to grab The Gentleman's wrist just as the blade reached his nose. A sliver of blood was drawn, trickling across his face.

"Fool."

Drake heard the words and feared the worst. This guy was some kind of trickster. He struggled to push the blade away, rolled to force the man off. His head spun from the blast, his body struggled to work. The Gentleman broke away, reached into the suit and came out with a short stick with two prongs on the end.

Pressed another yellow button and the prongs sizzled.

Gotta get moving . . .

Drake scrambled clear, but not before the cattle prod came down on his trailing leg. Instant high-voltage ran through his body, making him shake and sending him back to the ground. For a moment it all vanished—the heat, the sunlight, the arena and the stands full of jeering maniacs. Even the one corner of support receded fully from consciousness, the spot where his friends stood.

They were shouting encouragement now, spurred on by Dahl and Alicia. At first they'd been reluctant to take any part in this— but it was happening anyway and Drake needed something to shear away the veneer of agony.

He heard them. The terrible jolting had stopped but there was a pain in his lower rear calf. When he managed to twist a little and look down there his eyes met a horrific sight.

The Gentleman was slicing at his flesh with the edge of the cleaver; carefully, gently, as if stripping meat tenderly from the bone.

That's exactly *what he's doing!*

"Hey," Drake shouted.

The Gentleman looked up, inquisitive. Blood dripped from the edge of the cleaver.

"You missed a bit." He pointed where the strip of his flesh was still attached.

The Gentleman looked down.

Drake smashed him in the side of the head with his other foot, the boot slamming point blank in his ear. He fell over, the prod skittering away. Drake crawled back, realizing this was the best chance he'd get but unable to act quickly.

His body was still recovering and, like Alicia, his energy was already sapped.

Breathing deeply, he rose to his feet, allowing The Gentleman to do the same. Drake's head still rang from the blast; his vision slightly blurry. The harsh glare of the sun, beating down, didn't help.

"Hey," he shouted to gain a few more seconds of recovery.

"You got any paracetamol in that inside pocket?"

The Gentleman looked unsure, reached inside, and came out with a grenade.

Drake ignored the rush of anxiety, as his body knew it could not take another explosion. Calling on every moment of experience, he watched The Gentleman's arm, saw the flick of the finger when the pin was released, followed the arc of the throw.

Ran *toward* the grenade and met it bluntly. With his foot. He kicked the small round object away, then threw himself to the side. It was a good kick, the grenade curving up out of the arena and heading for the stands. Curses split the air and men scrambled out of the way. The grenade bounced down once and exploded.

Drake rolled and looked up.

A man was flung back by the blast, bounding off the rock-face and falling limply; another was cut by sharp fragments. Rubble flew indiscriminately and a minor cloud rolled into the air. Men rubbed and tried to repair nasty injuries, most of them sending deathly looks straight at Drake.

The Yorkshireman had other things on his mind. The Gentleman was already attacking again, slashing with the cleaver. Drake guarded the blows by blocking wrist against wrist, hoping one of the impacts might slam the cleaver out of the other's grip. He was pushed back, boots slipping in the grit.

Saint's voice interrupted them. "Round two!"

Several men threw objects into the ring.

Drake summoned a huge burst of energy, kicked out, and forced The Gentleman back, clearing space all around him. Several of the objects he recognized instantly. His own Glock. A knife. The club that had been taken out of the MMC's back. A sword. A battered old Uzi. A wicked looking machete.

No easy choice.

Drake saw confusion on The Gentleman's face. He hadn't expected this but, without the slightest pause, he ran for the Glock. Drake was less sure, assuming subterfuge on the part of Saint, and ran for one of the weapons that couldn't be misrepresented. The gaps between them were short; fitness essential.

Dropping the cleaver, The Gentleman scooped up the Glock and turned. Drake already had the knife. He didn't wait to see if he was right about the gun; just flung the short blade end over end so that the point embedded fully to the hilt in The Gentleman's throat. Reflex took over and the dying man's finger pulled the trigger.

Aimed right at Drake's head.

The hammer fell on an empty chamber.

Drake turned to Saint, said, "Fuck you."

And walked out of the ring.

CHAPTER TWENTY FOUR

Alicia was waiting for him, relief clearly evident on her face. "Nicely done, Drakey. For a moment there, I was worried. I mean, I've heard of Shish Kebab, but not Drake Kebab."

"Thanks." Drake took a deep breath, wiping the sweat from his face with both hands and checking the flesh wound. "What's the plan?"

Blank faces met his enquiry. Even Hayden looked stumped. "Survive," she said. "Survive and hope we get refreshments tonight."

Drake turned to Dahl. "Don't tell me you don't have a plan, Roxette?"

The Swede ignored the leg-puller and looked at the skies. "To be fair, I'm hoping for a lunch break."

"Shit. I'll explain one thing right here and now—we won't be allowed to go on winning."

"Not only that," Alicia added. "Our two best warriors have already fought."

A few protests sprang up, but the heat and their own exhaustion cut it short. Drake turned for the bottle of water he'd won and offered it around. The team looked bedraggled, Yorgi and Kinimaka sat at the back, staring at the ground. Hopefully, it was a way of conserving energy and not admitting defeat.

Mai finished off the last of the water. "Stay calm. Stay alert. An opportunity will always present itself."

"Yeah, well, it needs to hurry the fuck up," Alicia said. " 'Cause this sunburn is gonna be the death of me."

Saint wandered casually over to them. "Shit, it *is* toasty out here, girl. Luckily, I'm a surf dude, born and raised in sunny California. A bronze god from birth, you might say."

Shouts of annoyance pealed from the stands.

Saint bowed to their demands. "You want more?"

A general agreeable cry resonated around the rock bowl.

"Here he is then, the Mad Swede!" Saint swept into a bow and indicated that Dahl should follow him. Drake saw the gun barrels, unwavering, perfectly trained. The Swede walked into the ring.

"And fight!"

It happened fast. Two clubs spiked with dozens of deadly four-inch nails were thrown into the ring just as the MMC lumbered back out. Drake thought he looked refreshed or, more importantly, repaired. He moved easily, fast for a man his size, and bent down to pick up his club without flinching.

"Hey!" Alicia cried out in Drake's ear. "You got this, Torsty. I already softened him up for ya!"

Dahl picked up his own club and held it at arm's length, spinning the length of it. Some nails glinted in the light, others were too rusty. All had been hammered right through the club so that their points stuck out.

"Never forget!" Saint cried. "They killed our friends. This is *revenge,* men. Now . . . perforate that piece of shit."

Dahl didn't back away one millimeter. The Swede stepped forward, meeting the MMC's powerful downswing with a solid defense. The clubs struck, nails bending and catching, then grinding apart as their owners pulled hard. The two opponents came together again, another swing of the club and then a third. Neither gave ground. Neither tried to evade the impact, their back feet planted firmly into the ground.

The club-fight continued, unabated.

The mercs shouted for the MMC; the SPEAR team encouraged Dahl. Comments and observations were made; advice screamed at the top of several pairs of lungs. Dahl swung low, aiming for a leg-breaker. The MMC caught it and twisted fast, trying to wrench the club from Dahl's hands. The Swede's wrists were strong enough to resist the sudden wrench, pull away. He swing overhead and then to the side, overhead again.

He let the club drop.

And saw the feint work beautifully. Let your opponent think this was all you were, all you could do, and then strike hard. Strike fatally.

Dahl watched the MMC launch a huge overhead attack, and then danced to the side, swift as a gymnast and with ninja-like reflexes. By the time the MMC's swing would have struck Dahl's skull, the Swede was at the hulk's side, a completely unprotected flank in his sights.

He showed no mercy, sinking the club three times into the MMC, the swings full of power and might, wrenching each direct hit free of flesh and bone and instantly striking again. After three hits Dahl was almost spent, but the MMC was tumbling.

Fallen, dying.

Dahl threw down the club and walked away.

Alicia ran to throw her arms around him. "See, I told you I softened him up. Well done, Torsty."

The Mad Swede grunted. "You're all sweaty."

"Yeah, I get like that when I'm excited."

Kenzie was also waiting for the Swede's return. "A good fight," she said. "No quarter given."

Dahl put a big hand on her shoulder. "You can't show a moment of weakness to these animals."

Alicia pulled away. "You wanna get in here, Kenzo? The meat's a bit ripe, but it's really fresh."

Dahl turned away from them, eyes drifting over the rest of the team. Drake was just as worried. *Who would they choose next?*

"So, the MMC finally meets his match," Saint incited the audience. "That's Team SPEAR – three; you lot – zero! How about one more bout? Even the scores a little."

The cheers were violent, bloodthirsty.

Saint turned toward SPEAR. "Who's next? The giant? The boss? The thief? Nah, how about the relic smuggler? I fancy one or two of these guys know you, Kenzie. Maybe even worked for you. I hope you were a good boss."

"Hey." Kenzie squared up to Saint. "We've already jumped through your hoops. How about telling us why we're really here."

Saint waved down the guards that had lined her up in their sights. "You're here to die," he said simply and rather convincingly. "We were given carte blanche to kill you back at the temple, in the desert, in the street . . . whatever. We chose this because we want you to experience despair before you die. Listen to me now—you will never leave this place alive."

"Don't bet on it, pal," Drake grumbled.

"Who can save you?" Saint pointed out. "Who? You're all here."

Kenzie followed the man into the ring and waited to see who or what she might face. Drake gauged the surroundings once more. From his vantage point the bowl rose perhaps thirty meters, stepped, and was about half-full of mercenaries. The way back into the caves was up and to the left, a black arch overlooking it all. The ring itself was approximately twenty meters in diameter, maybe more, and the armed guards were stationed all around and well apart. They were also up in the stands. Drake knew his team could never hope to escape this place without losing some or all of their number.

Dahl leaned in. "Are you thinking what I'm thinking?"

Alicia overheard and nodded. "You mean Kenzie's ass? Yeah, it's sweet."

"No! I didn't even notice it. I'm trying to formulate a plan of escape?"

"Me too," Drake nodded, "only without the fancy description. I'm just looking to get the fuck outta here."

Kenzie flexed her muscles, waiting. A tense quiet stole over the arena. Even Saint shut up and started looking solemn. Minutes passed. The sun beat down in glaring waves, meeting shimmering heat eddying back up.

At last, a figure emerged.

A medium-sized man stripped to the waist, wearing a balaclava to hide his face and strips of cloth to protect his groin and thighs. A six-pack across his chest joined other rippling muscles and spoke of fitness. In one hand, he carried a sword.

"Survive three minutes," Saint said. "And you'll get one too."

Drake protested. Dahl walked forward, but a gunshot aimed close to his toes stopped him in his tracks. The man with the sword spun the weapon around in circles as he paced around Kenzie.

Saint affected a bow. "Meet Freddy Fergus. A genuine mad Irish bastard."

Fergus ran in, sword still gyrating in his grip. Kenzie watched intently and then side-stepped, keeping the distance between them. She let Fergus move in and rolled as he swung, passing by his left-hand side. When he came around, swinging again, she caught his sword arm and held it upright. Fergus cleverly let it drop, right into his other hand and jabbed at her with that. Kenzie leapt back at the last moment. Drake saw blood spring from a new wound in her abdomen.

"We have to stop this." Dahl gazed around desperately. "Are we just going to let them take us down one by one?"

Kenzie ignored the wound as Saint called out: "One minute left."

Fergus sliced the air apart less than a hand's-width in front of her head: two diagonal slashes. Kenzie skipped back as he came forward, looking to crowd her now. The ring worked to her advantage, giving her space to evade. She drew Fergus in even as he thought he was backing her into a trap.

Back against a guard, Kenzie sprang forward even as Fergus slashed. She caught his sword arm again, this time at the wrist, and held on. He sought to kick her but she swept that aside with an upraised knee. He tried to use brute strength to pitch her body around but she resisted. Finally, he wrenched back on the sword, trying to pull it from her grip.

She was already gone, darting past. His huge pull on the sword unbalanced him for several seconds. By then Kenzie had scooped up the sword that Saint, as promised, had hurled into the ring.

Now, the odds were even.

Kenzie attacked. Drake never expected anything else. What she didn't see was two guards grab Yorgi and also throw him, unarmed, into the ring.

Fergus saw it, staring over Kenzie's shoulder and a feral grin lit his features. He feinted a block as Kenzie swung and then pulled out of it, rolled past her and came up in front of a very surprised Yorgi.

Grit and dust from the arena's floor stuck to his bare skin, trickling to the floor.

The sword came up to disembowel the Russian thief, but Kenzie was far quicker than anyone realized. She'd seen the feint, spun instantly, and understood what was about to happen. Too far away she did all she could—hurling her sword end over end at Fergus. It hit hard, unfortunately the hilt end smashing into the side of his skull. He staggered. Kenzie leapt over and Yorgi fell back,

Fergus swung from the floor, the sword blade swinging in a deadly arc. Kenzie was in full leap but managed to twist her body so that only a small chunk of flesh was lost to the blade. She fell hard, gravel stinging her bare flesh, but scooped up the fallen sword and scrambled to safety.

Fergus met her. Swords clashed under the baking heat and bodies shed sweat in the shimmering still air. A dozen times they came together. Metal met metal and flesh slipped against flesh. Kenzie was wearing Fergus down; there was no doubting it. Her skills were greater, her speed more telling. Yorgi was the unknown factor. He stayed behind Kenzie but couldn't possibly predict her every lightning move.

Fergus must have realized his poorer standards and launched a desperate attack. He pushed her aside, slipped past and came hard at Yorgi. The Russian had no defenses and stood with his back to the SPEAR team. Guards sensed trouble and squeezed in around them. Yorgi backed away. Fergus came on, grinning with evil purpose. It was clear that Kenzie was too far away to help.

"Attack him!" Alicia cried out in despair. "Move!"

The distance between Fergus and Yorgi shrank quickly. Drake prepared to risk everything, despite the guards. Fergus slashed down the sword, straight at Yorgi's face.

But a guard struck him then, right at the very last second and, at first, nobody could quite work out what had happened.

Then the Mad Swede bellowed and Drake saw his hands outstretched.

"You crazy bastard, well done."

Dahl had hefted one of the closest guards off his feet and

propelled him uncontrollably into Fergus, effecting a major body strike.

Alicia scratched her chin. "Is that allowed?"

"Guard skittles is always free rein," Dahl said.

Saint ran up, unsure what to do, and seemingly amused with the outcome. Kenzie raced up to Fergus and stabbed him before he could regain his feet. Blood pooled across the arena floor. Saint took in the scene and held up his hands.

"Spectacle's done for now," he said. "I'm calling a half-hour break so we can get out of this dreadful sun." He threw a handful of water bottles at Drake and Dahl. "Get ready," he said. "You're staying right here. And it's going to be the worst afternoon of your lives."

CHAPTER TWENTY FIVE

Barely refreshed, the SPEAR team sprawled across the gravelly floor, arms across their eyes or propped up sideways. They weren't allowed to sit with their backs to the walls. Weren't allowed more water or any kind of food. They weren't allowed any kind of medication for their wounds. One of the guards explained they didn't want to waste medicine on dead bodies. He was wholly serious when he said it.

"Thoughts?" Hayden asked in a low voice.

"Our only option is a mass attack," Dahl said apprehensively. "We don't know where Crouch is, or even if he's alive. And there are simply zero odds that we will all make it out. Some of us will die."

"Then I guess it's better some than all," Hayden said. "The alternative is grim."

"Grim is our thing," Alicia said. "We've been in worse holes."

"Have we? When?"

"Umm . . . when we fought cannibals? Dmitry Kovalenko's attack on DC. That last man standing bollocks. Every time Kinimaka walks past something or Mai returns from a trip to Japan."

Even Mai smiled, if only slightly. "My personal problems have ended now."

"Oh yeah?" Kinimaka brooded. "That's the feeling right before the worst begins. Don't get too comfy."

Hayden reached out to him. "I'm sorry if I hurt you, Mano."

"Ah . . ." the Hawaiian stammered and then clammed up, surprised. The rest of the team were startled too, but turned away so the pair could have a least a semblance of privacy.

"Don't say anything," Hayden said quietly. "I'll prove it to you. I'll prove my sorrow and my worth and hope you can forgive me."

Saint appeared at the top of the channel that ran from the

cave system down into the bottom of the bowl. He brought a long, black whip with him and an enormous, frozen ice lolly, which he opened and started eating in front of them.

"How we all feeling? Refreshed?"

"So when are you jumping into the ring?" Alicia asked with interest.

Saint slurped at the lolly. "Whoa, this thing is juicy. Oh, darlin', you don't want that. You wouldn't last two minutes."

"Well, darlin', I'd be sure happy to give it a try."

"Hmm, well, let's see how the afternoon goes. The masses are wandering back in. Time to perform, kids."

Drake rose and the others followed suit, as much to prepare their aching bodies as anything. Lack of food and water would slow them enough. Nobody wanted to be caught out. Saint waited for the crowd to settle and then raised both hands.

"A nice spectacle to start the afternoon off," he shouted. "It'll be Mai Kitano versus Ronin the Samurai, and Mai Kitano versus the whip." He lashed the dirt floor with the whip, sending up a cloud of dust.

Drake gritted his teeth, wishing the day was already over. Mai walked through the team to sounds of encouragement. Drake knew she was the best warrior they had, but that didn't make her invincible. It only upped the stakes.

Saint smiled at Mai. "I think you're gonna enjoy this."

Mai Kitano waited patiently at the center of the arena, as calm on the inside as she appeared on the outside. It would do no good to get flustered. As she'd explained earlier, her life had become easier lately. Stiller. The personal issues were done with, the troubles all over and demons all met.

For that she was grateful. It was the main reason she had taken the step back with Drake. It was why she never challenged Alicia. Mai was content; she saw no reason to upset the good, serene fortune that had chosen to flow her way.

Now, Saint cracked the whip, the lashes landing in the dirt by her feet. It was a long, leather-handled thing with three thongs and Saint appeared to know how to use it. Of course, it would be the distraction.

Ronin came into sight. Wearing black robes, carrying a whip of his own. With long, black hair and Japanese features he was short and solid. He moved with grace, with purpose and paced toward her now.

Saint cracked the whip to get them started.

Drake found himself biting his lip until the blood flowed. Mai evaded three strikes of the whip, the weapon kissing the ground until clouds of dust whirled up. Ronin was too fast to directly assault; the whip always ready and the man constantly in motion. Drake watched hard, his eyes searing hatred at Mai's opponent until Alicia's cry made him whirl around.

"Michael!"

Crouch was dragged down into the arena and thrown among them. He was bloody, bruised and barely moving. Drake wasn't even sure he was alive at first, until Dahl checked for the pulse and nodded. The guards that had brought him down parted.

Another figure revealed himself.

The team ignored him, concentrating on making Crouch comfortable. Alicia acted as a prop for his back and head. Drake tried patting his cheeks to bring him back to reality.

"Michael. It's me. You okay, mate?"

"What did you do to him?" Hayden hissed, confronting the new figure.

"I questioned ridiculous English ponce," a long, drawling Russian accent came back. "But he . . . he has balls? Yes? For now. Same as all of you."

"I thought we were here only for revenge," Hayden said. "Your guy Saint there said as much."

"Revenge, amusement," the Russian intoned. "Diversion. We are happy with down time before next phase begins." He shrugged. "We get bored."

He came among them without fear. "I am Vladimir."

Drake ignored the figure, the words. He was staring between Crouch and Mai, alarmed for both. Mai had taken a whip-crack to the bicep, intent on catching the lash and reeling her opponent in, but Ronin had been a tad too quick for her.

Another attack resulted in Saint striking at the same time, partially unbalancing her, enabling Ronin to land another strike across her back. Mai's scar was already red, standing out angrily as the blood rushed through her body.

"I want to know what is the fourth symbol," Vladimir said. "I want to know it now or I will kill one of you. I will crush you underfoot as my men guard your friends with orders to shoot if they move. *I want it now!*"

Drake looked up at Vladimir, about to explain to him his place in the world. Crouch's eyelids fluttered open and he took a moment to study proceedings. "You are fighting for your lives now?" he muttered. "In a pit? God help us."

"That'd do," Dahl said. "We're open to anything right now."

Vladimir punched Smyth point blank in the face. Blood exploded from the soldier's nose. Vladimir kicked him in the side of the head. Hayden and Kinimaka made to move but gun barrels swiveled toward them. A bullet kicked up dirt once more. Vladimir kicked out at Smyth again.

"Tell me. You can stop this. Tell me."

Drake rose, ready to finish all this madness with one last all-out assault. Dahl read his mind and rose with him, the two shoulder to shoulder, head to head. Nobody could pick the time of their death, but right now, in this moment, they could pick who they decided to meet it with and how they went out.

"You stop that," Drake said. "Right now."

"You will tell me!"

"Yes," Crouch finally said through a hacking cough. "We will tell you." He caught Drake's eye. "It makes no difference to us. And it will buy us time. Rest. Respite."

Vladimir came over to him, a bull elephant charging through a pack and knocking everyone out of the way.

"Crouch, you are asshole. You do this now. I will make all deaths quick."

The ex-British soldier nodded wearily. "Deal."

CHAPTER TWENTY SIX

Mai Kitano ducked and sprang around the ring. The whip was a constant thrashing, side to side and occasionally across her body. Every time she got close to Ronin, Saint joined in but now she had learned to ignore him. He never made impact, but she thought she'd figured out a way to win. It was hard concentrating though, as Crouch was returned and then the new man—Vladimir—appeared, making his threats. She wasn't sure if she would be needed over there or here, or even among the crowd in the next few moments so she dallied, waited, prepared to move.

Then, something was agreed. Vladimir ordered a man to fetch an iPad and Crouch sat more upright, back to the wall. Hayden and Yorgi crowded around him. Mai saw it as an opportunity to finish this. The T-shirt she wore was already ripped and sweat dripped into her eyes. As Ronin swung the whip hard, sending all three lashes toward her, Mai dropped and spun under them, balanced on one leg, the rotation of her body bringing her to within an arm's length of her opponent. With the whip arm at full length, he was off balance. Mai was a flash of forked lightning, rising up and striking again and again with her clenched fists, eight times before he cried out. The last two were crushing throat strikes.

He collapsed, choking. Mai walked away from him.

Saint tried to calm the baying crowd.

Drake watched Crouch flick at the iPad. "It would have made better sense to wait until we found the bloody thing," he said to Dahl with Vladimir listening.

The Russian gave him a deadly look. "I work with what I can get," he twanged thickly. "You allow them special bikes to help with their mission, they get carried away." He shrugged. "What can you do?"

Crouch spoke as he worked, giving the Russian no chance to doubt him. "We cleared the upper level," he said. "Then went all the way down to the bottom to start there." A white lie to extend their time. "Your men came before we got started."

He studied the photographs of Hatshepsut's Temple carefully as Vladimir and his men looked on.

The SPEAR team took rest, managing to get four more bottles of water between them. Vladimir even allowed them bread to eat. Drake felt a surge of energy as he finished and his stomach begged for more. The intense heat was declining now, making the whole area a little more comfortable. With Dahl, Alicia, Kenzie and the others he sought a way out.

Crouch took an hour to search through the temple photographs they'd already studied. Then inexorably, he came to the final level, the level they hadn't examined.

"Last chance." He looked at Vladimir but the words were for his friends.

"You had better find it, English."

The team stirred ever so slowly, wondering what might happen next and not enthusiastic about throwing more of their number into the ring. The mercs, gathered around the stands, were like restless children forbidden to play.

Crouch looked up. "Got it."

Vladimir was already staring, having seen Crouch's initial hesitation. He studied the picture now, carved upon the base of a column at the bottommost level of the temple. "What is that?" he intoned. "A pyramid? Which one?"

Saint was watching them closely. "We can determine that," he said. "But now, you have to end this."

Drake and Dahl made ready. The team jumped to their feet.

"Throw these animals into the ring," he growled at the guards that held guns upon them. "Boys!" he shouted up into the stands at the hundred-or-so assembled mercs. "Have your way!"

CHAPTER TWENTY SEVEN

Before they could even think the guards were upon them, shoving and pushing, with guns raised. The team were already depleted, bruised and battered; the day's exhaustion slowing their reaction times as well as everything else.

Drake felt a boot to his spine, folded and rolled into the ring. Bodies fell all around him; his friends, sprawling head first or staggering left and right. Crouch was hurled in with them and lay groaning. The guards backed away and up the first few tiers of stands.

Mercs roared in their seats, grabbed weapons and started jumping and running down the steps and the channel, all converging on the fighting arena.

Drake struggled to his feet.

Alicia dragged herself up too. "This is not a good day."

"What is it they say?" Drake watched the oncoming blood pack. "Live every day as if it might be your last."

Dahl shaded his eyes. "Well, time to knock a few heads together," he said. "This should be fun."

Drake looked askance at the Swede. "A little warm up before taking Saint and Vladimir down?"

Alicia shivered. "And don't we bloody need it."

Drake smiled, the camaraderie lifting his spirits as they faced down a hundred mercenaries. "You guys fancy takeaway tonight?"

"Chinese," Alicia said. "And beer."

"Italian," Dahl said. "With wine."

Drake shook his head. "We're gonna have to work on that since my own choice would be fish and chips and Pepsi."

The entire team readied themselves as the mercs attacked.

*

Bodies struck hard, muscled men swinging in with everything they had. Drake blocked a blow, sidestepped another and kicked the first man in the chest. It did no good. He took the blow, grinned and came on. Drake used the only weapon he had—a rock he'd grabbed from the side of the ring—and smashed his adversary across the face. The man's nose smashed and blood flew, blinding a nearby merc so that Mai could get a couple of incapacitating blows in.

Great teamwork, Drake thought before a forehead flashed down into his own.

He fell back, seeing stars. The ring was large but not large enough for over a hundred people. The saving grace was that only about thirty mercs could attack at one time, but even that was more than enough.

Drake shook his head, ducking another blow. A boot struck his knee, folding his leg. He went down, caught himself, and threw his body clear of another attack.

Straight into an oncoming merc. The man brought a knee up. The non-stop blows were dizzying Drake, causing his focus to wane. Figures came and went through his vision. Dahl, slamming mercenaries from side to side. Mai, using her speed and size to precise purpose. The downed bodies of their enemies, in double figures already. Yorgi, on his knees, bleeding but still trying. Hayden, meeting men blow for blow and watched over by Kinimaka.

Was this SPEAR's last stand?

Drake pushed off one man to regain his balance. The arena was a total melee, just a chaos of men and women all trying to fight or defend or die. Guards had been stationed around the steps, just in case anyone tried to escape. Drake saw only death here.

But it wasn't his way to give up.

Yelling to fire even more adrenalin, he front-kicked a man into his partner, sending both to their knees. The first he kicked in the throat, the second he landed on with an elbow to the spine. Rolling off, he came up and headbutted another attacker under the chin with the top of his head. The guy never knew what happened: instant lights out. A blow came in from the left; Drake took it and jabbed at another nerve cluster, but the man evaded, coming in strongly again. Drake took more punishment. Dahl started throwing mercs around, but found even his incredible strength was sapped to a dangerous level. With the first three bowled over, he made sure they wouldn't get up. A crushing blow took even more of his energy, stopping him in his tracks, but that man was useful in defending against another. Dahl ensured both ended up with broken bones and writhing on the floor.

Alicia and Mai fought as one, moving forward slowly and protecting each other. Hayden and Kinimaka did the same. Kenzie helped protect Crouch and Yorgi with Smyth, but the duo were fighting a losing battle.

As were they all.

The attack flow was unrelenting. The merc weapons were inviting, but everyone knew with the first shot the guards would take no chances. They would pick the SPEAR team off one by one. So guns littered the floor, a temptation gleaming wickedly.

Drake and Kenzie found knives, and it aided them a little, but the bodies coming at them were still too many. It felt like they'd been fighting for an age, or at least until sundown, but Drake knew it was probably less than twenty minutes. The exertion was killing them as much as the telling blows.

Yorgi and Crouch were at the center as the SPEAR team instinctively came together in the middle of the ring. Smyth and Kenzie, Kinimaka and Hayden protected them. Dahl, Drake and Alicia moved around *them*. They held the attack back for longer than they could have imagined. The minutes ticked by.

Then someone stumbled. A merc struck a crippling blow, putting Alicia to the floor. Drake found his punches weren't filled with venom anymore. A headbutt to the face sent him falling back, landing in the grit, head spinning.

He crawled over to Alicia.

"Get up," he gasped. "Get up, get up."

She protected her body from blows, still recovering from the potent attack.

"I'm guessing no takeaway tonight after all," she said softly.

Drake reached out to her, touched her shoulder and held her gaze even as someone's boot rocked his ribs.

"We never could agree anyway."

Dahl dealt with Drake's aggressor, reached down and pulled the Yorkshireman up. Drake held on to Alicia, dragging her up too.

"Not the time for a bloody shag," the Swede growled.

"There's always time for a shag." Alicia palmed off a smaller, greasy man. "Just ask Kenzie. She knows what's important."

Dahl knuckled a twisted face, glanced over at the Israeli. "You know," he said. "The most important thing in life? Family. Or friends. Or both."

They held fast as a knot of four men hit at once. The impact rattled Drake's brain inside his skull. He blocked a punch, took another to the face, stopped a man getting past them. Kenzie threw her knife at Alicia, or so it seemed. The blade whickered past, embedding itself into the face of a man she hadn't noticed—a man that was about to smash a fist-size jagged rock into her skull.

"Helluva throw," Dahl said.

"And now she's defenseless," Alicia grunted. "Dumb as a bedpost."

But the nod she gave Kenzie was resolute.

Drake saw the mercs still lining up, over two dozen, all fresh, all desperate for a chance to get into the fray. A dozen more surrounded him. They were behind and to the side; they had put up the best fight they could muster.

"Guys . . ." he said, knowing he was battling with his very last reserves of strength.

"Don't say it," Dahl breathed, right there at his shoulder. "Team SPEAR will not go out this way."

"Cool." Alicia staggered under another strike. "What's the last-minute plan?"

The Swede knocked a man into unconsciousness with a single blow. "Last chance," he said. "We're done. Pick up the weapons and start shooting the fuckers."

"Good plan."

Drake spied a SIG Pro semi-auto and dived for it. Before he got there a random leg slammed into his right ear, sending him off-balance. The world turned. He landed, rolled and tried to push up.

The SIG was gone, kicked away.

Despair fought to take control of his mind. In that moment a shot rang out and he dived away, thinking it came from the guards. The arena floor scraped his flesh once more, or rather scraped the wounds where flesh had once been.

A merc fell nearby, shot through the head.

Who got the gun? Alicia?

With the mercs distracted, he rose, swaying in place. The scene was chaotic but also unbelievable. Men dressed in black, wearing jackets, helmets and carrying serious weapons were entering through the cave entrance. Fanning out, they raced down the steps and the channel, pumping bullets into every merc that turned to face them. Drake could tell from the way they held their HKs and fired with an economy of movement, from the way they moved, the way they signaled, that they were professionals at the top of their game.

Another team?

What the . . . ?

Smyth had found a handgun and fired three bullets into three mercs. Those still around looked around and took note. They saw their colleagues being killed in the stands, enemies pouring through the only exit.

Drake pulled Alicia back. Dahl followed. Together, the SPEAR team stood or sat in the center of the ring, watching proceedings with wary and unsure eyes.

The black-clad soldiers moved with deadly efficiency, picking off mercs even as they assessed their own danger. Some quicker ones engaged in the gunfight, but they were not allowed to leave. A few scattered standoffs emerged, but Smyth and Hayden helped by putting down those mercs they could reach from their vantage point. No bullets came flying their way, but only because the mercs were intensely focused on the newcomers.

Then Drake saw a familiar figure. "Oh, bollocks. That's not good."

He brought the thunder. The muscle-bound man they knew as Luther leapt down the arena stands throwing grenades left and right. They exploded at his back, framing him with fire and smoke but he never flinched nor lost momentum. Mercs cringed, fell away. The grenades were replaced with machine guns that smashed attackers aside like they were reeds in the wind. He cut a path right through the mercenaries, his men mopping up, and to the very front of the SPEAR team's new circle.

"You're coming with me, Drake. You and your team. Now move."

Desperate for anything but this, for shade, for water, for food, for a chance to recover, Drake and the others complied without even the slightest hint of reluctance. Luther herded them along as his men cleared the arena.

"Get these soldiers some refreshment," Luther ordered his men as they were approaching the cave entrance. "They've been through agony today."

Grateful though he was, Drake wondered if they'd just left the blazing furnace and fallen right into the raging gates of hell.

David Leadbeater

CHAPTER TWENTY EIGHT

The battle raged.

Luther and his men, twelve in total, may have had the element of surprise back at the arena, but Vladimir's men had regrouped by the time Luther broke back out and gave immediate chase.

The prospects weren't good. Drake had been herded into the back of one of two trucks—standard military with canvas covering the back—and told to sit on the floor. Half his team followed and half went in the other truck. Drivers stepped on the gas and they were away. Drake was thrown water and chocolate and then tied by one hand to a metal strut.

"Oh, love." He chomped hard at the thick bar. "This has to be one the best things that ever went in my mouth."

Luckily, Alicia was in the other truck. He sipped the water slowly, not surprised with the sudden vigor that entered his body but knowing it would take a while yet and some good food for everything to return to normal. One by one, they began to catalogue their wounds and the seriousness of them, sounding off to each other and yelling out to Luther's men that they needed antiseptic and bandages.

Both vehicles raced along the desert, hills and dunes to either side, as the mercenaries geared up to follow, pealing out in pursuit with four trucks. Luther's men had gained a five-minute head start.

Luther himself sat with them, back to the cab where a driver and shotgun-man sat. Two more crouched in the bed of the truck, peering through the canvas to gauge the pursuit.

Luther made a point of attracting Drake's attention. "You need us," he said. "For now. Don't fuck with us. Let us do our jobs."

Drake nodded and carried on evaluating his new enemies.

Luther got on the comms, talking to the other truck and

142

making sure they were following the plan. The desert rose and fell all around; mushroom clouds of sand and dust plumed into the air. Though the vehicles were traveling comparatively slowly it felt like they were moving at great speed, bouncing and jouncing around so that Drake's wrist again started to chafe as they rubbed against the new chains.

Dahl nudged his shoulder. "Captured twice in two days. That's a new low for me."

Drake considered it. "Yeah, me too."

"Really? Surely with the SAS it's just a Tuesday."

"Funny. Seriously though, this feels better."

Dahl shifted his gaze across to Luther; the enormous head with its long scar and intelligent, black eyes. "Depends what he has in store for us."

"The guy's Army, through and through," Drake said. "I'd like to know his orders."

"Well, if his orders come from the same guys that disavowed us it won't be a tea and biscuits invitation."

Through gaps in the canvas they saw flashes of the other truck, where Alicia, Hayden, Kinimaka, Yorgi and Smyth lay in chains, Drake assumed. It jolted along a few feet parallel to theirs, the figures and frames of their friends visible only briefly. If Drake shifted again he could see through the back.

The mercenaries were coming up fast.

"You couldn't get a faster truck, bro?" Dahl asked Luther.

A shrug. "White House is strapped for dollars these days. Everyone knows that."

Luther moved to the back of the truck with such physical presence it was like watching a lion stalking. Drake did not fancy trading blows.

"Pal?" he said. "Any more of that chocolate?"

"It'll make you fat." Luther studied the oncoming vehicles.

"We'll take the chance," Dahl said. "The conditions in that cave were somewhat taxing."

Drake snorted. "Taxing?"

"English understatement," Luther said, signaling one of his men to comply. "I like it."

Drake tuned it out as eating the sugary food became the highlight of the last twenty four hours. The engine roared in his ears, the tires rumbled like thunder across the desert. The heat was intense but frequent gusts of wind wound through the canvas gaps, making it more tolerable.

"Not good." Luther turned back to the truck. "This is not good, boys. Break out the candy."

Drake eyed Dahl and they both watched Luther's men crack open the large black box they had been sitting on. Reaching inside, they rummaged and then withdrew two RPGs, grenades, smoke bombs and other military paraphernalia. Luther crab-walked over to heft the first rocket launcher.

"Snyder, you ready with the smoke?"

"Yeah, boss."

"Do it."

The truck rumbled on. Luther approached the rear of the truck once again, then suddenly stopped and threw the launcher to the floor.

"Grenade!" he bellowed.

The driver heard, stamping on the gas. Drake saw the black streak flying toward them and ducked just as the driver wrenched hard on the wheel. The truck slewed, slamming into its partner and bouncing hard on the dust and gravel. The missile flashed by, burying its head into a mound of sand and exploding. The screen of expanding sand it threw up blasted far and wide, showering the passing trucks. Drake felt sand striking his back.

Luther rose and took position. "Firing!"

A rocket flew, just missing the passenger side wheel of a gaining truck. Drake now saw the second in line.

"Balls, that looks like it means business."

The truck sported a turret-mounted gun on top, like a tank, but Drake fancied it would move a lot quicker.

"Smoke." Luther reloaded the RPG.

Snyder stepped past him and hurled two grenades. Exploding as soon as they hit the ground, they spewed out thick, white smoke, blanketing the area. Luther crouched and hefted the rocket launcher across one broad shoulder.

Drake caught a good glimpse of the other truck. A man waited there too. He switched his gaze back to the smoke screen.

Two missiles flashed through the thin veil, straight toward them.

"Fuck!" Luther cried.

"Evade!" Drake shouted. "Do it now or we're dead!"

CHAPTER TWENTY NINE

To his credit, the driver moved instantly.

Flinging the wheel to the right this time, he made the speeding behemoth screech in protest. Joints rattled and clattered but held. Drake watched the enormous canvas cover tear free and flap off in the wind like a newly born pterodactyl.

A rocket impacted just behind their rear right wheel, sending up a large amount of dirt. The force of the explosion also lifted the truck at that side, forcing the wheel off the floor and the whole vehicle to tilt.

Drake held on with a death grip, more conscious now that the pursuing fighters would almost certainly kill them outright this time. Potentially, his life rested on the balance of the truck. The back end went high, sand and dirt following it in a rippling heap. His vision altered, now showing the sky. Luther tumbled back into the truck, losing his grip on the RPG. Worse, Snyder tipped over the side of the truck, tumbling over and smashing hard against the desert floor, unmoving.

Luther cursed as he moved against the truck's upward inertia, gripping a strut and staring fixedly at Snyder's clearly dead body. "Fuck!"

The big man then flung himself against the rising back of the truck, using his weight to help right the stability. The truck seemed to rise and hang in the air for hours as Drake held on but he knew it was mere seconds. The driver worked hard at the wheel, keeping it in line, and then it came down, ass first, back on the road.

Drake breathed in relief, then saw the other truck slewing left and right along desert mounds. "Looks like it evaded the missile and got stuck in sand," he said.

Another of Luther's men lay in its wake, dead.

The huge head fell. "Dammit, these kinda good men are hard to come by."

Drake offered him the rocket launcher with his one free hand. "You dropped this, mate."

Luther glared. "Give me the damn thing."

Another rocket came out of the box, a man called Nielsen throwing the object over to him. Luther keyed his comms. "How long to the road?"

He didn't like the answer, shaking his head again. "Time to light up the entire desert."

Drake saw four chase vehicles in total. Two standard and two with the wicked-looking turret. The latter two were leading the pack now, their guns lined up.

"You have to get off this road," Mai said tightly. "We're lit up like Chinatown."

"What I have to do is blow up one of those assholes," Luther said, loading quickly.

Drake saw the problem here. Luther was a blood and fury old-schooler. This was what he did. Realistically, it would come down to who had the biggest, meanest weapons.

"What else you got in that crate?" Kenzie asked quickly.

"We could help," Drake said. "We have as much riding on this as you do."

Luther merely snarled. "Once I've bagged my meat, it's let out only to be thrown into the oven. Sit tight."

Dahl sighed. "I don't think he likes you."

"Really? And he's such an accommodating guy."

A shrug. "So says Alicia."

"Now what's that supposed to mean?"

"A joke." Dahl and Drake watched Luther fire another rocket, missing the two lead trucks but hitting one of the followers. Flames and tearing metal marked the devastation, and a pump of the fist from Luther.

The loss only spurred the attack on. Both lead vehicles were close now, turret-guns trained and men visible in the back with rifles at the ready. Shells slammed out of the turrets, both missing by inches and sending plumes of dirt across both truck beds and the cabs. Luther bellowed crazily, picked up a semi-auto and started peppering the closest attacker with bullets.

Nielsen ran to his side, the two men unleashing walls of lead and seeing them bounce off bulletproof glass and metal.

"Grenades," Luther said.

When he turned to watch Nielsen fetch them, Drake saw a feral twitch to the side of his mouth, an agreeable expression across his face. Nielsen ran back and the two stood right on the back of the truck, lobbing grenades at their pursuers.

"Happy days," Dahl said with concern. "This isn't looking good, folks."

"Need to get free," Drake pulled on the cuffs again. "Nielson has the keys."

Ignoring the grenades, prepared to risk injury to gain the rewards, the chasing vehicle ploughed through each explosion, coming closer and closer. When it was near enough to jump aboard Drake could see the expressions of the men driving and of those in the back. The gun turret swiveled, but it was a distraction.

Through rear rails, guns were propped. The sudden sound of gunfire was ear-splitting.

Luther staggered and fell to one knee, holding his side. Nielsen was shot through half a dozen times, the bullet ripping holes in his back and deflecting past Drake and Dahl to slam in the cab, as the unfortunate man tumbled backward and came to lay dead, right in front of the SPEAR team.

Luther turned. "I need more firepower."

Drake saw the other truck under similar assault. Another hail of bullets struck right down the center of the truck. A scream from the driver sent everyone's nightmarish fears into overdrive.

The truck began to veer.

Drake and Dahl dived to the floor.

Luther protected himself just as the offside wheels veered into a sandbank and the entire vehicle tilted, slowed rapidly and fell over. The world tilted, everything shifted. Drake hung on once more for dear life.

And heard the mercs laughing hard as they pulled up, some firing for fun into the sky. He figured they had about thirty seconds to live.

CHAPTER THIRTY

Drake saw legs and torsos approaching the sideways truck. Luther was already prepared, machine gun lying along his right leg, aimed at the mercs. Drake patted Nielson everywhere before finding the keys, uncuffing himself and then handing them to Dahl.

"I know what you're doing," Luther said without moving a muscle. "Making one more mistake to add to the ledger. Don't."

Drake rooted through the upended crate, finding grenades and guns. "First time we've been free in a while, mate. Feels good."

"You are not free."

"I beg to differ," Mai said. "We hold all the guns. And they're trained on you."

Luther grunted. "It will do you no good, Kitano."

"Well, I'll give you this," Kenzie said appreciatively. "You sure do have balls."

"Like steel."

"But you are lacking in the brains department, my friend," Mai told him. "Surely by now you can see you need us."

Luther didn't reply for a moment; even from behind Drake could see his shoulders and muscles working as he struggled.

"I need no help from prisoners," he said. "Especially enemies of the state."

And, as the legs got closer, Luther opened fire, shearing some off at the knee and shredding others. At the same time he shimmied himself down the truck and through the tailgate, finally able to stand and face the enemy as he wanted to—head on.

They ranged all around him, at least ten men with semi-autos. Still firing, he waited for the hot death of a dozen rounds.

Fury smashed and burned all around him. Wounded and dying men, the fires and smoke of crashed vehicles, the evil thunder of gunfire; it was the very place where he'd been born to die, and he'd known it from around the age of six.

The HK fell on an empty mag. Never giving up, never resting, Luther whipped a new one out and slammed it home. By then, of course, a dozen men had him lined up in their sights.

Ah, shit.

And then glory stung the battlefield, and Luther's very soul, as the SPEAR team streamed around his left and right sides, a torrent of violence and surprise attack, a surge of death gunning for the very men that had incarcerated and tortured them. Luther stood strong at the center, picking attackers off one by one, and the SPEAR team lived up to every expectation he'd ever heard, chasing the bullets down, running into danger, facing the worst of the worst and tearing their ruthless lives to shreds.

Luther's second truck fared in a similar manner to the first, its disavowed occupants jumping into the fray after slewing to a halt. When Luther looked around, and all too soon, the second pursuing turret-gun vehicle was pulling up, closely followed by the one remaining standard truck.

"Go, go," Drake cried. "Into the desert. Run!"

Luther saw his two surviving people among the others. The kid, Pine, and the diva, Carey. It would be hardest for them.

"Move it!" he cried. "We have more safety in numbers for now."

Later on, he would re-evaluate that statement.

Drake aimed for the high desert mounds after checking everyone was together. The group didn't bunch in case Vladimir and his mercs decided to empty a mag in their direction. Drake ranged ahead, ignoring the sweat and the heat, the deep sand that dragged his steps down, the aches, pains, cuts and bruises he'd suffered in the arena.

This was desperation survival now; the end game to end it all.

"How far to that road?" he asked Luther, the man's huge head about all he could see on his right periphery.

"Last check had it two miles," came the low reply. "That way."

Drake altered the direction of his run. Behind he saw Alicia,

Dahl and Kenzie, followed by all the others, heads down and running easily. Crouch was being helped by Smyth and Kinimaka, but the Englishman looked to have perked up.

"Chocolate goooood," Drake called to him.

"Anything is good when you've been beaten, tortured and forced to fight for over a day."

Drake nodded, thinking: *It's not over yet, pal,* and slogged on. Behind them he saw Vladimir and Saint's frames vanishing in the heat haze, but noticed how the mercenaries were lining up.

"Bastards are giving chase," he said. "Vladimir must be scared of his masters. This FrameHub? What do you know of them, Luther?"

"Fuck off, Drake. We ain't friends."

Drake shrugged as Dahl chortled. "Our charismatic leader," the Swede said. "Working at the top of his game."

"Maybe I can help," Alicia panted from behind as they jogged up an incline. "After all, I'm pretty sure we've . . ."

"I remember you," Luther growled. "Yeah, it took me a while but I remember you now."

"There you go," Alicia said as if they were now all good friends. "Problem solved. Sometimes bumping uglies can be useful too."

"We bumped heads, not uglies," Luther said, legs pumping hard. "You worked for the other side back then, Myles. Seems you still do."

"I did?" Alicia frowned. "Stop being such a smug shit. America and all its covert agencies change sides every week. You're just an order taker, Luther. Might as well work at a restaurant."

Luther rumbled like an angered bear.

"Guys," it was Hayden speaking. "Can you stop trying to make friends? I thought we established that's not your forte."

Drake stopped at the top of the rise, shading his eyes as he gauged the lay of the land. The desert stretched to all sides, in places flat and in others composed of rolling dunes. Far away to the east he thought he spied a narrow black strip.

"There we go," he said. "Good call, Luther. I guess even a grunt can be right once a day."

"You got a problem with grunts now? We can settle this right here, asshole, if you wanna."

"I have no problem with grunts," Drake set off. "Just wankers that follow blindly."

"You were like that once," Crouch called over. "It's how they shape you."

"True," Drake admitted. "But then I was still a teenager."

Luther looked over as they ran carefully downhill. "Army man straight outta school?"

"Yep. Never knew nothing else."

"Same here. Parents almost killed me."

From the rear of the pack there came a shout from Mai. The Japanese woman had ranged back a little to get a feel for what was following.

"Twenty armed mercs, including Vladimir and Saint. Get a move on."

Drake was worried. The mercs were relatively fresh, trained and hungry for blood. They had their boss with them who, no doubt, was eager to finish and probably earn a decent pay day. Thinking it through, he decided the road was too far.

"Plan B," he said.

Dahl chuckled. "Not that old maxim."

"Always works," Drake said. Quickly, he shouted out a strategy and received a plethora of thumbs-up.

"How many rifles we got?"

Three shouts—Kinimaka, Smyth and Pine—one of Luther's boys.

"Can you handle it?"

Three affirmatives.

"Then do it. Mai, you hang back to supervise it."

Drake slowed as they found their positions. Kinimaka ran to the right, a hundred paces; Smyth to the left. Pine remained at the center and Mai watched over it all. They hunkered down on one knee, sighting carefully until the enemy were in sight.

Drake led the pack away at a steadier rate. Hopefully the

shooting would cause confusion and mayhem among their pursuers, bringing the road into the options scenario. Of course, it was merely a road and who knew how well traveled it might be?

The shooting began behind them. Measured, even shots designed to take out the lead runners. Kinimaka, Smyth and Pine were well covered back there, able to concentrate and fully trust that Mai had their safety as her priority. So far seven gunshots had rung out with no return. The signs were good.

"Wish we had comms," Drake said.

"Y'know," Alicia returned. "*That's* becoming the new proverb."

Luther ignored them and moved over to his remaining protégé, a woman called Carey. Drake heard him checking on her spirits. Carey seemed capable, but quiet, reserved. Drake wondered if it was her first outing with Luther.

Bad luck.

Taking down the SPEAR team was never, ever going to be easy.

Drake paused now, taking stock. The road was visible ahead and random cars were running along it. He wondered what Vladimir had done with the remaining vehicles. Carefully, he checked the status of those that guarded their backs.

Running now. On the way here.

Then we'd best be ready to help them. The wolves would be at their backs.

He wiped sweat from his brow in rivulets, looking at Dahl.

"Plan B worked," he said. "How about a C?"

CHAPTER THIRTY ONE

Karin Blake sat with her back to the tall white fridge, the laptop open in front of her on the scarred wooden table. Palladino and Wu sat opposite, legs propped up on tired-looking chairs, a bottle of chilled beer clasped in their hands. The house in the Californian desert was cool, due to cold snap sweeping through the state, and a tranquil breeze blew through the open doors.

"You relaxed enough there, Dino?" Karin asked the young soldier.

"Oh, yeah, I'm good. I could get used to this."

Wu saluted his friend. "Me too, bud. Me too."

Karin shook her head, but it was for show. Truth be told something had just popped up on her computer screen that she didn't want them to see.

Am I really seeing this now? I really don't want to see this now.

Plans were already prepped. Arrangements made. Time was ticking and she didn't have long before they were due to head out. It had taken awhile, even for her, to sift through Tyler Webb's maze of secrets, draw out the useless from the perverted and the plain silly to those skeletons in the closet that might just rock the world.

Three she classed as megaton blasts, but one of these was in play even now—the American splinter group that had disavowed SPEAR without anyone's knowledge and were pursuing world-domination of their own, codename: Tempest. It was an attempt to amass the most terrible weapons that had ever existed—the weapons of the gods. Two more were imminent, but it was the Tempest riddle that she had to unravel first.

It would do no good if they succeeded.

So, the enigma presented itself. She and SPEAR were on the same side, at least for a week or so. Another issue that made what had popped up on her laptop rather timely and interesting.

"You checking up on Drake again?" Dino asked. "Hey girl, you still on board with the plan?"

"I am." Karin nodded. "They're somewhere in Egypt right now chasing down the seven seals. Last I heard, seal four was down and then they vanished off the radar. Even our radar. Luther was closing in." She shrugged. "Maybe it's all over."

"We need to get going soon," Wu said. "Enough of this waiting around. We end this, and then we can move on. *You* can move on. We're a team, right? You ready?"

"Give me thirty," Karin said. "Still a few things to finish off."

Guiding her plan to fruition had already caused great heartache, and the dangerous part was yet to come. Since the day Komodo died on the streets of Tokyo, since Drake found a place for her in the army training camp . . . since then the wheels had never stopped turning. In truth they'd been turning long before that—when Ben died perhaps—but not so loud that they consumed her every waking and sleeping moment.

Tyler Webb had owned a wealth of secrets. Karin and her team had appropriated them a short time ago. Now, she knew.

She knew everything.

One member of the SPEAR team was dying.

And Drake? Well, his secret would have to wait. She didn't know whether she hated the man or admired his tenacity, but when all the people he proclaimed to love died around him and still, pigheadedly, he forged on down the same path, the reasoning had somehow become lost.

But she felt for Lauren Fox. Felt deeply. Living with what she knew could happen at any minute was one of the worst nightmares imaginable, and Karin admired the New Yorker. Her attention was then taken again by the image bobbing around her computer screen.

An ultra-confidential invite to meet FrameHub face to face and talk about becoming a Fellow.

The language of it told her what to expect. Calling it *ultra*-confidential envisioned an organization of young know-it-alls that bristled with self-importance; that knew very well how clever they were. She assumed a 'Fellow' was a sworn-in club member, another arrogant term. She'd worked with male geeks before. Back then she had tolerated the looks and the sniggering. Now, she'd maim them for it.

Still . . .

It came at entirely the wrong time, but joining an organization like FrameHub was a lifelong dream come true. There, she could make a difference. There, she could fight in the way she really knew how. But what about her bloody plans?

So long in the making, perfect in the execution. This was the endgame.

This group were behind the deadly ransom demand of Egypt, Greece and Turkey. It didn't make perfect sense, but she assumed there was another motive behind it. Perhaps they were involved in the seven seals hunt for the ancient doomsday weapon. That made a kind of sense—geeks would think it cool and want to own it, they would see it like some kind of game. To them, knowledge was power and the ancient seals and the machine without doubt offered some kind of all-powerful knowledge.

She thought again about all the threads, slowly coming together. Drake and SPEAR. Egypt. FrameHub and their ransom. The splinter cell. Tempest, all the weapons of the Gods. Lauren Fox now in DC. Luther.

Her world was no longer her own, and was moving on at a frightening pace.

"Wait for me," she said. "Make ready to go. I have a final call to make."

She rose, grabbed a bottle of water and walked across the kitchen and out the back door. A rather nice desert breeze caressed her face, telling her what she was about to miss.

"Shit."

She tugged out her cellphone and dialed a number.

"Yes?" Robotic, the voice answered on the fifth ring.

"This is Karin Blake. I just received an invite from you."

CHAPTER THIRTY TWO

"This is Karin Blake?" the robotic voice answered. "Are you sure?"

"Last time I checked," she said, squinting at the desert and dirt road ahead.

"Voice recognition is good, but why are you calling on this cellphone?"

Karin saw their confusion. "Ah, you can see my location, right? A silly mistake that Karin Blake would never make. Don't worry, I'm leaving as soon as we end the call."

"And the cell?"

Karin breathed deeply. "I'll feed it to the first coyote I meet."

"Good." No sense of humor then. "Your Web footprint *was* hard to track but nothing eludes us for long. Do you know who we are?"

Karin was tempted to say: "The psychos holding three countries and millions of innocent people to ransom?", but curbed her ire. The potential here was too appealing to waste on sarcasm.

"FrameHub? Yes, I do. The whole world knows of you." She smiled, knowing the right words to plump their egos.

"Yeah they do." The excited robotic voice sounded ridiculous. "We're the hottest property on the planet right now . . ."

Karin cringed a little.

"But hey, what better time to reach out to a bi . . . um, girl like you? Seriously, we are the masters of this universe. Digitally, together, there's nothing we can't do. Nothing we can't own. *Nobody* we can't own. We're friggin *gods*."

"You just proved that with the demonstration." Karin fought to keep her voice amicable.

"Yeah we did! Wasn't that fuckin' mega? How that missile exploded over the tops of all those houses, showering down like fireworks? I bet the people on the ground were crapping themselves, am I right?"

Karin closed her eyes, breathing deeply. FrameHub were looking less and less appealing—in particular as this guy had been chosen to be their spokesperson—but this kind of offer rarely came around in a lifetime.

"I'm listening."

"We want you to join us."

"I realize that. Why me?"

"Are you kidding? I have pictures. Also, you're more intelligent than the average lumbering mammal out there. Phonetic memory. Keyboard wizard. First class coder. I have to say—you would further our cause."

"Be clear here. What *is* your cause?"

"We can talk more of that when we meet but, on a basic level, we're playing a game. FrameHub versus the world. Ain't it cool?"

"And you think I can help?"

"We know you have secrets, Karin. We know you went after the stash left by that corkscrew, Webb. It was on our radar too, but—and admittedly this is one of our problems—we didn't have enough people to spare. We were all involved in configuring the ransom game."

"You want me for my secrets?"

"Some of them. The most wicked. I mean, I may not be a social butterfly, but I do know that's how the world works, right?"

"For some," Karin admitted. "There are some that just like to get along."

"Really? What are they called?"

"Humans. Look . . . I'm interested. I have schemes and designs of my own but, I am interested. Where do we go from here?"

"We meet," the voice said. "We talk. We audition you."

Karin didn't like the sound of that. "Audition?"

"Yeah, check out your talent. What do you excel at? Are you a *hacktivist* or a 'denial of service' girl? How are your back-door capabilities? Do you like a Black Hat or White, or both? Can you form a botnet? Do you enjoy some keystroking, how big a Trojan would you prefer, and what's your favorite payload?"

Karin shook her head to the vast desert, knowing he was getting off on the terminology but not quite hating him for it. "I get it, I get it. Nice speech, but it did sound rehearsed. You already know my talent or you wouldn't have contacted me. Where do we meet?"

"Where you headed?"

She hesitated, then decided honesty might help in this case. "Surprisingly . . . Egypt."

"Land of blood and sand. That's good. We're not far. I'll call you when you get in."

"No, sorry. We're going in undercover. I'll have to contact you."

A robotic snort. "Don't be ridiculous. Expect my call."

He cut the call, leaving Karin to wonder about modern freedoms for just a moment before the screen door slammed and Dino padded out to meet her, a look of concern on his face.

"You good, Blake?"

"C'mere, Dino." She waited for him to approach and then grabbed him in a headlock, forcing him down and kissing the top of his head. "What a bunch of dorks we are, hey? We were soldiers. There's so much bad out there . . . in the world . . . and here we are, months into plotting some kind of twisted revenge."

Dino struggled out of her grip, red-faced. "What the fuck, Blake? Since when did we kiss?"

"We should probably do it more. Maybe we'd be better people."

"Crap, are you coming on to me?"

"For fuck's sake." Karin kicked at the dirt. "Do I look that desperate? And, you know . . ." She laughed, a twinkle in her eye. "You'd only wanna win anyway."

He grinned and turned away. "I am better than you."

"You ready to prove it?"

He looked wary. "In what way?"

"Egypt, mate. We're going to Egypt. Finally. This is it, Dino. The plan is in motion. The endgame. We're gonna do this!"

"I'm ready. So long as we sleep in separate rooms."

"With Wu?"

"I didn't mean it like—"

"I know. You don't trust my wandering hands. Maybe I'll sleep with Wu instead."

"You think you're the hot one that can take her pick, eh?"

Karin gave him a radiant, sexy smile. "What do you think?"

"It'd rather take a crate of beers."

Karin laughed and punched him on the shoulder. Dino winced. She felt almost as close to the young solider as she'd once felt to Ben. Dino was the brother and Wu the close friend. The three of them had formed a bond, unbreakable, entwined until death. Until now, the path had been relatively straightforward and easy. But the hard work was coming. She expected both Dino and Wu to form the solid wall at her back.

"Ready for Egypt?"

Dino nodded. "I've been ready since we deserted."

"Everything set?"

"Yeah. The money we appropriated from Webb's accounts paid for a nice private jet. Passports are fake, of course. We're good, Miss Blake."

"Excellent, Mr. Palladino. Shall we go and kick some arse?"

"Ass, you mean ass."

"I guess we're in America, so I do." They headed back into the house, picked up their packs and Wu and headed out to the car.

No turning back now.

CHAPTER THIRTY THREE

Plan C appeared to be working.

When two vehicles appeared, following each other down the blacktop, Drake and Dahl put their misgivings aside and pointed their weapons at the drivers. Happily, they were both male and young and didn't appear too traumatized as a dozen soldiers crowded in alongside them. Of course, they never saw Vladimir and his men coming over the hill at their backs. With the entire team barely inside the cars, hanging out of windows, wedged so tight even their bones hurt, they made the break for freedom.

Smyth drove one car, Kinimaka the other. Drake was squeezed in beside Luther, with Crouch alongside.

By design.

They talked about the fifth seal. "Of course I remember," Crouch said indignantly. "I remember the design. The pyramid is from Saqqara, the earliest burial site of the nobles of the First Dynasty. One of the common traits of this mission has been the age of the objects in question. Perhaps this doomsday machine is the earliest of all."

"Because it is a weapon of the gods?" Kenzie asked. "And thus came first. It makes perfect sense."

"Why not recap that curse again?" Drake said, for Luther's benefit.

"Find the seven seals for seven tombs and settle the fate of men. Follow the lost symbol that entombs the Ancient Doomsday Machine. Break the seven seals of Egypt and start the End of Times."

"No matter how many times you hear it," Alicia said from the front, "that always sounds nasty."

"The same could be said of you, bitch," Kenzie, crammed next to her, said.

"Shut it, skunk."

Drake urged Crouch to continue. The older man was happy to

take his mind off aching bones, bruises and raw wounds.

"Saqqara is in the north and where we should go next. If we can't stop FrameHub, the CIA and possibly this splinter group fighting for and getting the doomsday machine then we're all in big trouble."

"Is it a big place?" Drake knew they all needed rest and to head blindly into some ancient vastness was just foolhardy at this point.

"Relatively. And our rivals will be headed there too. Saqqara comprises underground galleries, funerary tombs, monuments. It's also famous for having the oldest comprehensive stone building complex throughout known history. It remained significant to the Egyptians for more than 3000 years. Such incredible history . . ." Crouch tailed off, shaking his head in wonder.

Dahl shouted something back through the open window. Drake had to strain to catch it.

"Any thoughts on why FrameHub would want the weapon so badly?"

"Just the obvious," Crouch said. "They're a new entity. Though why they're clouding the issue with this ransom demand is unclear."

"That's exactly what it is," Drake said. "Muddying the waters. Flooding Egypt with mercs. They aim to steal the weapon in the chaos and use it when they fancy it. They're kids, spoiled kids at that. It will be another ransom, another game. At least, that's my take."

"Sounds feasible," Crouch agreed.

Luther was listening intently, but remained on mission. "I may be grateful for your help, and all, but you guys are coming in with me. All of you."

Drake admired his tenacity. "It may have escaped your knowledge that we outnumber you five to one."

"Doesn't matter. I never fail."

"Neither do we," Dahl said, half out the window and catching some serious airflow. "I'd advise you to re-evaluate."

"Orders are orders," Luther said. "Can't change 'em."

Drake gestured for Crouch to continue. "Well," the Englishman said. "I recognized the pyramid at Saqqara. It's from the third Dynasty, called Djoser's step pyramid, world-famous and with a rectangular base. We're getting very close to the seventh seal now, my friends, so we really must hurry. Whoever gets their hands on that machine . . ." He shuddered.

For the first time, Luther glared at him. "You keep talking about a machine. What is it?"

"Nobody knows. The curse of the seven seals leads the way to, supposedly, an ancient machine that could destroy the world. Don't get me wrong here—we know this is an olden-day piece of writing and comes with the undesirable tag-word *curse*, but we started out skeptical too. But so far, each tomb or monument has led us to the next. It may all be hoax, but what if it's not?"

"I hope it's a hoax," Dahl said. "Better for everyone."

"Agreed," Drake said. "But we can't afford not to find out." He fixed on Luther. "Do you understand that?"

"I'm no thinker. No strategist. I'm a bloodhound—they point me in the direction they want me to go and slap my ass. I'm tenacious. Raw. I get the job done without relying on fancy gadgetry. So no, Drake, I don't understand it. And even if I did you lot would still be my prisoners."

"Look." Alicia struggled to turn around and look the big man in the eye. "Whilst I like the imagery of you being slapped on the ass, you—my old-style, simple, loutish beast—are talking up a steaming pile of crap. Open your damn eyes and wake up to the fight. Soldiers shouldn't deal in black and white anymore. There's adversity in much of the world right now, most of it caused by the people that pull your strings."

"And dude," Drake added, "it's not as if they try to hide all of it."

Luther couldn't twist his body in order to address Alicia, but replied to Drake. "You think I haven't heard this before? A hundred, desperate times from outta the mouths of a hundred desperate criminals? Shit, I could have made the speech for you."

Kenzie groaned. "Well maybe some of them were telling you the truth. So what does that make you?"

Luther hesitated just for a moment. "You guys came outta hiding to chase down some ancient weapon that may or may not exist? Why the hell would you do that?"

"Now that—" Alicia banged the seat "—is a great question. Drake?"

"You're asking me?" Drake felt defensive. "We all agreed. Even Smyth. We all agreed."

"I came with you. You came for Crouch. Kenzie came for Dahl."

"No. We all came to help."

Alicia shrugged. Kenzie tried to catch Dahl's eye through the window. "She's right, Torst. I'm not here to save the world."

Drake heard the outer shell at work and ignored it. Dahl called back inside whilst nobody could see his face.

"We are not together, Kenzie. We never will be."

"Now I know that's not true. You wouldn't lead me on all this time."

Drake heard the warning note in her voice and how Dahl fell suddenly silent. A taut silence filled the car.

"Did I lead you on?" the Swede finally asked.

"Stop it with the jokes. You're scaring me."

Drake frowned at the tone of her voice and the heat in her eyes. Kenzie had proven she could care and that she could fit in with the good guys. He hoped this wasn't some kind of degeneration.

Smyth, driving the car, spoke up then out of nowhere. "It was me," he said. "Luther? It was me, anyway. You shouldn't be chasing these guys."

Drake both saw and heard the guilt. "Shut up, mate. This isn't the time."

"I'm willing to accept any judgment."

"There were circumstances," Drake said. "And the guy was a murderer. Nobody should ever shoulder another man's sins."

"This is interesting," Luther grumbled. "But what are you talking about?"

"Nothing," Drake said. "Sunstroke has made the dumb American delirious."

"Ah, great. And we're good with him driving the car?"

Crouch stepped in, seeing a chance to gloss over it all. "The fifth seal is the pyramid and we must go there in all haste. There's a lot of ground to cover. Of course, these tombs are still being excavated. Almost eight million dog mummies were found a few years ago. Who knows what else lies beneath those sands?"

The car slowed as they reached the outskirts of a town. Drake thought this might be the perfect chance to procure an extra vehicle and maybe dump Luther and his two comrades. In all honesty though, what he wanted was something entirely different.

"Luther," he said. "I hate to tell you that you're working for the bad guys. I hate to tell you that there's a rogue cell in the American government searching for terrible weapons. I hate to see your loyalty, your faith and your training betrayed at the highest level. So I'll say this—find someone you trust in DC and ask them to check. Stick with us whilst it happens. Call a truce. And if, at the end of it you still think we're all guilty of treason, then we will come quietly. You have my word."

Drake held his hand out.

Alicia practically squawked a rebuttal. Dahl tried to wriggle back inside but couldn't get near. Drake had chosen the perfect time.

Luther considered it. "We stick with you? We have full weapons? Alone time?"

"Yes, but no communications. We don't want have the Air Force dropping down on us."

"I always go dark," Luther reminded him. "Only chatter is between the team."

CHAPTER THIRTY FOUR

The Pyramid of Djosser, built in the 27th century BCE, was fashioned by the great Egyptian architect, Imhotep. It stands at the center of an immense mortuary complex surrounded by grand structures and ritual adornments. By building this, Imhotep himself was laying the groundwork for all those greater structures that came in later dynasties, including the Great Pyramids of Giza.

Three cars arrived, all air-conditioned and with extremely grateful and weary soldiers resting inside. When the vehicles pulled up to a tire-grinding halt nobody moved for an entire minute. About an hour ago they had pulled over to the side of the road, nursing and cleaning cuts and wounds, tending to bruises. Their injuries were painful, but not debilitating.

"Oh, my legs," Alicia groaned, having just finished off a sandwich and a Pepsi, wedged in the front seat. "I can hardly open them."

Kenzie snorted comically. "A new first for the English harlot."

Drake was with Alicia, nursing a dozen aches and pains, and still nowhere near fully recovered. They had weapons, and bullets were in good supply but T-shirt and camo-trousers would have to fulfil the dress code.

"We must be extra careful," Hayden told them. "These injuries will affect our reaction time, our range of movement and, hell, our pure damn skill. Take care out there."

Crouch was out first, a testament to the man's desire for the job. Drake struggled to follow but had the fun job of yanking Alicia out of the passenger seat.

"Ow, ow, be bloody careful! Kenz, is that my ass or your face? Never can tell. Whoa, steady Drakey!"

"You'd think dehydration and hunger would shut her up for a while." Dahl stared at her speculatively. "Maybe a day at least."

"There's a reason they called her Taz." Mai laughed and

mimed a spinning devil, never stopping, always moving, even though it had no idea where it was headed.

Alicia offered to help Kenzie out of the car, face neutral. Surprisingly, the Israeli refused and pulled and pushed herself out.

The team gathered in the heat, to the front of the parking area and with Djosser's pyramid in plain sight. It was large, stepped and flat-topped, different to the pyramids common in modern culture. Drake raised his face to the breeze, enjoying the coolness on his skin and the chance to slow down for just a moment.

"Let's reccy the tomb," Hayden said, and the moment was gone.

From afar, splitting and acting like tourists, they viewed the pyramid from every angle. Drake and Dahl walked with Luther, Pine and Carey; Mai close behind to help watch for any sign of trouble. So far, the conventional crusader had taken it easy, watching and taking no sidebars with his colleagues. The entire team met around the front of the tomb and compared notes.

"We're good," Crouch decided. "I'm headed inside."

Drake went with him as Hayden assigned Smyth, Mai and Kinimaka to stay outside with Luther and his soldiers. Luther declined the offer, wanting in, but acquiesced to Pine and Carey staying back. Crouch was already inside, Yorgi and Kenzie trying to keep up. Drake studied the dark entrance to the tomb, checked around with suspicion once more and then ducked inside.

It would be good to have five on the outside. Safer.

Crouch was searching by flashlight, scanning the inner walls of the pyramid and wandering toward the funerary chamber. Yorgi backed him up with Kenzie checking ahead. It was quiet down here, cooler and secluded. An atmosphere of ancient repose filled the passageways, as if this place might see humanity out and then the next upstarts. A fitting resting place for what some may once have seen as a god.

Drake knew all about men elevated to the status of gods. He'd come across it and proved it during the Odin thing, and later by discovering more tombs and more evidence. Did it disprove the theory of real gods?

No, not really. But maybe they went the same way as the people with *real* wealth and power. Nobody ever knew who they were.

"I have it," Crouch said at length. "Just down here."

"You have what?" Luther asked. "Let me see."

Drake was pleased he was taking an interest. Crouch took a picture and then let Luther in. Drake stared at the image.

"What is that?"

"The capstone," Crouch affirmed. "And a coffin laid by the banks of the River Nile. I think the contours here—" he pointed at a peculiar bend in the river crowned by a peak "—tell us the location."

"And they've all been like this?" Luther asked, still staring. "I guess they're clearly timeworn, of Egyptian origin and potentially indicative. You guys managed to follow four of these already?"

Drake nodded. "And now five, once we decipher this picture. Mate, I was cynical at first too. The only reason I came was because Michael here—he has a reputation and is rarely wrong. Now, it doesn't sound unreasonable that the Egyptians left a trail for someone to find, does it?"

Luther rose now, shaking his enormous head. "Nah, I guess not. The issue comes when Michael here brings up an ancient doomsday machine."

"There are precedents," Crouch asserted. "Archimedes for one. He designed and built the Iron Hand, a weapon that withstood Roman invasion for three long years. He also tried to build a death ray out of mirrors. Nikola Tesla did the same and called it the Teleforce. Aristotle spoke, quite plainly, of a doomsday machine, so what did he know back then? The capstone is the right size, has the heritage and the ancestry. It follows the pattern. "

Luther didn't answer. The group began to walk, in single file, back toward the daylight. Luther stopped them just before they reached the exit.

"Look here," he said, face open and honest. "I'm nothing but plain-speaking. I see you as fellow soldiers. I realize I'm just like you. I *am* you, but better." He grinned. "Naturally. I don't entirely trust you, but once . . . I had a similar problem."

"You were burned?" Alicia asked.

"Not exactly. But I submitted to the suits and found a way through. You could do the same. But you run from me and I will come back down on you like Nemesis, the Greek god of vengeance. I ain't exaggerating when I say you will feel my fucking wrath."

Drake let out a long sigh. "The men that sent you are corrupt. They have parted ways from your government, and real society. They're using you, Luther, using your team. If it wasn't for them your friends would still be alive today. We are not the enemy here."

"I know you believe that, but—"

They exited into the sunlight, an overpowering glare. Crouch put a hand out close to Luther's arm. "What if they could prove it?"

Drake tried not to look surprised. *How can we . . .*

"Give them a scrambled satphone," Crouch said. "I know you have one. Not for reporting in to the suits, but for reaching out to vital contacts. Believe me, I'm in exactly the same boat. Sometimes, it's the only way to move forward."

"A satphone?" Luther looked surprised.

"To call our woman on the inside," Hayden said. "To call Lauren Fox."

Luther struggled with it for a long minute, but then perhaps understood they'd seen fit to take him into their confidence. A little reciprocation couldn't hurt.

Taking a black phone from a backpack, he handed it to Dahl. "Knock yourself out."

The Swede didn't hesitate, but turned his back to Kenzie and walked away. They stood by the cars now and their surroundings were clear, bright and peaceful. Whichever enemies were abroad today were not here. Life had gifted them a good day.

Drake listened to Dahl and watched Kenzie. The signs were not good.

"I miss you all. God, I can't wait to see the kids again, and you. We will sort it, I promise. Just hang in. I'll be home soon. Kiss my girls . . . kiss Isabella and Julia for me . . ."

The Swede ended the call then, since he could hardly form another syllable. Kenzie glared at the floor as he walked by, her face set grim. Smyth plucked the phone from Dahl's hands.

"Is that wise?" Hayden asked him. "We need Intel."

"I will get Intel," Smyth snapped. "But I'm talking to her."

Drake and Alicia stood by Luther and Carey, chatting comfortably about recent missions and scars. Dahl joined them after a while and then Mai, conversing like the old friends that they were. When Smyth had finished, Mai went away to call her sister and Yorgi joined Drake.

It was peaceful, nice for a short while.

Luther loosened somewhat, telling a story of his own, but Carey never spoke, this being one of her peculiarities. Her eyes followed everyone though, and took it all in, and occasionally her lips curled.

Smyth broke it up to report Lauren's status. "They set her free," he said anxiously. "Finally. They let her go and she's been wandering randomly for a day, checking for tails. Seems there are none."

"Lauren's in the clear?" Hayden said. "That's great news."

"For your proof?" Luther asked.

"Aye," Drake said. "See, now you can relax. We concentrate on finishing this seven seals bollocks and then we'll have your proof. How does that sound?"

"Apart from the gibberish—I can live with it."

"Sweet."

"I think this is the place." Crouch held up his cell and displayed a map app. "See how the river bends and that mountain lies right in its lowest curvature? I think the place was chosen on purpose. Landscape like this never changes."

"How far?" Drake was acutely aware of time constraints.

"Thirty minutes." Crouch was happy. "North toward Cairo and the Giza pyramids and then a fifteen-minute drive east."

"Great news," Yorgi said. "We could finish this today."

Hayden padded over to Kinimaka and the two enjoyed a quick private conversation. Drake hoped they might make it back together, he knew how deeply they cared for each other, but Hayden had hurt the big Hawaiian quite profoundly. She would have to work hard and show sincerity to make it happen.

Then Luther dropped a bombshell.

"I just realized something," he said. "There's only one hour until FrameHub's deadline."

"It really makes you wonder," Alicia said. "SPEAR would have been all over their operation. I really believe we would have destroyed it. If the same splinter group that took us out also burned many more similar teams—who's now protecting the people against threats like this?"

Hayden came over after hearing Luther's words. "Nobody," she said. "That's why FrameHub haven't and won't be stopped."

"Then two of those poor countries is about to become hell on earth?" Kinimaka asked.

"I'm afraid so. It's gonna be Dark Age stuff. Or post apocalypse. And there's nothing we can do about it."

"Do we know which ones?" Yorgi asked. "Since we have a vested interest?"

Luther had popped a set of earphones in and was listening to the news on his cell. "Not announced yet," he said. "They're holding what they call an awards ceremony in twenty minutes." He shook his head. "Crazy, crazy men."

Dahl came running up. "Hey, I was patrolling the perimeter. The mercs are here, but they pulled away over to that side. If we leave now we can probably sneak out without being noticed."

Some good fortune for a change. Drake smiled.

"We should go anyway," Luther said. "If your coffin's a thirty-minute drive away we should be there before FrameHub potentially launch a devastating strike on this country."

Together, they marched out.

CHAPTER THIRTY FIVE

Alicia listened as Drake, Dahl and Hayden worked on Luther to try and get him to see things their way. He was one tough nut, but then Alicia barely expected less. His protégés, Pine and Carey, were hardly less resilient, the first never cracking that boyish face and the second never speaking. Pine reminded her of Zack Healey, who had died in the Caribbean recently. Healey had been a fine warrior, a trusted friend. Maybe Pine would be too.

The minutes ticked down; time drifted away. Their mission was fraught with anxiety now as FrameHub's deadline drifted inexorably closer. Alicia recognized it as one of the few times she had felt truly helpless. Usually, they were the team running toward the death threat, fighting in the shadows for those that never truly knew, but on this day they could do nothing about it.

All they could do was wait and see.

Alicia held memories and friends close to her heart. "Hey." She leaned through the front two seats. "Are we there yet?"

Dahl glared back at her. "Sit still. Another ten minutes and you can have a reward candy."

"Thanks, Dad."

The landscape changed as they drove through a small town and approached the banks of the River Nile. The streets were clean and narrow, full of people brightly dressed. Young children carried and traded handmade necklaces to all that passed. Every man and woman, it seemed, called out to every other, seeking something. Men sold piles of oranges off the back of carts. A man walked his child along the street because there were no sidewalks. As they approached the banks of the Nile the landscape flattened and Alicia got her first view of the longest river in the world.

Sparkling under the sunlight, its waters were wide and fast-flowing. What she could see of the river banks were sandy and rock-strewn, just like most of Egypt, she reckoned. Crouch, at the wheel, continued to pick his way through the streets, following his app and aiming for the place where, earlier, he'd dropped a pin at the best vantage point he could find.

"Three minutes," he said. "Get ready."

"What are we looking for?" Alicia asked.

"Anything tomby," Drake said. "And capstoney."

"That's a great help, thanks."

"No worries."

Crouch guided the car to the place he'd dropped the pin and braked, staring out the windshield. From here, the banks of the Nile were wide open due to a gap in the buildings. Dropping many feet from the top to the flowing river.

Crouch commented as he switched off the engine. "It's possible were looking at a Tombs of the Nobles situation."

Alicia raised one brow. "Totally."

Crouch cracked open the door. "The Tombs of the Nobles lie on the west bank of the Nile, about halfway down the slope that leads to the river. The entrance stares over the width of the Nile. Could be the same here."

"You got that view pinpointed?" Luther asked.

Crouch raised a thumb to gauge the distant peak, then checked his phone. "I do."

"And they knew it would stay this way for all time?" Luther sounded supremely skeptical.

But Crouch had no problem rounding on him. "Y'know, stop being such a bloody wet towel. No, of course they couldn't be sure. People build tombs and raise buildings every single day, hoping they stand the test of time as some kind of memorial. But they don't know. What they have—is faith. I'm so sick of hearing people like you repeating the same old bloody mantra. Nobody knows what will survive a thousand years or even ten, and for the relatively few treasures we *do* manage to find I bet you now there are hundreds we don't."

Luther held up both hands, letting Crouch have his day, then as he turned away caught Drake's and Dahl's attention.

"Your time is almost up. I gave you leeway; you're just about

out. Best get ready to come quietly, boys."

Alicia was standing quietly behind the big soldier. "And there I was thinking we'd managed to sway you slightly over to our side."

"I see no gray area," Luther said. "I got tasked with bringing you in. That's about to happen. Like I said before, fight your case with the suits. Maybe you'll win."

Drake didn't want to lock horns with him. "How about the proof we promised?"

"I don't see nothing."

"You're a bloody pig-headed brute of single purpose," Dahl groaned. "Refusing to see the truth and shouldering a lifetime of regret."

"I have no regrets." Luther gazed into the middle-distance where the glimmering sunlight met the waves. "That's why there's a chain of command and you boys are enemies of the state."

"Depends what day of the week it is," Alicia said. "Next week—we'll be heroes."

"And like I said—I wouldn't regret that either. This is the sixth seal right?"

"Yeah. This should show us the location of the weapon." Alicia felt the familiar rush of adrenalin returning now as they all recovered from their arena ordeal.

Luther pursed his lips. "I can promise you another hour, but not much more than that."

Drake looked like he wanted to argue, but Alicia saw him shrug and mouth "what's the point?" He was right. Luther was a hound with dogged, unwavering ideals. The mission, the orders, could never be compromised.

Right?

Hayden's voice cut through the tension like a bullet through parchment. "How much longer until FrameHub's announcement?"

Luther checked his watch, and planted his earplugs in. "Ten minutes."

"Best to get a move on." Kinimaka followed Crouch to the edge of the road.

Alicia followed, knowing the storm of storms was coming and wanting to take her mind off to a different place. A treasure hunt with Crouch should do the trick. It had worked before.

The team joined them near the top of the slope that ran down a sandy bank to the lapping waters. The incline was steep but still negotiable. Crouch shaded his eyes.

"Nothing obvious."

Of course, there wouldn't be. Hayden had already crosschecked the area to see if anything important had ever been found. Crouch aligned his position with the picture as best he could. "Moment of truth," he said. "Wish me luck."

Alicia followed him over the edge. "Don't be silly. We're all coming."

They started down the slope, inches at a time, balancing uncertainly on the rocky, shifting ground. Shales of grit ran away from their heels, ending up in the Nile. Sunshine glared down upon their heads and blinding lights shimmered off the water. Alicia felt the breeze rushing along the Nile like a racehorse around a track and welcomed the cool respite.

From above, Luther called out. "You have three minutes."

Crouch picked up the pace, almost fell and then steadied. Drake came alongside him. Alicia stayed above, scanning left and right for any kind of jutting rock or alcove. So far, all they could see was endless rock.

Mai ranged furthest to the right; Kenzie to the left. Those in between searched with increased desperation and doubt.

"Not looking good, Michael," Drake said. "Are you sure this is the right place?"

"It matches the symbol," Crouch replied. "Like no other contours along the entire Nile. I guess the picture, being old, could depict anywhere along this whole stretch."

Luther called down to them, signaling to the buds in his ears. "Time's up. FrameHub are broadcasting."

"Is it really going ahead?" Kinimaka asked, fearful not for himself but for those that would undoubtedly be caught up in it.

Luther nodded. "They getting to it. Some kinda juvenile speech about toeing the line and doing as you're told. Sounds like a parent telling a child off." He glanced over at Pine without thinking, giving Alicia something to ponder on. "Everyone had the same chance, everyone had the same amount of time. Blah, blah, frickin' blah. Shit, they're promising to lay waste to certain areas and cripple others."

Luther looked down at them. "I hope to hell they're bluffing. This could get real bad, real quick."

Alicia thought about the town they'd just driven through, the civilians going about their daily business, many of them having no clue who FrameHub were and what they were threatening.

Luther tensed. "Just naming the countries now."

Alicia looked up at the man, her friends and colleagues alongside. For a moment nobody breathed.

"Greece," Luther said. "And . . . Egypt. The countdown has begun."

A knot of tension roiled inside Alicia's stomach. With everyone else she turned her gaze to the skies.

"Ten, nine, eight . . ." Luther counted it down.

And eventually: "One."

CHAPTER THIRTY SIX

The nightmare turned into reality.

Drake felt his face slacken and his eyes close as rockets took to the air. He saw vertical and arcing ones; heard one explode out of a bunker only a few miles away and scream into flight. He saw the lovely, peaceful waters of the Nile and the air filled with death high above it.

Luther breathed a running commentary. "Egypt have SCUD launchers, at least ninety of the Project Ts with increased range. They have FROG-7s, purchased from the Soviets with a seventy kilometer range. They have M270s from the United States." He stared in horror. "This is . . . Armageddon."

Drake counted eight on their way to a terrible devastation. FrameHub had challenged the world, and no one had managed to stop them.

Did anyone even try? He wondered how many other teams were scattered around the world now, watching this in torment and utter helplessness.

"It wasn't all about the missiles," Hayden reminded them. "FrameHub promised a countrywide breakdown. Infrastructure, utilities, everything."

In moments the missiles had vanished and the sky was clear. Drake made out several spiraling clouds of smoke toward the direction of Cairo and other cities, and could only guess as to the devastation.

"We get this done," he said. "And then we get FrameHub done."

Alicia nodded. "They can't get away with this."

Hayden agreed. "And just as importantly—they won't *stop* this. How long until the next ransom demand?"

Drake, for once, felt powerless. Usually, they were at the tip of the sword, saving the day. But now . . . somebody in America had taken on a wealth of sins today and, soon, they were going to pay.

Luther sat down at the top of the slope, body language showing distress and disbelief. He stared at the floor, ignoring the SPEAR team.

Drake said nothing, just continued searching along the rocky bank. The team spread out in silence, each lost to their own thoughts, and when Crouch and Mai stumbled across something it took three low-key shouts to gather everyone together.

It wasn't a splendid Egyptian tomb, nor even a marked burial site, just a hole in the side of the hill, covered over by a three-foot-thick slab and hidden by years of silt build-up and gathering sand. It had to be dug out. The only reason they continued in the light of everything was that this hole lay exactly where the depiction said it would be, and the thick plank overlaying it spoke to the fact that it had been made to last. Even the occasional Nile flood wouldn't wash away the murals, and this site may never even have been flooded. The ancients knew what they were doing.

Drake's fingers were bleeding by the time they finished removing sand. Then Crouch tried to wriggle into the hole and found he was too large. As ever, it was Alicia that turned to Yorgi and flashed a grin.

"What say you, Yogi? If anyone can get in there, it's gotta be you."

The Russian thief stepped up, dropping down into his belly and wriggling into the tiny alcove.

"You know what you're looking for?" Crouch fretted, always anxious to be at the center of the hunt, inside the actual chamber.

"Got it," Yorgi said a little thickly, concentrating hard. "I see darkness."

Alicia looked like she was about to crack a witticism, then Drake saw her glance at the far-off plumes of smoke and let it die right there on her lips. He felt the same.

"Take my phone," Crouch said, handing it over. "Just don't lose it."

"I will try."

Yorgi struggled inside the narrow recess, forcing his body

further and further into the hole that it concealed. The hole itself was behind the rock, invisible to the naked eye unless a person climbed down and dug it out. Crouch voiced the opinion that if they hadn't found the picture and knew where to look, it would have gone unnoticed for many more millennia.

Slowly, and with a steady patience, Yorgi forced first his shoulders and then his torso into the gap. He moaned constantly, scraping flesh even under clothes. Drake saw his legs wiggling and then he was gone. He pressed forward.

"You okay?"

"Yes. I forget flashlight. Please pass down."

Drake managed to reach in and hand his down. Yorgi wriggled off into the dark, leaving the team alone. Drake sat down, staring at the horizon and Alicia landed at his side.

"We can't save everyone, Drakey."

He nodded. "We should be trying," he said. "Being stuck on the outside like this . . . it's fucking unbearable. Totally undermining."

Many pairs of eyes stared with undiminished dread and distress into the clear distance, wishing they had been able to help. This was what it felt to lose then, to be cut off and forgotten. Drake hated it.

In time, Yorgi reappeared. The climb in and out had exhausted him, and Dahl was called upon to help drag him out. Even then his sides were bleeding and, without a word, he collapsed into a heap, breathing shallowly.

But he held up Crouch's phone.

The Englishman plucked it deftly from Yorgi's grasp, turned it around and stared hard at the screen. At first, he seemed confused, then unhappy.

"Oh dear," he said with typical understatement. "I think we may have to go back down."

Drake winced. Who else could even fit down there? Mai? *Pine?*

Hmm, an interesting conversation. He caught Luther's eye and beckoned him down.

"We have a little problem."

Luther stopped. "No," he said. "We don't. It is the people over there, those on the sharp end of this hell. We are fine."

"Agreed, mate. But—"

"Wait." Yorgi finally found breath to speak. "It *is* what you see. It is. I did not believe what I saw but stayed and stayed and looked and looked. I took pictures from every angle. Look at them. Look! *It is what you think it is!*"

Crouch backed away from them, the horror and fear on his face mirroring that which had crossed it when the missiles flew. "We came all this way, went through everything we did, and the answer was right in front of us all this time."

"What are you talking about, Crouchy?" Alicia waved at him. "Snap out of it."

"The seventh seal. It's been there all along. We missed it. I missed it. The doomsday machine. No, oh no, it can't be. There has to be some kind of mistake because, I see it now, and it's horrendous."

Drake was almost hopping. "C'mon, mate. What do you bloody well see?"

Crouch sent a dismayed face to the horizon, unable to speak. Drake followed his gaze, beyond the columns of smoke, beyond the mayhem and the twisting Nile and the mountains.

All the way to the giant pyramids of Giza.

CHAPTER THIRTY SEVEN

"The seventh seal and the key to the doomsday are inside the pyramids of Giza?" Luther asked in disbelief.

"*The* pyramid," Crouch said. "That's the Great Pyramid. And it does sound odd, since the capstone has been missing since before records were taken."

"What could it be?" Kinimaka gazed at the horizon.

"But that's impossible," Hayden said. "The Great Pyramid has been explored already."

"Ah, that's not strictly true," Crouch said. "It has been discovered quite recently that there are at least three passages inside that are still unexplored and, possibly, another tomb."

"But why? Why would they not investigate it?"

"That," Crouch said. "Is a very good question. I suggest we head that way and find out."

To a person, the whole team followed his hand gesture at the distant pyramids.

"And into Cairo," Drake said.

"I'm counting three hits," Dahl said quietly. "And if the infrastructure has failed that's going to be one hairy ride."

"Gonna be some frightened people in there," Luther said. "It will help to see some American military ride through."

Alicia goggled her eyes at him. "Dude, that's some scary blind faith you got there."

"What are you talking about?"

Drake knew the American soldier was going to prove the hardest nut to crack and held out no illusions that it was even possible. "Y'know," he said. "We should go there. That's where we should be. Even if we help only one person or one family it's the right thing to do."

They walked away from the ancient tomb, leaving it now for some adventurist or local fisherman to 'discover'. Who knew what other riches lay down there?

As Hayden came over the top of the slope and Crouch headed for the car a cellphone started to chirp.

Kinimaka tapped her. "That's you."

"Yeah, I thought so, but it can't be."

Drake heard the incredulity in her tone and hesitated. "Why?"

"Because it's . . ." She pulled the cell out and stared at the screen. "Kimberly Crowe."

If the team had been struck by a missile at that point they couldn't have been more surprised. Mai summed it up: "This can't be good."

Luther latched on to the name immediately. "Secretary Crowe is calling you? Now? Can you prove it?"

"How about this?" Hayden jabbed the answer button and then the speakerphone, holding the cell in the palm of her hand.

"Hello?"

"Hayden Jaye? Is that you?"

"It is. I'm surprised to hear from you, Madam Secretary."

"I'm surprised you still have this cell, Miss Jaye. Can't it be traced? Even by your own ex-CIA colleagues?"

"I have a special chip that reroutes my location five times every second. I installed that in case you ever wanted to get back in touch."

"Oh, well that's fine. That's fine then. There are no words for what has been done to you, so I'll say nothing. My hands have been tied but now I'm starting to find options. Do you know Tempest?"

"It's an operation, I believe. Something about finding the weapons of the gods."

"It's not an operation, Hayden, it's the codename of the cabal behind your team's quiet disavowing. And others, I might add. Their *goal* is to amass all the remaining weapons of the gods."

"To what end?" Drake asked.

"I haven't figured that out yet. But they're influential in all governments. They're like the worst damn weed in your garden. It has roots everywhere."

Hayden looked momentarily taken aback by the Secretary's

language. Luther took the opportunity to bob his head toward the phone.

"Is this really Secretary of Defense Crowe?"

"Who is this?"

"Luther. I mean it is Luther, Madam Secretary, sorry." The soldier looked embarrassed.

"*It is Luther,*" Dahl mimicked, grinning, and Drake looked away. Luther gave them both a stone-cold glare.

"Luther?" Now Crowe sounded astonished. "The same soldier they sent to kill you? I feel like I'm dreaming here."

"No dream," Luther said quickly. "We've apprehended the suspects and are bringing them in."

"That's not strictly true," Drake said. "Right now we're unclear as to who has apprehended who, to be honest. And we're stuck in a mutually co-operative situation."

"A what? Wait, it doesn't matter. Luther was sent by Tempest which somewhat compromises me. Do you hear that, Luther?"

"I do," Luther said stonily. "My orders came from . . . a five-star general, Madam Secretary. I know nothing of this Tempest."

"Look here, son . . ." Luther's eyes widened at the title. "I've been hoodwinked more times in the last few weeks than in my entire life. I'm facing down men with agendas upon agendas, schemes that would make your hair curl. Not many, mind you, but enough to develop a nasty, deep scourge within this good government. I'm fighting against it . . . carefully. Because these people—they go after you, your family and your friends. Now you hear my name, you keep your damn mouth shut. And you trust these good people. They're trying to do right. Got it?"

Luther appeared a little chastised. "Ah, yeah, I guess. Madam."

"Is this why you called?" Hayden was mindful of the time they were wasting.

"Partly, to reassure you that you have a friend in DC, yes."

Drake was pleased nobody mentioned Lauren. At this point, they couldn't properly trust anyone except their own team mates.

"But also . . . to urge you to get out of Egypt and meet me.

There is a great and terrible danger to the world. Tempest have started it and they will not stop until they own every weapon, and the means to destroy or rule it all. They're evil. Plain evil, in the old-fashioned way. I cannot stress enough how bad it will be if they get their hands on those weapons. Meet me. Soon."

Drake saw that even worse things than those they had already endured were in their future. But if they didn't stop it, who would? The entire FrameHub disaster was proof enough.

"How many teams were burned?" he asked. "How many good people?"

"Out there, now? At least a dozen. Probably more, all like you. Look, I can't come clean. I can't nip up to the White House and shout in Coburn's ear. In some way, I was complicit. Nobody will believe that I didn't know what the hell was going on. And .. . I have my family to worry about."

"Are you thinking we might contact them?" Dahl asked Drake.

"Twelve to twenty teams like ours?" Drake's eyes brightened. "That'd be a once-in-a-lifetime thing. An army to end all wars. I'm excited."

"Me too," Dahl agreed. "An incredible spectacle."

Crowe went on: "I need to speak face to face and we need a plan. Tempest is moving ahead very quickly. The Sword of Mars is being sought as we speak. This doomsday machine in Egypt is also considered a weapon of the gods. Many others that were taken away from the tombs you all discovered. I need your help. Your countries need your help, and your loved ones too. Come to DC now."

"All right," Hayden said. "We can do that. We can talk. But right now . . . we have to go. This needs finishing first."

"Yeah," Drake said, watching the spiraling smoke as it drifted among the clouds and studying the ancient Great Pyramid where all the secrets and death quite possibly crouched, waiting.

"Yeah," he said again. "Just . . . give us a minute."

CHAPTER THIRTY EIGHT

Cairo has become one of the most famous cities in the world and has the largest metropolitan area in the Middle-East. It lies close to Giza, the ancient city of Memphis and the incredible Nile Delta. Pollution, traffic and overcrowding are just a few of its daily demands.

Drake viewed its environs as they closed in. All the way from the last tomb both he and Dahl had been working their magic on Luther and, at this stage, they'd almost given up.

"Even Secretary Crowe?" Dahl put real disbelief in his voice.

"If that *was* Secretary Crowe. And my orders come from the general. I can't go committing treason."

Drake pressed. "Do we *act* like evildoers to you?"

"Soldier like you should know they come in all forms and sizes, bud. You never drop your guard."

"He's right." Dahl eyed Drake. "Did they teach you that in the SAS?"

"Piss off, Dancing Queen. I don't know what to do with you, Luther. You're a bloody brick wall."

"I like you all. Even you, Drake. But I gotta say: ord—"

"Don't say it." Alicia held up a hand. "Orders are orders, right?"

Luther clicked his fingers at her. "You got it, sunshine."

"Aww, cheers. Now I gotta think of a nice nickname for you."

Dahl put their case as succinctly as possible. "Decision time. We're entering Cairo right now and heading for those big, pointy rocks. No doubt, FrameHub's mercs will be there. Tempest's agents too. Who else? Maybe the Chinese, the Brits, the CIA. The question is: will you help us?"

Luther looked like he didn't know whether to help or kill them. Drake kept an eye on the streets, already seeing the signs of a city in chaos. Sidewalks and roads were thronged with people, some running blindly toward danger and some away.

Buses and cars were strewn everywhere, most abandoned. Shopfronts were boarded or barred. Screams and yells rang out constantly, like a plaintive chorus of those trapped in Hell. Drake saw men with half-face masks already strutting around.

"It's gonna get ugly," he said, "before they turn this around. How does a country recover from this?"

"Depends if it was a Denial of Service attack, or something more sinister," Hayden said. "Egypt have a world-class IT section. They'll turn it around pretty quick, but applying that to the real world?" She shook her head. "Months."

"With FrameHub still out there," Drake said. "Should we really be turning our attention to Tempest? Feels wrong."

A rubble-strewn street showed signs of a missile attack, bricks lying in heaps, smoking, with mini-fires all around. Drake stopped the car and ran to help a nearby wandering man, his face so bloody he could not see, and shepherded him along the street to a medic. Dahl forcibly removed a family huddling close to the brick pile, explaining that there might be ruptured gas pipes and other dangers. Luther was quick to jump in too, helping to carry an older woman out of harm's way.

The team drove on, stopping time and again to help the afflicted. Nobody, not even Crouch with his desperation to reach Giza, not even Smyth with his anger and fear for Lauren, could drive on without helping these uninformed innocents. Twice, Drake and Dahl faced down looters but it was all a mere drop in the ocean. They could not prevent coming atrocities over the next few days.

Another fail, right on the back of the first.

In the end, they could not reach the pyramids by car. They abandoned the vehicles and continued on foot, realizing the distance from outer Cairo to the pyramids was rather more than they'd expected as an hour passed by.

The flames receded and the running people thinned. Out here, groups rested or took stock, fearful of being inside the city now. Drake knew they were waiting for someone to tell them what to do. For an authority figure, for information. He gave as much news as he could, translated by Kenzie, and moved on.

They ran and they walked, Luther at their side, and their rations and weapons were supplemented by the big man.

"Giza," he'd said. "The last seal. Get to this weapon and then we'll have our talk."

Drake had sighed with relief whilst, at the same time, dreading the "talk." Somehow he didn't think it'd be a reprimand.

The bright yellow rolling desert surrounded the Giza pyramid complex, a trio of ancient structures the largest of which—the Pyramid Of Khufu—was the oldest of the seven ancient wonders of the world and remained the tallest manmade structure ever built for almost four thousand years. *Not a bad final résumé,* Drake thought, *for a structure that took twenty years to build even if they moved eight hundred tons of stone a day.*

To complete the task the builders would have had to move twelve blocks into place, every hour, through day and through night. For twenty years. The math was mesmerizing.

And it certainly looked impressive as they drew closer. Drake knew the outer cladding had been stripped away through the years—once a casing of highly polished white limestone wrapped the entire pyramid, only part of which remained today around the lowest courses.

Crouch shaded his eyes as they approached, the supply of sunglasses running out before they'd reached him. Drake was glad to see his wounds were not affecting him and appeared to be healing nicely. It was the same for them all, although the trauma of the arena would never fade.

"Wait," Dahl said, gazing hard at the foot of the pyramid.

They paused almost beneath its great shadow. "I see it," Kenzie said.

Guards lay around the side and at the entrance to the Great Pyramid, and the ground near them was saturated with blood.

"Somebody's already here," Mai said.

"Then we'd better be quick," Crouch said. "Let's move."

CHAPTER THIRTY NINE

Outside the Great Pyramid of Giza they came under attack, in the bright light of day. Whoever had killed the guards had left sentries of their own behind who had been patrolling to the left, around the funerary chamber. Now, as SPEAR openly approached, they came running, shouting, threatening with guns.

Drake and Dahl ducked their heads, raised their rifles and fired. Bullets sped across the plateau, embedding in stones and structures and the scattered police cars. If the dead guards had called in a warning it hadn't been heard.

Crouch ran to the entrance and covered Mai and Yorgi as they raced to join him. Drake and Dahl ducked and covered and ran from shelter to shelter, raising their heads and sights briefly to squeeze off bursts of ammunition. First one sentry and then another fell back, arms akimbo, blood bursting out of their chests. A third dug in, but Luther smoked him out with a flash-bang and Pine ended his life.

"This way." Crouch waved them toward him.

Drake signaled and called that he was moving. Dahl, Smyth and Kinimaka remained to cover him, wary of more threats, leaving their posts one by one to join the rest of the team at the entrance to Khufu's Pyramid.

Dahl joined them last. "Moving."

Crouch ducked in, leading the way. The inner passage was narrow and led down an incline to start with, presently presenting them with two options.

"Upward, to the Queen's and then the King's Chamber, or continue down to the subterranean chamber. Input here would be good."

"Where were the secret passages found?" Hayden asked.

"Heat anomalies saw passages at ground level, the first course of the pyramid and in the top half, above the King's

Chamber, leading to the apex. Nobody knows what was found or if they even looked."

"Odd. All the other depictions were found low down," Mai said. "I would say we try the subterranean chamber and passage."

"Or the King's?" Kenzie put in. "Him being important and all. Plus, I'd like to know if that secret passage goes all the way to the top."

They hesitated. In the end the decision remained moot as soldiers began to fill the tunnel below them. The first pointed them out and then the bullets started flying. Crouch and Yorgi crowded into the upward tunnel and the rest jumped in after.

"No room to fight," Drake said. "We got a problem here."

Bullets whistled past the opening to their tunnel, non-stop.

Dahl waved an arm out, firing his weapon blindly. A scream paused the hail of gunfire for a while and Drake risked a peek out.

"I'm counting eight," he said. "And they're moving pretty fast."

"We got more trouble," Kinimaka said, looking up. "They're coming from both directions."

"Sounds like my prom night," Alicia said. "This is gonna be a slaughter."

It was indeed a kill box, Drake saw. Nowhere to go and two enemies coming at them. Kinimaka decided the way they would go. He was in front and charged at the descending men. A bullet flew past his head, dislodging rock, and then another displaced a large, jagged chunk that plummeted onto his temple stopping him like a rocket would stop a rhino, forcing him to his knees.

The oncoming mercs cheered, still coming. Kinimaka was down, head hanging, groaning and winded.

"Let 'em have it!" a voice rang out.

Then Mai was in action, running, planting a foot firmly on Mano's back and using him as a springboard to launch her body among the mercs. She landed hard and true, scattering their weapons and unbalancing them. Instantly, she kicked out whilst they were already unstable, toppling one headlong into the griping Kinimaka and another in his wake. The one above her landed on his tailbone, yelping. She grabbed his gun, twisted it in his hand and shot him three times with it. The fourth bullet went past his head as another man sought to target her. The fifth made sure he collapsed back into the man above, head blown away.

Giving her clearer sight of the tunnel above. The mercs were bunched up, hampered beyond measure, and she added one more body to the mix, killing the next visible merc and making him fall among his comrades.

"Close quarter combat," Luther breathed in an impressed tone. "Now there's a specialist."

Drake backed Dahl as they slowed the oncoming mercs in the other direction. Effectively, they were guarding the exit and the mercenaries were trapped. The dubious factor was that the mercs were leaving.

What had they found?

Overheard transmissions told him nothing except they had radioed in for heavy machinery, which could mean absolutely anything. It was clear though that the mercs were in a desperate hurry. They were sacrificing their number just to get close to the exit.

Kenzie jumped after Mai, looking to help. She dragged the first dead man away, let him slide past, then used the close-set walls as a fulcrum to jump over the next. She kicked him down until his body slithered into Kinimaka. The Hawaiian got the message, heaving upright and wincing even as he threw the dead men past him.

All the way to Drake, who rolled them out into the downward passage.

Communications flared between both mercenary groups. Drake could hear one team telling the other to fall back, to let them take the lead, to get the hell out of the way.

"*We found it!*"

His heart leapt as he heard those words. Crouch zeroed in on it too, coming to Drake's shoulder and listening.

"No way we're gonna lift that mother," someone shouted into

a walkie. "It's almost thirty by thirty and weighs about six tons. We got a stallion en route, but someone gotta smoke these fuckers first."

What's he talking about? Drake mouthed at Crouch.

"Must admit I'm stumped. I thought all we were here for was a wall painting, a mural. Could he be talking about the weapon itself?"

Drake guessed it was possible. "These men are clearly FrameHub's mercs. If Tempest and the others were ever here they've been dispatched. Maybe that's why the mercs are in such a rush—to safeguard what they found."

"Sounds likely," Crouch said.

The incredible close-quarter battle continued inside the Great Pyramid. Drake saw a dead policeman thrown in front of the upcoming mercs, positioned as shields, and gritted his teeth in hatred. Another was thrown from above, striking Kenzie and knocking her to the floor. Mai resisted a concerted attack, breaking a man's knees with her gun and watching him stagger past into the arms of Kinimaka.

Today, not kind arms.

Mai fired up at the next, using each man as a shield to reach around. Twice bullets ripped through clothes but passed her by.

Drake and Dahl braced as the mercs inched closer. They had lost eight of their number but still retained at least that many, uncompromising with their advance. The time was approaching when they would push past the upward passage and that was going to present some problems.

For all of them.

"Make sure you're fully loaded," Drake shouted. "Here they come!"

CHAPTER FORTY

An unknown quandary faced them. Nobody had ever fought in such close quarters against so many armed men inside an ancient pyramid before. Alicia pointed it out, and the rest had to agree.

Luther was halfway up the incline, helping Mai, drawn to her courage and skill. Pine and Carey were at his back. That gave the rest of the SPEAR team chance to ponder the mercs coming from below.

They couldn't step out into the line of fire. They could hardly let them pass. But they found they could not stop them either. At least eight mercs attacked in a line, carrying their dead and at least one man not-so-dead, with them and forcing them against the hole where Dahl and Drake crouched. Their bullets struck the dead bodies; the dead bodies fell upon them, their number weighing everyone down. A flapping skull struck Hayden, felling her. A lifeless, weighty frame came down on Drake, pinning him to the floor. A slim man pushed up at Dahl, rocking him back on his heels and then another was added to the weight and the makeshift barricade, forcing him back and allowing more mercs to slip past.

They did get some shots off, and through, heard cries of pain. Bullets found their mark. Some came through the other way too, one almost felling Kinimaka for a second time.

"Not again," was heard as he went gasping to the floor, shocked at how close it had come.

Drake wriggled free of his obstruction. Another landed atop him, slithering across the man above and adding its weight. Drake was trapped. Perhaps the ascending mercs could have made more of that chance, but their heads were pointed in one direction only, their orders to escape as fast as they could.

Mai fought tirelessly, dragging down the last of the mercs and throwing him over her shoulders. Luther caught him in mid-air and slammed his head against the bedrock, only dropping him when all life had departed the body. When Mai had checked for stragglers she turned and caught Luther gazing at her.

"You," he said, "are one incredible conflict diamond. And I mean that in the best possible way."

"I know how you mean it." Mai acknowledged the compliment with a nod.

"If I weren't such a gentleman I'd ask you to accompany me on your next available date . . ." He left it hanging.

Mai picked her way through the dead. "And are you a gentleman?"

"Depends what your answer would be."

"No, it depends on what you intend to do with us once this is finished."

Luther took in the scene with fascinated eyes. From the bodies strewn up the incline that led to the King's Chamber to those Drake and Dahl and the others were throwing off further down. "This is . . . captivating."

"For us, mate, this is normal," Drake said. "Now help me lug this big moose off Alicia."

"That *is* Alicia," Kenzie said.

Drake almost fell for it, glancing twice, but caught his natural instinct at the very last second. Once Alicia was free and the way cleared, Dahl took a tentative look back up the tunnel, toward the exit.

"Looks clear. Ready to move?"

"All good."

"Wait." Crouch stopped them. "This merc is still alive."

"Well, what do you wanna do?" Alicia said. "Nurse him? These guys made their own . . . tomb. Let them lie in it."

"You're not wrong," Crouch said. "But he may have information and, people, that is just what we need right now."

He knelt alongside the faintly gasping man, cradling his head and helping him to achieve a more comfortable position. "Listen up," he said. "Your own men shot you, used you as a human shield so they could escape. All I want is one answer—*what did you find?*"

"I am *not* with them," came the soft, indignant reply. "I am . . . professor at Akhet . . ." Crouch knew this was the museum of natural history in Cairo. "They . . . forced me to come along and . . . help." He coughed hard. "Then . . . they use me as human . . . shield. The wall painting," he said. "It was the same as the last which we found already opened just an hour ago . . . the capstone . . ."

Drake closed his eyes with the frustration. They had lost the race here simply because they had stopped to help people. Because the cars had gotten snarled up and the mercs had access to helos. Having said all that, he wouldn't have changed a moment of it.

"The same?" Crouch repeated. "We know the capstone is the weapon. Please do not tell me those mercs are now headed to where it's hidden?"

"The last depiction showed a section of the lower wall highlighted. The kids with the brains—and the mainframes—took a gander. They used thermal scans and say the whole thing lit up. There's a passage, a big one, inside this pyramid, hiding the capstone."

Crouch blinked. "Which capstone?"

"*The* capstone. The capstone of the Great Pyramid. I'm sure you know—the one that's being missing for thousands of years?"

Crouch couldn't stop himself shifting in utter amazement. "Here? I find that . . . incredible. You're saying it's been here the whole time?"

"Along with all those passages the Egyptians knew about and never bothered to excavate. Yes."

"We have to go," Dahl urged. "They already have a five-minute start."

"Wait a minute," Hayden said. "If they've found the capstone here, inside the pyramid, are they now able to use it as the doomsday machine?"

"Lady," the professor said, "I was there, greatest moment of my life, finding and ogling the missing capstone, so it took me a while. But let me help. The capstone isn't the weapon. You're standing in it."

Hayden glanced at her feet, then back at the professor.

Crouch looked like he'd been hit with a car tire, but recovered fast.

"Dahl's right. We must get moving. But we can't. We need this man's knowledge. I believe I know what's happening now. It's one of those legends nobody really knew was real because the only way to properly test it, *was to turn it on.*"

"I don't follow," Dahl said as he started to run. "Turn it on?"

The professor shifted uncomfortably, still bleeding despite Crouch's and Drake's best efforts. "The fantastical legend is real, it seems. As far back as the nineteenth century the British inventor, Siemens, was allowed to climb to the top of the pyramid with his Arab guides. On hearing stories that other guides heard an acute ringing noise when they raised their hands with outspread fingers, Siemens did the same. Bear in mind this is the founder of the Siemens Company, of course." The professor paused for a hacking cough, face turning paler by the second. "Siemens raised his index finger up there and felt a definite stinging sensation. After that, he raised a wine bottle that he'd brought to drink from and received an electric shock. Being a scientist, he moistened a newspaper and wrapped it around the bottle to create a rudimentary capacitor."

Crouch looked dumbfounded. "I read about this but thought it farfetched."

The professor nodded. "And I. But Siemens was not a joker. Holding the bottle up, he saw it charged with electricity, sparks being emitted from it. When the Arab guides attempted to stop him he pointed the bottle toward the Arab and gave him such a shock that it knocked him to the ground."

Hayden frowned, helping Kinimaka stand as the big man struggled with a head wound.

"I don't understand."

"It's not the capstone, it's the pyramid," Crouch said. "The Great Pyramid of Khufu is the ancient doomsday weapon."

Drake urged the team to rise and make ready. "What do we need to know, Professor? I'm sorry we can't save you, but to help us, to save countless lives, what do we need to know?"

"Physicists throughout time have studied the Great Pyramid with painstaking detail. They concluded it could have been designed to gather, amplify and gel energy emissions from a particular target and return them with the exact same harmonic frequency. Opera singers can do it—smash glasses with their voices by matching the basic harmonic vibration of the glass. It causes a shift in the glass's natural vibratory rate and makes it shake until it shatters. You've all seen it happen. In 1997, I think, the US government conducted research into acoustical weapons. They also analyzed the Great Pyramid and determined that the configuration of its chambers, and the placement of its passageways, could be used as a great loop, generating sound waves which could then be directed at a target. It was thought to be the most powerful weapon that ever existed on earth. Amplified energies." He wheezed. "Enormous force. It would neutralize all electronic equipment and detonate all explosive devices, including nuclear bombs. It would directly kill every living thing, including viruses. In truth, it is the way the chambers are placed and the passages built, the inclusion of shafts that lead nowhere, the precision with which it was built, metal pins attached to doors that look like electrodes, that made people look at the pyramid as a machine, rather than a tomb. The placement of the capstone will . . . switch it on."

"Right," Drake said. "Grab the capstone. That's all you had to say."

In another few minutes the professor's life had drained away, taken by the heartless, merciless men he had been forced to help.

Crouch bowed his head. "At least he paid them back in the end."

"Let's hope," Drake said. "We do this for him as well as the rest of the world."

They raced toward the pyramid's exit, surrounded by bedrock and ancient majesty, the ghosts of long-dead workers still haunting these halls, the labor they had undertaken an epic endeavor that would resonate through time. The Great Pyramid soared above them, a mass of six million tons perceived and crafted by the hand of man; extraordinary.

Is it really all just a big coffin?

Drake shut the thought down, listening to Crouch as he yelled out an explanation. All the while, the exit drew closer.

Dahl slipped out into the light, backed by Smyth. Drake came next, quickly shifting his body in all directions and scanning the area for hostiles. They moved swiftly and carefully to the right, heading toward the eastern side, since that was where the hidden tunnels had been found.

"Here we go," Dahl breathed.

Mercs were waiting for them, dug into the sand. Drake dived forward onto his stomach, landing hard but keeping his head up, his gun up, and firing blast after blast. Sand kicked up around the mercs. They scrambled behind some ruins, several low walls that were left to crumble with time. Bullets destroyed some of the stone, tumbled others. Drake rolled in the sand and dirt, firing potshots at the enemy. One was hit and then then second, precious minutes passing, and then they were up, running hard for the eastern corner of the pyramid.

The sun beat down hard. Weariness was a predator tearing at their limbs. Drake hit the side of the pyramid hard first and waited for the others, concealed, just waiting to sneak a look around to the other side.

"Moving?" he asked.

"Ready," they said.

He peered around the wall, eyes going wider and wider as they encountered one of the craziest, most astonishing scenes he'd ever witnessed.

CHAPTER FORTY ONE

In all his days Matt Drake never expected to see anything like this.

About thirty mercs stood against the wall of the pyramid, guns raised and tough looks stretched across the granite-like faces. Most of them were shouting. A helicopter hovered close to the ground and off to their left, further away from Drake's vantage point. A big one. *A Sikorsky,* he thought, *capable of lifting enormous weight.* Three more civilian choppers rested behind, their rotors idle for now.

Sunlight flashed from every surface.

Standing before the mercs, facing them down, were just four people. Drake wanted to rub his eyes, cartoon-like, just to make sure they weren't deceiving him because one of those people was Karin Blake.

Words, and thoughts, failed him.

Alongside her were two young men, standing like soldiers and with guns perfectly poised. Maybe they'd graduated from the same school?

The fourth figure took even his breath away.

"What the fuck is that?" he breathed.

Intrigued, the entire team came around the corner. No longer wary, they didn't need to be. The mercs' attention was completely engaged.

The fourth figure was crazy looking, a large behemoth dressed in robes and rags, all draped and wrapped around his torso. Around his face he wore more rags so that only his eyes peered out. His legs were clad in knee-length shorts and on his feet he wore brown sandals. One hand held the biggest machine gun Drake had ever seen, over 15mm diameter and heavy as hell. The flesh Drake could see was corded and brown. It was the other hand that drew his attention. He'd seen something like it before, but never quite as vicious looking.

"Oh, that," Luther suddenly said. "That's my big brother."

Dahl gawped at him. "You have a *big* brother? Fuck me."

"I sure do. His name's Molokai. But don't speak to him. He'd just as soon spit down your severed neck than shoot the shit, if you get my meaning."

Drake couldn't tear his eyes away from the right claw—a mechanical, knife-edged appendage instead of a hand, all steel and carbon-fiber, and gleaming in the sun, fingers opening and closing mechanically, edged by blades and dripping thick red blood into the thin covering of sand by his feet.

Dahl shook his out of it. "Get moving. We need to help them."

Luther laughed. "Ha, ha. Not with Molokai. He's a weapon. Just watch."

Drake didn't listen. "This team doesn't spectate," he said. "It helps."

Before they even sprang into motion the battle began. The helicopter hovered and the mercs fired their weapons, the amplified sound immense beside the Great Pyramid. Karin and her accomplices dived to the sides, firing accurately and cleverly, using broken and crumbling steps for cover. Molokai raised the gun that was about the size of Yorgi and opened fire, the clack-clack of its chambers resounding as deep down as Drake's very soul.

Bullets tacked a line across the mercs, each bullet killing a man and blowing a large hole through his torso. They shattered large chunks from the pyramid. In just seconds Molokai had ended ten men and was walking forward, into the fire. He didn't go unscathed, taking bullets to the chest, but he somehow walked through the barrage, withstanding the pain. When a bullet struck a part of his body that was not protected by Kevlar he ignored that too—shrugging the through-and-through off with an irritated twist of the mouth.

Half the mercs were finished. Drake now found himself confronted with the unknown scenario of the SPEAR team being forced to simply watch the last battle. They were normally a full part of it.

So this is retirement? he thought ironically. *Watching? I don't like it.*

Bullets clattered and struck hard. Karin and her two comrades fought economically and with a minimum of risk. Molokai did resort to taking cover but only when a bullet took off his ear lobe, causing that appendage to start bleeding profusely. Luther grunted with humor at the incident.

"Kai won't like that."

The unorthodox fighter dug his clawed hand into a body and threw it at the remaining mercs, shredding it with bullets. It was distraction enough to take out another two. Drake and Dahl were on the scene then, followed by Luther, and finished the mercs that remained.

There was a lull, a strange nonentity of action that lasted half a minute. During this time the big chopper continued to hover.

Drake ignored Molokai and walked over to Karin. The last surviving Blake stared at him with neutral eyes, letting him get close and not dropping her gun.

"It's me," he said, wondering if she had a head injury. "Matt."

"About time," she said. "We've been waiting for you."

"Where have you been?" he asked. "Why now?" A thousand questions hovered at the tip of his tongue.

"Not now," Karin said. "After the battle."

"We just finished it." Drake laughed.

"What, them? No, they were just the guards. The real force of mercs is coming. They were waiting out front." She jerked her head in the direction of the Sphinx. "Do you know what they're chasing?"

"Yeah, the capstone." Drake shelved his questions for later, turning to the arriving team. "Fighting's not done."

"Oh, thank you for that." Alicia sighed loudly. "I thought we'd missed out."

Hayden, Kinimaka and others greeted Karin carefully as the black-haired girl looked on. She smiled, nodding, but Drake thought he detected something else there. Maybe it was the training.

"Hey," he said. "Don't worry. You can get close again. With us. If you want to, that is."

Karin motioned at her friends. "Meet Dino and Wu. New friends of mine."

Luther brought Molokai over, seeming intent on introducing him. At the last moment Molokai stepped back with Luther; Pine and Carey fanning out.

"We can take it from here," Luther said. "And we can take *you*. I wasn't sure I'd need backup to take you, Drake, but called my big brother here just in case. Do you really wanna tangle with both of us?"

They leveled their guns and the standoff began.

"Bloody hell, Luther. Why can't you see past the trees?"

"Because I have the luxury of not having to. Now lay down your arms, all of you."

Drake worried, thinking of everything Crowe had said about Tempest and what Lauren might have discovered. If they fought back now, some would die. A glance at Karin told him she hadn't been expecting this; so she wasn't in on it.

"Tempest," he said. "The weapons. The other teams. Luther, we have too much at stake and so does the world."

Luther waved his handgun. "Down. Now. You have until the count of—"

The whistle started low but grew very quickly, becoming a thunderous roar. It came out of the sky, a missile fired by FrameHub, precisely monitored so that it struck at the exact angle and the exact point. Drake threw himself headlong. The missile struck the Great Pyramid and exploded, throwing rubble out into the air along its first and second seams, blasting a hole in the side.

The huge chopper still hovered; out of the blast radius.

Over the hill came a running horde of mercenaries.

"Weapons!" Dahl cried out.

CHAPTER FORTY TWO

Shattered pieces of Khufu's tomb landed all around them and upon them. The team sighted the attacking mercs and unleashed a hail of gunfire, but the force was too strong and reckless, overcoming them in minutes. The helicopter at their back repositioned slowly, moving until it hovered outside the great hole that had been blasted in the side of the pyramid.

"They're going for the capstone," Crouch said. "They just breached the secret passage."

Drake guessed as much. He smashed a running merc in the face as he raced past, then braced for a return punch of the production of a weapon, but none of the men were fighting. They were running straight for the still-smoking hole.

Chains dangled from the bottom of the helicopter, curled in a heavy iron mass for now. The quicker mercs grabbed hold and began to unfurl them, dragging them into the new hole. More soon joined, lending their strength to the task. Some fought with Luther, Molokai, Mai and Kinimaka, but only a few, causing a distraction. Others took cover and took potshots. The area was in chaos; frantic.

Drake slid over to Crouch. "Ideas?"

"I don't bloody like it, Drake! FrameHub have researched this. Acting on Intel received inside the pyramid they blew a hole in just the right spot. Now they're planning to drag it free. This is the same alliance of nutter that just sent Egypt to the Dark Ages."

Drake caught his drift. "You think they're gonna set the capstone up top?" He raised his gaze to the apex of the currently flat-topped structure. "No way. Even FrameHub aren't so stupid."

"They're gamers. Juvenile madmen with incredible power at their fingertips. And they're ghosts, gods. I think they'll do it just for the kicks."

Drake took it all in; the hovering heavy-lift chopper, the twenty or so men attaching the chains; the way the others were pinning his people down; and then: something else.

Vladimir and Saint stood just inside the ragged hole, supervising their men. As he watched Vladimir turned to the chopper pilot and gave the sign for two minutes.

And then he gave the sign for up.

Maybe it meant something else, but Drake wasn't taking any chances. He spun, took a deep breath, and screamed at the team.

"Forget them! We have to grab the capstone. These madmen are going to start up the machine."

Most of the SPEAR team turned, Karin too. Luther and Molokai continued to take out hidden enemies. Pine was looking over and so was Dino.

He gestured again. "If the pyramid is the weapon, the capstone is the key. Once placed, it'll power up. We can't afford to let that happen!"

He surged forward, running headlong into danger. Dahl was at his heels, Kenzie too. They evaded bullets, dodged a grenade. They went through three men as if they were made of dough. Alicia joined them and then came Smyth and Hayden. They were deadly karma, angels of death.

They passed by the chopper just as it began to thunder, rotors spinning harder, rising slowly off the floor. From inside the tomb came a terrible and tremendous grating roar, the sound of age-old stone being moved, being dragged, being torn out of its resting place. The pilot poured on the power. Mercs came surging out of the hole, desperate not to get crushed. Vladimir and Saint came with them.

They ran straight into the SPEAR team.

Drake met Saint head on, not even slowing momentum as he timed a headbutt to perfection. If he'd been wrong even by a millisecond it could have ended disastrously but it ended with Saint recognizing him and receiving a shattered nose bone and cranium at almost the exact same time.

Saint fell instantly, the shortest bout in history.

"That's how you fight." Drake spat on the jailor and fight

orchestrator. "*That* . . . is how you fight."

Dahl rammed into Vladimir, taking the merc boss right off his feet and carrying him ten paces before using that incredible momentum to throw him into the jagged pyramid wall. Vladimir struck hard, twisted, and screamed from the pain caused to his back. He went down like a sack of spanners, inert. Dahl leapt over to ensure the job was done.

Drake fought more mercs, sending a punishing blow to stomach and then chin. But again, they chose not to engage; all running past him without acknowledgement.

"This is becoming annoying," Alicia said. "Are we even visible?"

"Well, they're sure feeling us." Kinimaka wrenched his hand out of a folded merc's stomach, moving aside as the man dropped at his feet.

Another bunch ran past. Drake fought with one and then the most horrendous screeching that he'd ever heard rang out. The chain grew taut, the chopper strained, its engine groaning. It rose by the meter. The huge chains grumbled. And then, through the hole, Drake got his first glimpse of the ancient capstone that had been formed to top the Great Pyramid.

It came through the hole, dragging blocks and showers of mortar with it, a small pyramidion in contrast to Khufu's but looking large and deadly to Drake. It swung free, lifted by the chopper, passing close to Drake's flying body as he dived aside. Kinimaka ducked under it, caught in its shadow for many seconds, leaving Drake with the paradoxical wish both for the chains to hold and to break—but not right now.

The capstone, still shining, still covered by white polished cladding, swung under the chopper and then began to rise faster as the pilot learned its weight and dimensions. The mercs fought hard now, their primary job done, and the SPEAR team communicated as best they could.

In battle.

The capstone rose higher. Drake looked to their last chance; the grounded choppers.

"Dahl!" he cried. "With me!"

CHAPTER FORTY THREE

Drake and Dahl, Alicia and Mai raced together for one of the black helicopters.

They passed Luther and saw him nod, acknowledging their perilous bravery and offering support. They passed Hayden and Kinimaka, the big man back to back with his oldest living friend, striking mercenaries left and right. They passed Yorgi and Crouch with guns, keeping men at bay and helping the others. They passed Smyth and Kenzie, one looking like he wanted to get this fight out of the way as soon as possible and the other wishing she had joined them.

Even took a step their way.

But Smyth needed help and she jumped back in, supporting him.

Perhaps there was a major hope for her yet.

Drake climbed into the pilot's seat of the first helicopter; Dahl the second. As one they fired up the engines, letting the rotors turn. Alicia pointed out a stockpile of weapons in the back that the mercs hadn't even used—RPGs, grenades and loaded guns.

Above, the giant capstone moved up the side of the huge pyramid, hefted by the big-lift chopper. Drake moved the cyclic controls so that his own bird lifted and then took off. They took to the air, chasing the capstone up the sloping wall, aiming to get alongside the big helo.

Alicia, watching as they drew closer, said, "Y'know, I'm quite excited to say this, Drake. Just put me on that big chopper."

"Bit busy now, Alicia."

"Oh, har har, Quick as a flash, Drakey." She readied her gun, slamming a new mag in and pointing the barrel out the window.

"Not bothered about saving them," Drake said. "Take the pilot out if you can."

"On it."

Dahl came up too, visible in Drake's eye line, his helicopter rising up the other side of the Sikorsky. They passed the capstone and then the bulk of the bird, drifting around to the cockpit. Below, Drake could see a sandy plain of death, blood and battles to the death. Up here, it was all noise, concentration and maneuvering.

Hayden fought in the midst of it all, stopping mercs where they ran and watching Kinimaka's back as much as he watched hers. They pivoted, spun as if on a hinge, a well-rehearsed, experienced dance. As best they could they watched out for the other members of the team.

Yorgi and Crouch stayed put, well defended, but the others moved frequently, not wanting the enemy to grow comfortable with their position. Smyth crawled along some ruins, the wall barely taller than his back, with bullets glancing off it. Occasionally he would bob up, squeeze off a few rounds and then shift to the next place. Kenzie used her speed and skill, stepping up to an enemy, wrenching his gun aside and breaking his nose with the barrel.

Hayden knew these men had lost their leaders—she'd seen what Drake and Dahl had done to Vladimir and Saint—but concluded they must have been promised some final bonus, something extra if the capstone met the top of the Khufu pyramid.

She made them pay dearly for that decision.

Kinimaka was moving slower than normal, still in pain from the bullet strikes. She sympathized but this wasn't the time for pity. When he faltered she was there for him. When he winced in agony she took the man that was targeting him.

When he fell to one knee, she used his immense shoulders as a bench to rest her gun.

She saw Drake's helicopter riding high, chasing the big Sikorsky and the swinging capstone up the giant pyramid. The capstone shone so brightly it blinded her, glorious white light shimmering as it played backward and forward with the sun. Kenzie cut across her vision then, again using a merc's weapon as a club and no doubt missing her sword. In truth, the SPEAR team were well dug in. It was the mercs that had made themselves exposed.

And what of Karin? Hayden saw her running and switching positions in perfect routine with her team. But where had she been until now? And why was she so suddenly here? The questions would have to wait.

Luther fought at the fringes with his team. Pine and Carey ran in tandem, perfectly in tune, covering each other's backs and communicating with ease. Molokai raged among a knot of mercenaries, taking bullets but ignoring the impact as if they were made of foam, not lead. Hayden had to assume he'd gotten hold of some new kind of body armor. Even a glancing bullet should stop a man, but she'd seen it in the past where Drake had ignored a bullet impact and kept going on sheer adrenalin. But Molokai . . . the man was savage.

The metal hand was a brutal claw he used to devastating effect. One touch or grip of that hand signaled the end for the man on the receiving end. In the other, a high-caliber weapon pumped lead into everything nasty that moved. Hayden saw three men mown down in just a second, and then three more. Molokai held a man up by the neck, his terrible claw constricting his throat until his legs stopped kicking.

"Not keen on our new playmates?" Kenzie asked as she slid to a sandy halt a meter to Hayden's left.

"That is a different level of fierce," Hayden pointed out. "Luther and Molokai are . . ." She shook her head.

"Exactly as advertised," Kenzie reminded her. "We were told their reputation. Well, Luther's at least."

"I guess."

Hayden focused on the moment, rather than watching Luther and Molokai's rampaging. The band of mercenaries was thinning out now, and several were hanging back, shading their eyes as they stared at the topmost height of the Great Pyramid.

Hayden looked that way too, just as Kinimaka and Kenzie gazed up. The capstone was approaching the top; the doomsday weapon minutes from being completed. Drake and Dahl

David Leadbeater

struggled to get close, beset by gunfire and buffeting winds. Where it all ended up from here was anyone's guess.

Hayden stayed close to Mano.

Gently, Drake feathered the stick and floated alongside the pilot's window. He saw a skinny white man with grizzled hair and a thick moustache. Drake saw the dirty yellow teeth when he bared them.

The pilot stuck a HK casually out the window.

And opened fire.

Drake pulled back, letting Alicia return the favor but not wanting to lose the engines. It wasn't the fall that bothered him, it was losing the chance to prevent the enemy laying the capstone.

The Sikorsky continued up slowly as if nothing was occurring, an incredible spectacle against the Great Pyramid with Drake and Dahl's black choppers flying alongside. Guns poked out of many windows and gunfire was exchanged. Bullets laced the skies and indiscriminately sprayed holes in the metal sides. And now Drake saw one more anomaly—a black drone with mini-cameras mounted on its sides tracking the Sikorsky and watching.

Watching everything.

"Fucking FrameHub," he said. "They're recording all of this."

"Teenagers at play," Alicia said. "Don't worry, we'll get 'em."

Drake looked askance. "Will we?"

They had reached the very summit of Khufu's pyramid. Drake took his chopper away to give Alicia a clearer shot. Her bullets passed by as the Sikorsky pivoted to get directly over the top. Dahl and Mai struggled to get a better shot, beset by a gunman nestling in the other chopper's rear seats.

"Grab the controls," Drake heard Dahl's voice over the headphones.

"What are you going to do?" His voice was wary.

"Just be ready."

A crosswind buffeted the birds, battering their sides and tail rotors. The capstone was now directly over the top of the

208

pyramid and began to descend. Drake saw the very top of the Egypt's great wonder of the world, a flat gray plateau of rock.

Dahl kicked at the door of his helicopter, and watched it break free and tumble to the desert far below.

Drake tutted. "You know there are door handles?"

Dahl didn't answer. Mai was behind him, using the stick to keep the bird as stable as possible. The Swede sighted one of the RPGs over his shoulder and rose to full height, balanced on the skids.

Mai had one hand holding his belt. Her head was low.

The Sikorsky saw the weapon and tried to evade, but it was too late and far too slow. Dahl allowed an extra moment for the weapon to balance, for the air to still, for his mind to dispel all other distractions.

He breathed.

Then pressed the trigger. The backdraft blew out the door behind him. The grenade flew unerringly at the Sikorsky, exploding against the side and sending a billowing surge of flame through the entire bird. Within seconds it was disintegrating, blazing, falling out of the skies. The chains holding the capstone folded and the unblemished pyramidion was falling out of the skies, catching the light and shining like the sun as it tumbled and plummeted, plunging through flaming bits of fire as it fell, smashing aside broken lumps of metal, destroying the Sikorsky's blazing cockpit as it, the heavier object, fell faster, approaching the desert floor at terrible speed.

Drake watched Dahl climb back inside and then flung the chopper into a dive, desperate to get back on the ground. He saw the horrendous impact of the capstone, the hard, sandy ground buckling beneath it and sending out waves of force and a plume of dust that spiraled into the sky.

He landed the chopper quickly and jumped out almost as soon as their skids touched the ground. Alicia was tooled up with some of the new weapons and threw a fully-loaded HK to Drake as they passed the chopper's tail-rotor.

Dahl landed a moment later and caught up.

"That is one big-assed coping stone." He laughed as they

jogged past the fallen capstone. "Gonna look good on somebody's gate post."

The black drone currently hovered over it, no doubt streaming the scene in real time back to FrameHub's lair. As they passed, Mai took a bead on it.

"Wait," Alicia said. She walked right up to the drone, nodding amiably as it angled toward her. Slowly, she sighted it up with her new Walther PPK. Leaning forward, she spoke slowly.

"Hashtag this, motherfucker."

She pulled her trigger, blasting the drone out of the sky and into a dozen pieces.

Death, fire and blazing fury surrounded them. They saw none of it, but raced through the turmoil to help their friends.

CHAPTER FORTY FOUR

When the capstone and the helicopter came crashing down, the leaderless mercs lost their nerve and their courage.

Luther helped chase them off, backed by Molokai, Pine and Carey, helped by Karin and her crew. They took out another half dozen before they managed to jump into their vehicles and race back for Cairo, tails firmly between their legs.

In the aftermath, Drake walked carefully to the side of the Great Pyramid, sitting and waiting until the SPEAR team gathered around him. That seemed to be the cue for Luther and Karin to join them, followed by their colleagues.

"It was a close call," Yorgi said with a straight face.

Crouch planted himself down in the sand, still feeling the effects of Vladimir's torture. "I think a few months off now would be good."

Drake nodded, but eyed Luther. "I guess that all depends on the big man."

Luther looked torn. "What you guys did here today—it's truly heroic. Never seen the like of it. Trouble is, if I don't follow my orders then I become a fugitive too."

Alicia held up a water bottle. "Cheers. It's fun."

"You all do seem to be happy with your lot," Luther admitted.

"Sure," Alicia said. "Every day I get to wake up, laugh with and fight alongside my friends. What could be better than that?"

"Not much for a soldier," Molokai admitted, checking out his metal claw and flexing it to ensure it hadn't been damaged in the battle.

"I bet you have some story," Alicia said.

"Much more than you could ever imagine."

"Oh, I dunno, I can imagine some pretty wild scenarios. Just ask Drakey."

Molokai partly unwrapped the rags from about his face, showing skin partially eaten away and hanging loose. "Do I win?"

Alicia whistled. "Yeah, pal. I can't even imagine what happened to you."

"Leprosy is what happened, but that's a whole different story."

"You're a leper? I didn't . . . I don't even know what to do with that information."

"I *was* a leper," Molokai said. "And I appreciate the honesty."

Drake watched the big Sikorsky burn, looked over the bodies of dead mercs and heard rubble falling from the ragged hole that now existed at the base of the pyramid. The sun was looking like it might finally be thinking about setting, but that didn't bode well for the good people of Cairo.

"FrameHub," he said. "Have a big payload of sins to answer for. Tracking them won't be easy."

Karin Blake stepped up. "I can help with that. I want to. Those bastards have gotten in the way of my agenda, but I can't stand by and see them do again what they've done to Egypt and Greece. Ending them must come first."

Drake wondered what her *agenda* might be, but agreed. There would be time to talk and discuss later. The thing he found hardest was sitting alongside a man he'd just fought with, bled with and admired—the same man that was threatening to end his freedom.

"You game for it, Luther?"

"I have to say," Hayden spoke up before the soldier could answer. "We should talk to Secretary Crowe first. She put herself in danger contacting us and her wishes were somewhat different."

Everyone nodded, including Luther.

Soon, Crowe was back on the line, enervated when they explained what had transpired at the pyramid. Again she reiterated her views on Tempest and the weapons of the gods that they sought.

"The Sword of Mars," she said. "The Chains of Aphrodite. The Flail of Anubis, The Dagger of Nemesis, the Waters of Neptune, The Key of Hades, The Forge of Vulcan, and more. It's a global hunt, no holds barred and utterly deadly. Believe me, nothing you've encountered so far will come close to this."

"We're somewhat up against it," Dahl said diplomatically.

"The splinter group, Tempest, are incredibly well connected. It says a lot that the US Secretary of Defense has to creep around, making covert phone calls. I couldn't even get next to the President without arousing suspicion as I believe one of his aides to be a mole. But I do know that if we let them gather the weapons of the gods, we're all dead. Or may as well be."

"Where would we even start?" Mai asked.

"The weapons were either stolen or given away. You will have to hunt them down."

"There are ways," Hayden said. "Remember . . . we located the Sword of Mars ourselves."

"And what about FrameHub?" Karin asked.

"I hate to say this, but they come second to this. Nothing in this world could be more important now than those weapons. They literally have the power to crack the world in half."

Drake listed to the somber silence, the weary surprise. "Do we have allies?" he asked.

"Maybe," Crowe said. "The other burned teams. The Brits—I have a source there in the SAS. Maybe others."

Drake thought it might be fun hooking up with the SAS one more time. Crouch caught his eye and smiled, knowing exactly what he was thinking. The Yorkshireman watched Karin. "Secretary Crowe," he said. "I believe we may have a way to take out FrameHub. We don't want to fail there. Perhaps we could multitask."

"Perhaps. Now, start making plans. I'll be in touch later."

"One thing," Drake said. "What are we supposed to do with Luther?"

"He's there? Oh well, bring him with you. He's useful."

"At the moment, he'd rather clap us in chains."

Crowe was silent, then said. "Give him the phone."

Luther looked surprised, but held out a hand. "Hello?"

"I'll tell you one thing although my every instinct says I shouldn't. One of the leaders of Tempest is a man called General Gleeson. Do you know him?"

"Ah, yes, Madam Secretary, he's the man that sent me after SPEAR."

"I know. Look, Luther, as the end of the day it's your call. But you've seen first-hand what these people can do. You've fought alongside them, bled with them, risked your life with them. Deep down, you know what they are. They're soldiers, Luther, just like you. All they want to do is help normal, down-to-earth, ordinary people live their lives as freely as they can. They're not American traitors; they're international patriots. Save your damn soul and give them a chance."

Luther handed back the phone and glanced around the team finally alighting on Drake. "I trust her. I don't trust you, quite yet. I have my team; they're coming with us."

The Yorkshireman grinned. "We're teaming up?"

"I'll let you tag along in case I need my gear cleaned."

Alicia clicked her fingers. "Can you be more specific about that part?"

Kenzie nudged Drake. "Better watch your bitch, Matt. Sounds like she needs soothing."

"I'll get right on it."

"It?" Alicia raised an eyebrow. "And not right here you won't. Too sandy."

Mai rose and walked over to Luther. "Look forward to working with you, my new friend."

Luther eyed her respectfully. "You are the best warrior I have ever seen."

Dahl reminded them of his own aerial heroics. Hayden and Kinimaka moved to sit slightly apart, saying little but allowing each other to enjoy some new, and some old, familiar company.

Dahl stretched his legs after a while, leaning this way and that to ease out the kinks in his back. The team were having a last few rations and swigs of water before moving out. He wanted to wander just for a moment and ponder over what might be happening back home.

What he might be missing.

In the end, he didn't want to miss all of it.

So, when Kenzie came up, all smiles and innuendo he

grabbed her arm and pulled her to the side.

"I can't do this," he said.

"What? You mean me? Us? I won't accept that."

"You have to," Dahl said. "And the sooner you do, you will move on."

"Hey." Her voice rose. "*You* said you saw something in me. Something better. *You* said I had a heart. I believed you. I followed you. This is where it has brought us."

"I can't help your past, Kenzie." And he wouldn't apologize for it either. "Life is a game of chance. You work hard enough, stay straight, and good things will happen to you. Forget the billionaires so power-stricken they've lost their humanity. Forget the ones that don't seek redemption, but wallow in corruption. Live a good life."

"I can. With you."

"I am already spoken for," Dahl said. "And I do love my wife. I will not risk her and the children with you. Whatever you think we have, Kenzie—" he started to walk away "—whatever you think this is, it is now over."

His words hung in the air behind his back, stunning her.

It is now over.

Dahl didn't look back. Drake guessed what was transpiring and watched his friend's back carefully, still not fully trusting Kenzie. What would this new development do to her? He was ready, fingers poised over a Glock, in case she acted.

She didn't. She walked back to the crew, face blank, eyes far away. Drake couldn't tell if she could get past it or let it destroy her. Alicia was watching Kenzie too, a knowing wariness in her eyes.

Bloody hell, he thought. *What comes next?*

The toughest quest of their lives, searching for the weapons of the gods? A journey with the old-school blood and thunder warrior and his big brother? The return of Karin and her unknown agenda? FrameHub? Tempest? Dealing with the dreadful knowledge that they had been burned and were, essentially, still being hunted along with more than a dozen other teams?

He stood up today, ready to heal quickly and face the world with a little laughter and a good deal of camaraderie.

Tomorrow, and its oncoming, unstoppable nightmare, would be here all too soon.

THE END

For more information on the future of the Matt Drake world and other David Leadbeater novels please read on:

The next Matt Drake novel will be called *Weapons of the Gods*, and should be released around February 2018. It will feature the climax of the current arc, so we are able to move on to the next.

Next up, in November 2017, will be another instalment of the very popular Relic Hunters story, where the new characters will be greatly expanded upon amid another edge of the seat archaeological thriller, this time centering on Atlantis. In case you didn't know, Relic Hunters 1 won the Amazon UK Kindle Storyteller Award on the 25th July 2017, picked from a panel of 6 judges, and I would like to thank everyone that bought the book and left a review.

If you have enjoyed this or any other books of mine, please leave a review. Even a short line or two helps to ensure future releases.

Other Books by David Leadbeater:

The Matt Drake Series
The Bones of Odin (Matt Drake #1)
The Blood King Conspiracy (Matt Drake #2)
The Gates of Hell (Matt Drake 3)
The Tomb of the Gods (Matt Drake #4)
Brothers in Arms (Matt Drake #5)
The Swords of Babylon (Matt Drake #6)
Blood Vengeance (Matt Drake #7)
Last Man Standing (Matt Drake #8)
The Plagues of Pandora (Matt Drake #9)
The Lost Kingdom (Matt Drake #10)
The Ghost Ships of Arizona (Matt Drake #11)
The Last Bazaar (Matt Drake #12)
The Edge of Armageddon (Matt Drake #13)
The Treasures of Saint Germain (Matt Drake #14)
Inca Kings (Matt Drake #15)
The Four Corners of the Earth (Matt Drake #16)

The Alicia Myles Series
Aztec Gold (Alicia Myles #1)
Crusader's Gold (Alicia Myles #2)
Caribbean Gold (Alicia Myles #3)

The Torsten Dahl Thriller Series
Stand Your Ground (Dahl Thriller #1)

The Relic Hunters Series
The Relic Hunters (Relic Hunters #1)

The Disavowed Series:
The Razor's Edge (Disavowed #1)
In Harm's Way (Disavowed #2)
Threat Level: Red (Disavowed #3)

The Chosen Few Series
Chosen (The Chosen Trilogy #1)
Guardians (The Chosen Tribology #2)

Short Stories
Walking with Ghosts (A short story)
A Whispering of Ghosts (A short story)

Connect with the author on Twitter: @dleadbeater2011
Visit the author's website: www.davidleadbeater.com

All helpful, genuine comments are welcome. I would love to
hear from you.
davidleadbeater2011@hotmail.co.uk

Made in United States
Troutdale, OR
09/30/2024

23265825R00126